"Bradley and I feel blessed to have met you, Special Soldier Montgomery."

Joel cast a thoughtful expression at her. "Can I, uh, get your contact info?"

"Okay." Amber's heart thudded warmth onto her face.

"You know, for updates on Bradley. And stuff."

He stared at her with sincere intensity. "It was truly an honor to meet you, too, 'Special Teacher' Stanton. I won't soon forget you."

Suddenly, a weird panic seized her that she might never see him again. Her heart and mind raced. Amber reached up as far as she could and hugged him.

Bulky arms wound around her, pulling her close. She marveled at how he could be strong and tender at the same time.

When Amber pulled back, she instantly missed the comforting beat of his heart.

Joel's eyes twinkled. "Wow. What was that for?"

"For giving Bradley something to live for. A reason to hope."

CHERYL WYATT

An RN turned stay-at-home mom and wife, Cheryl delights in the stolen moments God gives her to write action- and faith-driven romance. She stays active in her church and in her laundry room. She's convinced that having been born on a naval base on Valentine's Day destined her to write military romance. A native of San Diego, California, Cheryl currently resides in beautiful, rustic southern Illinois, but she has also enjoyed living in New Mexico and Oklahoma. Cheryl loves hearing from readers. You are invited to contact her at anavim4him@gmail.com or P.O. Box 2955 Carbondale, IL 62902-2955. Visit her on the Web at www.CherylWyatt.com and sign up for her newsletter if you'd like updates on new releases, events and other fun stuff. Hang out with her in the blogosphere at www.scrollsquirrel.blogspot.com or on the message boards at www.SteepleHill.com.

A Soldier's Promise
Cheryl Wyatt

Steeple
Hill®

Published by Steeple Hill Books™

STEEPLE HILL BOOKS

Steeple
Hill®

ISBN-13: 978-0-373-81344-5
ISBN-10: 0-373-81344-9

A SOLDIER'S PROMISE

Printed in U.S.A.

Be devoted to one another in brotherly love.
Honor one another above yourselves.
—*Romans* 12:10

Dedications

To Mom, who always said I could.

To my favorite soldier, Dad, who always said
I could do it better.

To Lisa, who always said she could do it better. Grin.

To Billy. Not one soldier marching around my imagination
could occupy the place you've secured in my heart.

To Granny Nellie and Aimee. I could not have done this
had you not stepped in while I went MIA from my
Hide-N-Seek posts to write.

To Mag, Eno and Randa. I love you to infinity.
Ready or not…here I come!

To my editor, Melissa Endlich, for handing me
this dream in the form of a contract.

To my agent, Tamela Hancock Murray of Hartline,
for seeing promise in my work.

Thank you, Lord, for remembering our dreams
even when we feel they're long lost.

I love you all beyond what words can express.

Acknowledgments

To fellow author Anne Greene and her personal hero,
Colonel Larry Greene, U.S. Army Special Forces, Ranger,
and the other military contacts (you know who you are)
who've helped me validate research for this series.
May the Lord watch over you and your loved ones as
you watch over our country. Thank you for serving.

To Lynette at Lifeway in Carterville, Illinois. Little did
we know when you led me down the Christian fiction aisle
that God used you as a traffic director to walk me into my
destiny as an author.

Chapter One

"Sure you wanna do this, Montgomery?" Fellow U.S. Air Force Pararescue Jumper Nolan Briggs asked above the engine hum.

"I'm sure." Joel shifted away from the window as the luxury jet broke through wispy Southern Illinois clouds on descent to the one place on earth he never wanted to see again.

Refuge. The irony made him snort.

Nolan leaned close enough for Joel to inhale toxic doses of mafia-strength garlic. "'Cause if you don't, we'll handle it."

Teammate Manny Peña joined Nolan in the passenger aisle. "Yeah. Nobody'll know if you don't make the jump, dude."

Joel fastened a gaze on his well-meaning friends and fellow PJs, and aimed a thumb at his sternum. "I'll know."

And so would that kid.

"It's gonna be tougher than you think," Nolan said.

Hardest mission of his life. Especially on a cold Friday in September. Joel laced his boot. "Nah. Piece of cake."

"Right. Like running a catering service with an Easy-Bake." Manny clicked the overhead bin open.

"No sweat." Joel tugged his chute pack from under the seat.

"Not a drop," Nolan agreed. "But the offer still stands."

"He asked for me. I can't let him down, guys." Joel retrained a determined gaze on the small town peeking up at him. Recognition of his old neighborhood clogged his throat. He clenched his jaw against a surge of unwanted emotion. He looked away from familiar landmarks. "I'll be fine."

As long as he steered clear of that house, and the uncle who'd destroyed his family, he'd be fine.

A chorus of unconvinced faces stared back at Joel when he looked up. A torrent of vulnerability rushed through him at their perception. He torqued his gaze out the window. True. They could do this without him and spare him the pain.

Except for one thing.

He tugged the letter out of his chest pocket. Unfolding it, he eyed the elementary attempt at cursive.

My name's Bradley. I'm eight and I have cancer. My teacher called Dream Corps who said I should write a letter about my wishes since doctors say I might not get a transplant in time. I want to meet a Special Forces soldier more than anything. Well, almost anything. Having a family would be nice. I heard a PJ grew up in my town. It would be awesome if he'd come see me but I know he's kinda busy with wars and rescues and all. Anyway, if you find him, tell him he's my idea of a hero…

Words blurred. Joel blinked, refocused and read:

Thinking of soldiers who fight terror helps me be brave and fight mine. If me and God win our cancer war, I promise to plug my nose and eat my stinky call of flower so I can grow up strong and come help the soldiers win theirs. Love, Bradley Tennyson. Refuge, IL U.S.A.

Joel folded the letter Dream Corps had forwarded to him. He crimped along the crease and came back with blue fingertips, probably from one of those messy erasable pens. He rubbed fingers on a hanky, but the ink didn't come off. Weird, since it had transferred from the paper with no trouble.

Ink imprinted his hand, but scribbled wishes stained his heart. *Family.* The very word stung. Joel couldn't help the little guy with one, but he could make the other a reality. No matter how hard the next hours proved to be, Joel's discomfort in coming back to the site of his most painful childhood memories would be a speck of dust compared to the earth of hurt this kid faced.

Joel pressed thumbs into the corners of his eyes and lifted his face. He swallowed, but his voice box didn't seem to want to loosen and let him speak.

"I appreciate you guys offering me an out, but…" He met and held each man's respect-filled gaze, drawing courage from the admiration in each one. "I *need* to do this."

Grins erupted all around, revealing to Joel they wanted him to conquer this every bit as much as he did.

Nolan tossed Joel his goggles. "Don't tangle up on a power line before you hit the ground, Montgomery. It wouldn't bode well to fry your fanny in front of a load of little kids."

Joel smiled back at the grinning faces before refastening his gaze on strings of pinpoint runway lights rising to meet the Dream Corps aircraft. "All right, you platoon of goons. As soon as we hit tarmac, load the choppers while the pilot flies me back up into a holding pattern. I'll jump when you hover on the school lawn. Fastrope down when I flare my canopy. Let's go make this little guy's dream come true."

A chorus of "Hoorah!" shouts punctuated the end of his sentence, and a dozen fists shot up.

He'd parachute in, spend a few hours with the kid, then get away from Refuge for good. It would be as easy as that. What could possibly be simpler?

* * *

"What on earth is that?" Special needs teacher Amber Stanton grasped the desk and held her breath.

Her best friend and co-teacher, Celia Muñez stared at Amber as if she'd morphed into a snail. "What?"

"You don't feel that?" Amber whispered.

Ebony eyes waxed blank and oblivious. "Feel what?"

Leave it to her zippy friend to be in the middle of a natural disaster and not know. Had Amber imagined it? No. The rumbling vibration beneath her feet strengthened. Ripples pulsed across the surface of the water in the small fishbowl on her desk. "Shh—" Amber leaned in. "Listen." The windows gave a faint rattle. "That!" Amber clutched Celia's shoulder in a pinch grip.

"Cool it with the claws, will ya?" Celia peeled fingernails from her blouse. "It's only—"

"I know. Let's get these kids outside."

"You know?" Now Celia looked properly stricken. "Who told?"

"Shh. I don't want the children frightened. Let's go."

Celia tugged Amber back. "Hold on. They all know except Bradley. If you keep yapping, you'll ruin the surp—"

"Class—" Amber moved from Celia's grasp. Why didn't Administration ring the bell? "Line up at the door please."

Celia yanked Amber hard back behind the desk. "Not yet!"

"Sit!" Celia waved the class down with choppy arm motions. Children sat, giggling as crayons jittered off slanted desks.

Amber's chest tightened. She turned a fierce gaze on Celia. "Obviously you have no idea how dangerous they can be."

Celia screwed up her terra-cotta–toned face. "They?"

Amber helped children from seats, then leaned close to Celia's ear. "Do not panic or react outwardly to what I am about to tell you, but I think we are having an earthquake."

A sharp laugh yelped from Celia, causing Amber's face to jerk back. Celia slapped a hand to her mouth.

Amber glared at her and ushered the class down the hall like a kiddie cattle drive. "Stay together, guys. Good." Amber kept her teacher voice calm and helped stragglers along, including Celia.

"Though this is frightening, it's only minor and should stop any moment. I moved from California to get away from these things," Amber said out of student earshot.

"Looks like they followed you here." Celia spoke in a wry voice. Amber's pulse spiked. Did Celia forget Refuge sat atop the New Madrid fault? Amber pushed her feet against fear that weakened her knees. *Please, Lord. Not now. Not here. Not even a thousand years from now. Not these children. Not on my watch.* Celia maneuvered Bradley up to Amber as she flung open the double doors and stepped outside into—

A war zone? Talk about shock and awe. Bradley gasped and froze beside her as a blast of cheers erupted. She grew cognizant of little hands shoving them forward into a sea of noise and green. Military stuff—everywhere. Amber and Bradley moved down concrete steps to grass where the entire school, sans her class, waited. A bugle charmed the air with a patriotic tune, and drums danced a rhythm with Amber's pulse.

Mouth agape, she peered at Celia, who winked.

"Whoa!" Bradley's voice cut through the chaos.

Amber realized the roaring vibrations were military helicopters hovering above the school, fumigating the air with a sharp exhaust smell. Camo-fatigued men slid from ropes hanging out. One after another, they dropped to the ground. Helicopters lit on the lawn like twin gigantic metal grasshoppers. Thunderous chopping abated as the blades slowed to a halt.

Bradley drew in a sharp breath. "Look! Look at him!"

Amber followed the trajectory of the finger Bradley jabbed at the sky. She gasped. A uniformed man dangling from a white parachute etched with a blue USAF insignia penetrated clouds above them. How could a person jump from such heights? Amber tugged Bradley's shoulder to move him back but a large hand halted her. She turned.

A wide grin peeked at her from a dark face painted in calico earth tones. "Don't worry, ma'am. He's never landed on a lady's head. Yet." The camouflaged man chuckled then directed her class to join with others as if this were…

Planned. Suddenly she knew. Her phone call. The letter. Dream Corps. Bradley's wish coming true in a spectacular way.

Slammed with a tidal wave of emotion, Amber sprawled fingers over her lip to smother a tremor.

Celia's hand circled her wrist, tugging it back down. "It's okay to cry happy tears, *chica*. You've shed enough sad ones for him. Don't quench the enormity of this moment. Revel in it." Tears glistened in Celia's eyes, too, though she prided herself on never crying. She pressed paper in Amber's hand.

Celia peeled the backing off a flag sticker and placed it on Bradley. Amber lifted hers and read the preprinted font:

Welcome to Refuge. My name is Ms. Stanton. Faith Elementary, along with Dream Corps International, wish to thank you for your service to our country.

Chills marched down her arms as the words took hold of her.

"Oh!" Her head snapped up and her shoulders back as the parachutist landed mere feet in front of them. Bradley stumbled backward.

The soldier grinned, took three steps forward,

dropped to one knee, putting him nose to nose with Bradley, and saluted.

Bradley sliced a clumsy hand to his forehead, causing his glasses to topple. The soldier righted the lopsided frames on Bradley's nose.

Amber laughed, recalling her earnest prayer the day she'd called Dream Corps. "I asked for one, and you sent…fifty." She roamed a deeply thankful look over each soldier who'd answered this very special call.

But it was the one brandishing a heart-seizing grin, the most piercing blue eyes, and parachute material falling around him in billowing waves, whom she couldn't extract her gaze from.

Chapter Two

As Joel knelt on clean-shaven lawn, Bradley's eyes widened through bottle-thick glasses perched haphazardly atop his nose. His eyes traveled up Joel's body.

His mouth gaped like the nine-pound bass Joel hooked yesterday. "Whoa! Dude! Who're you?"

Joel offered his hand. "Senior Airman Joel Montgomery, little sir. You must be Bradley."

Awe and trepidation flowed over the child's gaunt face. "H-how do you know my name?" He shook Joel's hand, pumping as if it were the handle of a water well.

Joel grinned, tapping the patriotic sticker on the boy's bony chest. "Says so right here."

Bradley's gaze hit the sticker the way heat seekers locked on target. He lifted his shirt, twisting material to view it. "A flag tag! With my name!" His gaze skittered to Joel's shoulders. He stuck a tiny finger out and poked his bicep. "Are those real muscles?" *Poke. Poke. Poke.* "They are! Dang!"

"This is a private Christian school, kiddo. You sure you're supposed to be saying that kinda word around here?" Joel asked.

Bradley jerked his head around, rapidly scanning the perimeter as if they'd just come under heavy enemy fire. "N-no. I ain't supposed to. Good thing the playground patrol's not—"

"Right behind you, Bradley?"

Bradley stiffened as if stabbed in the caboose with a bayonet. The sweet-timbred voice belonged to a very attractive woman with night vision–green eyes. He flashed his best grin and offered a hand to her. "Joel Montgomery."

She reached forward. "Amber Stanton."

From the air, he'd mistaken her for a student because of her petite frame. Closer observation confirmed she was all woman. He continued the handshake past the edge of proper, enjoying the flush that crept up her neck.

"Pleasure to meet you, ma'am. How do you know this brave guy?" Joel tousled Bradley's hair, which lay unusually sparse in places.

"I'm his teacher."

So this is her.

Joel rose to face the reason he was here today. Her phone call had deployed six military units to a hundred-student school in a middle-of-nowhere town.

"So, *you're* the one."

She started at his words. He wondered about the blush invading her cheeks until he realized how his statement could have been misconstrued. He dipped his chin to his chest, laughing at himself. Half-embarrassed, he looked back up. "You're the one…who called Dream Corps?"

She laughed then nodded. "I am." She smiled again. Cute mouth. Nice teeth. The kind that spoke of parents who'd forked over some hefty dough to orthodontists.

"Miss Stanton, you knew about all this?" Bradley's words rode out on the winds of an awe-induced whisper.

The riot of auburn curls framing her ivory face bounced as she looked from Joel to Bradley. Childlike mischief frolicked in her eyes as she surrendered a secret wink to Joel. "Not exactly."

He admired the way she pretended not to notice how hard Bradley attempted to simultaneously push his shoulders up and his chest out as far as Joel's. The jerky movement came out looking more like a barnyard bird with Parkinson's.

Joel watched her study Bradley, enthralled with the level of loving care in her eyes.

Eyes that seemed to glow with interest when they came to rest on Joel. He bit down on his cheek to keep from grinning over the possibility of the attraction being mutual.

Pink infused her cheeks when he didn't break his

focus except to travel lazily down to her left ring finger before returning to her face again. The gesture was far from covert, as he'd intended to gauge her reaction.

Her blush deepened. Butterfly-delicate hands fluttered across her forehead before coming to rest atop Bradley's shoulders. "Shall we walk?"

Bradley clasped her hand, then Joel's. He had the feeling she'd wanted to slip out from under his assessing gaze but Bradley trapped her. He grinned. This couldn't have worked out better had he planned it himself. The threesome trekked past soldiers talking with huddles of enthralled students.

Around the east side of the school Bradley led them through a garden gate to a huge oak tree. An anklet of yellow flowers surrounded it. Bradley pointed to one whose color seemed muted. "That's mine. Planted it myself."

"Each student in class planted one," Amber explained.

Another teacher motioned Bradley to the gate.

Joel remained beside Amber. Concern troubled her expression as she eyed Bradley's flower, then the ones flanking it. Joel brushed fingers along the droopy petals. "Hey, I'm sure it doesn't mean anything."

She blinked and smiled. "It shocked me to see the wilted condition of his compared to the others."

Joel pushed his fingers in the soil surrounding Bradley's flower, then eyed the other stems intently. "I'm no botany expert but my mother was an avid gardener before she died. She taught me a thing or two. Seems to me Bradley's isn't planted in the soft dirt like the rest. If it doesn't perk up, maybe transplant it into better soil so it can take root and be healthy. It might thrive then."

"Thank you." Amber stood, tracking Bradley, who grinned at them from the gate. "I think he's waiting for us."

Joel chuckled. "I think so."

The fence chinked as Bradley bounced against it. "Miss Muñez says a special show is coming."

"Okay, catch a bathroom break and take your seat with the other students," Amber said.

Joel adjusted his waterproof Luminox watch with the PJ emblem and motto So Others Might Live engraved on the band and peered at the face. Ten minutes until the hour.

"Where'd you get that cool watch?" Bradley turned Joel's wrist around, peering intently at it.

Joel slid his cuff up. "It was a gift from one of my boys."

Bradley's shoulders slumped and his grip on Joel's wrist slackened. "Wow. Your kid sure is lucky. How many you got?"

Joel caught Bradley's hand before he pulled it away. "I don't have children. By *boys,* I meant one of my teammates." Joel gave Bradley's hand a comforting squeeze as compassion for the little guy consumed him.

"You gonna have any kids?" Bradley swung their arms back and forth like a hand clasp pendulum.

Miss Stanton put a firm hand on his shoulder. "Bradley, it's not polite to ask personal questions."

Joel looked at her and shrugged. "Doesn't bother me." He met Bradley's gaze once more. "I don't think being a dad is in God's plans for me, buddy."

Bradley squished up his nose. "Why not?"

"Enough, Bradley." Miss Stanton's voice carried a sternness that made even Joel perk up.

Bradley dipped his head. "Sorry, sir."

Joel inched Bradley's chin up with his finger. "No sweat, buddy. It's all good, but I think it's okay that you know. I didn't have great examples for parents so I'd probably be no good at it."

It struck Joel suddenly that his uncle Dean had been more of a father figure than Joel's dad had been. Joel hadn't thought about that in years. He certainly didn't want to start thinking about it now. Despite Joel trying to sweep thoughts of Dean from his mind, they clung like stubborn dust.

The latent question of years ago resurfaced. Why had Dean gone out of his way for Joel? Were his actions motivated by guilt for cheating on Joel's dad with his mother?

Or was there something else?

No matter. Joel had little mercy for a man who trampled on another man's wedding vows. He didn't want to disappoint Bradley in case the kid got some wild notion about hoping Joel would want him. A career military dad was the last thing this kid needed. He relinquished Bradley's hand.

"Will I get to talk to you again?" Bradley asked in a small voice and twisted his shirt hem.

Miss Stanton smoothed his fidgety hands down.

"Of course. I'll be here all day unless something happens. Tell you what. Save me a seat after the show and I'll sit next to you. I'd feel honored if you'd be my best buddy today."

Bradley's face ignited with joy. "Cool! Did you hear that, Miss Stanton? He wants me to be his best buddy today! I'm going to be a PJ just like Joel when I grow up. A man of integ—"

"Integrity," Miss Stanton enunciated. Pain flashed across her face with Bradley's words. Joel doubted Bradley saw because she quickly hedged it. He determined to put his prayer pedal to the metal so that Bradley would get to grow up.

"Integrenary." Bradley skewed his face.

"In. Teg. Rit. Tee," she repeated. "Bathroom, tater."

"Okay, gator." Bradley ambled toward the building with an unsteady gait.

"You sure he'll make it up those steps without falling?" Joel eyed Bradley until double steel doors swallowed him.

"Probably not, but he'd be mortally wounded with embarrassment if I helped him in front of the other students. Mr. Montgomery, I apologize for Bradley's personal questions. He hasn't been raised with the best of manners or social skills."

Joel shrugged. "Kid's just curious. Besides, it's no secret to those who know me that having children is not on the radar for me." Joel wanted to laugh at the curious look that flashed in the teacher's eyes. It seemed to him that kids usually just spoke aloud what adults only had the guts to think.

He considered that he felt so mesmerized by her a blessing. Without knowing, she was keeping his mind off why he hated this town so much. It also helped that the school sat miles from the house on Haven Street. The spot where his life had unraveled, beginning with the breakup of his parents' marriage and ending with his mother's desertion of him. Then the fatal accident on her way back that snuffed out her life, and his hope of ever seeing her again.

Joel scanned the streets past the school yard where he'd worn out many sneakers and bicycle tires. Some good times, yeah. But the bad overshadowed and overtook them. In short, this wretched place haunted him with too many painful questions.

The only person with answers was the last person Joel ever wanted to speak to or see again. Questions like why his mom had been on her way back to Refuge from wherever she'd gone after abandoning him at age seven. Was it to come get Joel as she promised? Or even better, to reconcile her marriage so they could be a family again as he'd prayed and imagined night and day for three years?

"I understand you were born in Refuge. Do you come back here often?" Amber's gentle voice tapped into his thoughts. Joel blinked a moment, figuring out how long he'd been staring like a lost astronaut into space, probably with a hopeless expression that matched the dismal chasm this town opened in him. His teammates had been right. This was tougher than he'd anticipated. He didn't like not being in total control of his emotions and thoughts. He pondered how to answer her.

"You're right. I was born here." He hated the crack in his voice and forced a smile he didn't feel.

He could tell by her concerned expression that she wasn't fooled by the hedging veneer.

Another part of his mind rippled with pleasure that she had retained that bit of personal information about him. Her smile and soft voice eased the sadness of missing his mother. He cleared his throat. "I don't recall hearing the Stanton name growing up here. So what about you? What brought you to Refuge?"

Her eyes lit with wit. "A car brought me here. I want to know why you're avoiding my original question."

Joel chuckled. She joined him as they walked along the grass. He'd forgotten how it felt to laugh with a lady.

"Well?" She lifted a brow; the smile never left her face.

He bent to pick up a gravel pebble, staring first at the chipped ridges, then at her. "I haven't been back here since I moved away."

Surprise shone in her eyes. He handed her the rock. "Memories live here that I've spent a lifetime trying to forget. I have a longtime rift with a family member who still lives here. So I try to avoid the place."

He didn't want to dredge up the memories by talking about them. But something in her eyes called to him. She placed the rock back in his hand then pulled out a stick of red licorice from her jacket pocket and peeled the plastic wrap off it. "Then it was truly a sacrifice for you to come here for Bradley. That speaks well of your character. Want half?"

He took the licorice, loving the smell, but hating the memories it evoked. He didn't want to hurt the teacher's feelings. Uncle Dean kept bowls full of red licorice at his house. "He used to give me one every day after school," Joel surprised himself by saying.

She nodded. "I think I know the man in question."

Joel nearly choked on the candy. He stopped chewing and stared at her, feeling his jaw harden like the rock in his palm. "Excuse me?"

"Dean DuPaul. You're the spitting image of him. How long's it been since you spoke to your father, Mr. Montgomery?"

Joel shook his head. "He's not my father. He's my uncle, my father's brother. They had different fathers, so their last names don't match. Dean betrayed my family and I have no use for the man." The words felt bitter even with the layer of sweetness coating Joel's mouth. She nodded again, eyeing him with what Joel interpreted as concern. He needed to stop looking into those compassionate, compelling green eyes. Doing so made him want to get all soft and talk about it.

He forced his eyes to an about-face and his feet to march ahead as he motioned with his hand. "Let's move on." Hopefully she'd get that he didn't want to talk about it further. Relief melted the tension from his jaw and shoulders when she fell into step beside him.

They meandered toward the ranks of Bradford pear trees flanking the concrete walk leading up to the school entrance. "Tell me about Miss Stanton," Joel said, really wanting to know.

"There's not much to tell." She tugged her shirt hem much the same way Bradley had earlier.

Joel bit back a smile. "Reàlly?" He leaned closer.

She looked everywhere but at him. "Really."

He had a hard time believing that. Her chin lifted and she squinted her eyes at a yard scuffle erupting near the jungle gym. Another teacher blazed in, looking intent to deal with it.

Joel stepped off the path to a patch of sparse lawn which reminded him of Bradley's thinning hair. He kicked a dirt clod. Dust layered the toe of his boot. "What kind of cancer does Bradley have?" Joel cringed inwardly, wishing he'd eased in instead of crashing into the subject.

Amber stopped and stared somberly at the scattered dirt. "Leukemia." Emotion thickened her voice. "Without a successful bone marrow transplant, he'll be––" she paused, swallowing "––gone by the end of the school year. I know God can step in and intervene either way. Regardless of whether his time is long or short, I intend to make it matter." She lifted her face to meet his. "So, thank you very much for coming here today."

Joel's respect for her went up a notch. It took a unique person to teach children with special needs. Then to champion the task of making life matter to a dying child—he admired her big-time.

She shifted her stance as Bradley emerged from the brick school. Joel clenched his jaw. *No need to cry in front of the kid, right?* Today was supposed to be his dream come true. Joel was determined to go all out to accomplish that. Fact was, Bradley had already bunkered down into Joel's heart. "Kid's cute."

"He knows it, too." Pleasant laughter trailed her words.

Bradley hobbled up, darting his gaze from one to the other, making google eyes. Joel tugged off Bradley's glasses, handing them to Amber. He swooped him up on his shoulders and galloped around more gently than he would if he were toting a well child. Bradley squealed with laughter.

Joel set him down and adopted a conspiratorial whisper. "Wanna hear my brilliant idea?"

Bradley leaned in, mimicking the whisper. "Yes."

"How about we make you an honorary PJ for the day?"

Bradley's shouts pierced the air then he ran off to tell his friends.

Over the next two hours, Joel felt anchored to Miss Stanton like a tether strap. He could mill around. Should even. Had no desire to. Completely fascinated with this small-town teacher, he soaked up her presence like drought-cracked earth after rain.

Too bad she lived in this tree-infested town. He'd like to get to know her better. Besides, in his line of work, long-term was tough. Not only that, her persona blared *maternal!*

The crackle of an ailing sound monitor preceded the high-pitched *screech* of toe-curling feedback. Joel shifted toward the announcer.

"I'm Mr. McCauley, the principal of this school. Though it's daytime, students wanted to welcome our military visitors with a fireworks display and a special program, followed by our national anthem to be sung by one of our students." His gaze sparkled with pride as it roved over the crowd of servicemen.

He swept his hand in an arc. "Gentlemen, we welcome you."

Bottle rockets, lit by students with the assistance of teachers, streaked into blue sky. Screaming whistles zinged through the air, leaving spirals of twirling white smoke in their wakes. Cardboard cones on a concrete pad shot multicolor fire streams in regal hues.

Joel pivoted to observe Miss Stanton watching students interact with his teammates. The kindness in her face captivated him. That must be the appeal, he figured as she regarded each child with a tender smile. He shouldn't stare. His good manners whispered, *look away,* and he would in a second…or two.

Hairs on the back of Amber's neck stood at attention. She tilted her face upward. The intensity of the soldier's gaze siphoned breath from her lungs. The sparks in his eyes were more electrifying than the fireworks.

Fireworks. She summoned strength to rip her eyes from the man and return them to the sky. Three muffled pops birthed sparkling red, white and blue alternating starbursts that sprinkled themselves across the sky before raining dozens of miniature plastic parachutes toward earth.

Children scrambled to grab them. As Joel turned to watch them, an eye-sized tattoo peeked at her from the back of his neck, just below the horizontal buzz of inky black hair. Her heart warmed at the sight of the Christian fish symbol with the Greek letters IXOYE in the middle of it.

But if he was a Christian, why would he harbor unforgiveness against someone, especially a blood relative?

Amber determined to pray for this soldier. If he was as stubborn as he looked, it would take someone bigger than her to convince him that reconciling was best. She knew firsthand what postponing forgiveness could do. She didn't want this softhearted soldier to fall prey to bitterness. When he'd smiled, she'd been shocked just how much his cheeky grin resembled his uncle's. Dean had mentioned Joel fondly in prayer requests at church.

She felt bad for assuming Joel was Dean's son. She guessed now was not the time to tell Joel that Dean had been the one to stuff her pockets with gobs of licorice last Sunday. "For those special students," he'd said. But she didn't have to deal with the soldier on a sugar high the way she did her class and was glad to have someone else to give the red twists to.

When he rocked back on his heels, Amber shunted her stare back to the display. What was wrong with her today? She hadn't even realized she'd been gawking until he'd turned and nearly caught her. She had no business scolding Bradley when she couldn't keep her own manners in check.

Still, she couldn't help wondering about this man who'd mentioned his mother in past tense with a twinge of sadness in his eyes.

And what had he meant by saying that God didn't have children in his future?

She couldn't fathom a person feeling that way. She couldn't remember a time when she didn't look forward to being a mother more than anything. But a California quake had shaken her life, leaving that dream in ruins.

Had it not happened, though, she might not have considered adopting a child. She could do that without a man and spare herself from heartbreak.

A concussive thump broke into her thoughts and ear-piercing whistles accompanied by dozens of gold and silver shooting stars that completed the show caught her attention.

When frenzied cheers and clapping subsided, a cocoa-skinned girl with dark, curly tresses whom Amber had seen around school stepped boldly to the microphone.

Palms to hearts and hats in hand, servicemen and parents stood to honor three students as they marched respectfully across the lawn with homemade flags bearing the words, Freedom, Liberty, and Just Us Four All, in glittery paint.

A laugh flew from Amber's throat.

Joel, hands pocketed, leaned over and bumped her shoulder with his. "The children mean well." Baritone laughter rumbled from his chest.

From an open side door, fifty students emerged, each waving a small American flag. T-shirts choreographed in order—one red, then white, the next blue, and so on all the way to the end. Well, almost to the end. Amber giggled. Two children must have gotten out of order, disrupting the color sequence.

Her heart melted as Joel and his rough-and-tumble cohorts' expressions turned tender as they watched two students run back to help a lagging third with Down syndrome catch up. So the sequence went red, white, blue, red, white, blue, darting red, tugging blue…toddling white.

In a soulful alto, the little girl sang, and every voice became her chorus. On her ending note, the principal stepped to the podium and adjusted the microphone back to his level. He patted the little girl's back as she stepped into the lawn of applause amid a standing ovation.

Just then, a dozen different beepers went off like cicadas all over the school yard. Silence dropped like a bomb.

A platoon of quiet murmurs and confused glances rippled as students, parents and teachers studied the serviceman closest to them. Palpable tension swarmed the air as each uniformed man pulled beepers from various places and peered at numbers.

Concern floated across faces one by one as numbers and codes registered, before they quickly recovered, controlling facial reactions. She doubted anyone else noticed. She probably wouldn't have, either, had she not known sign language which attuned her to lipreading and nonverbal communication.

The military personnel met each other's eyes, passing invisible signals like some sort of ominous code. Dread slithered up Amber's spine. Thoughts spun like the twin chopper blades. Reason scrambled like the spotted men.

This many beepers. Not one silent. Every branch of the military. Every available soldier. All Special Forces. *This is no coincidence.* Fear entrenched itself in her chest and burrowed deep. Something major. Something global. Something terrible had just happened in the world.

What? Her mind screamed.

What?

Chapter Three

"Yo, Montgomery!"

Amber stepped aside as a man in desert camouflage sprinted over with a cell phone in hand. "CO Petrowski's callin' you back on this phone in twenty."

A flurry of activity erupted as military personnel packed up display items and loaded gear into the choppers, which roared to life. Their blades swooshed her hair like monstrous fans, and ended conversation. Despite that, Amber picked up on a few words passed between Joel and the other officer. *Unprecedented magnitude. Tragic destruction. Thousands trapped.*

Something about a large rescue, relief and recovery operation, and their team being on standby for deployment.

"Let's be ready to roll just in case." Joel bent as Bradley neared—to hear over the *thwumping* helicopters, she supposed. Clay-colored dust clouds turned the air into a sandstorm.

Bradley looked like a poster child for despair. "Am I ever gonna see you again?"

Amber wanted to ask the same thing.

"I sure hope so, lil' buddy." Joel circled Bradley's waist with one arm.

"I sure hope so, too." Bradley's chin quivered. Amber drew closer, hand to Bradley's back.

"You promised I could be a hairy PJ for the day." Bradley fingered an emblem on Joel's uniform.

Honorary, Amber corrected mentally.

Joel tilted his face and coughed into his hand and pulled Bradley closer. Amber wasn't fooled. Moisture sheened Joel's eyes before he'd blinked it away.

Hands sidling Joel's face, Bradley leaned nose to nose. "You promised, and PJs don't break promises, right? That means you'll be back. You only rescue people. No one really ever shoots at you, right?"

Joel's Adam's apple bobbed as he regarded Bradley. "Let's make a pact. You promise to fight this cancer as hard as you can and hang on till I get back, and I promise to be the best rescuer and bullet-dodger in the world. Deal?"

Bradley's smile reached his eyes. "Deal."

Chills danced up Amber's scalp as Bradley transformed before her. *Hope.* She hadn't seen it on his face since his diagnosis. Bradley hugged Joel hard. Joel held Bradley tighter. He pulled a maroon beret from his side pack and placed it on Bradley's head. After swiping tears at the gesture, Bradley made Joel pinkie-shake on their special deal.

At the last bell, a horn sounded in the parking lot.

Amber brushed Bradley's arm. "Your ride is waiting, tater."

A frown beset by a flash of irritation drew Joel's face tight as he glared at the car, a dilapidated source of incessant honking which Amber deemed Bradley's ride.

Bradley stole one last hug, then shuffled off like a slug in the slow lane. Joel watched him, looking coiled and ready to pounce should Bradley stumble.

The car door swung open and a barrage of female screeching tumbled out. Compassion settled on Joel's face.

"What makes his gait unsteady?" Joel asked.

"His illness," Amber replied.

He eyed the car and its driver with what she interpreted as disdain as it jolted forward. It sped from the lot, leaving twin tire trails and poufs of silvery-white dust. "Car muffler's obviously MIA. That his mom?"

"No. Bradley's birth mother abandoned him."

Joel twisted to peer at her. Had his skin blanched a shade lighter with her words?

He flicked a glance down the road. "Who picked him up just then?"

"His foster mom."

"That the best they can do for him?"

"There is a court hearing scheduled to secure a better arrangement for Bradley." She glossed over the fact that the woman was one violation away from losing her foster license and custody of Bradley. Her answer must not have pacified Joel.

With pinpoint accuracy and acutely unnerving silence, Joel stared into her eyes like a sniper to a scope.

Amber brushed hair behind her ear. "We suspect she's neglectful on many levels."

His brows crinkled. "He's still with her, why?"

"Because we need concrete proof, and she's the person his mother left him with."

"Why doesn't she let someone adopt him? He's an adorable little kid. Though I suppose with his illness, most families wouldn't want to take him."

I would. "Adoption requires consent from his biological mother. After a two-month quest, we located her, hoping his diagnosis might spur her to want time with him."

"Did it?"

"No. She signed over rights, saying she couldn't deal with a healthy kid, much less a sick one. His caseworker and attorney subpoenaed paperwork to determine where things stand legally with the foster mother, and whether he needs to be a ward of the state."

Joel peered at his watch, then to the choppers.

"Do you need to go?" She wondered what the page had been about. Had to be something big, but she didn't want to put him on the spot if it were something top secret.

"Not yet. The page earlier set us on standby alert. We're packing up just in case we get deployed. We're a quick reaction force, so I like to be ready." He dipped his head toward her collar. "I forgot to give his glasses back."

She looked down, and tugged them from her pocket. "That's okay. It'll give me an excuse to run them by his house."

Joel lifted a boot to the school yard slide. "You need an excuse?"

"His foster mother can be…volatile."

He stared at the glasses in Amber's hand. "No wonder he wished for a family. How can they allow a questionable individual to be a foster parent?"

"I gather she put up a good front at first. Lately, not so good."

"Poor guy's got a lot on his plate." Joel lifted hands to soldiers gathering tiny flags the children had left them. He caught one they tossed. "You said *we*. Are you involved in the process as his teacher?"

She nodded, about to clarify she had applied for a foster care license to take Bradley in. Something stopped her. "I spearheaded the search for his mother—"

Joel's reaction silenced her. He first looked slapped, then detached as he faced the swings. His head dropped forward toward the ground and he swallowed. His expression like a flint, he set his face skyward, as if searching for something. As if suddenly remembering Amber, he swiveled toward her and their eyes locked.

Her breath hitched at the bold, compelling intensity. Amber couldn't tell his thoughts. He didn't speak, just stared. She stared back, wanting badly to know what in the world was happening. Not just here between them, but globally. A shrill jingle made him blink.

She flinched, the moment lost.

He flipped the cell open. "Yes, Commander... I am aware, sir... We anticipated that and are only ten from liftoff... You're welcome... I know, sir. I'm praying, too."

Joel closed the phone, dropped it in his front pocket. "Can they spare you a minute?" He darted a glance at the school.

"For a few minutes." Amber followed. "Can you tell me what's happened? We're all understandably frightened."

"It's all over the news. An earthquake hit Asia, causing floods in the tsunami zone."

"Earthquake?" Amber blurted.

"Thousands of South Indians are in dire need along the coastline. My team will be part of the humanitarian mission."

Amber deflated, glad World War III hadn't started. Then guilt assailed her. The tragedy might not have struck her world, but it had struck someone's. Lots of someones. "How horrible." She held Joel's empathetic expression.

He nodded. "Listen, I intended to make things real

special for Bradley, but literally the ocean came up. Will he understand?" Uncertainty flickered behind the calm in his eyes.

Was he kidding? "Oh, Joel. You have no idea the impact of what you've done here today, do you? All these soldiers, those helicopters, your jump…unbelievable. Bradley has never experienced anything so profoundly amazing." *Neither have I. The world needs more men like this one, Lord.*

The glimmer resurfaced in his eyes. Not tears really, just tangible emotion. "That's good. I hate to cut this convo short, but I should help pick up." He moved toward soldiers who passed by, loading supplies. They waved him back, so he retrained his gaze on her. She guessed this was goodbye.

"I feel exceedingly blessed to have met you, Special Soldier Montgomery." She stretched her hand for a departing shake.

He didn't budge except to blink down at her palm before casting a thoughtful expression at her. He scratched a finger over his temple where tanned skin melted into an onyx-shadowed buzz cut. "Can I, uh— can I get your contact info?"

Her heart thudded warmth onto her face. "Um… Okay, sure."

"You know, for updates on Bradley. And stuff."

Stuff? What constituted stuff? "Of course." She patted her pockets for something to write with and on.

So did he, and came up with a blue splotched paper.

"That's Bradley's letter," she said.

He eyed her head and grinned. "And this—" he tugged the blue pen from behind her ear "—is the culprit."

They shared a laugh as she wrote down her contact information. Fending off a snicker, she slipped the pen between the paper folds while he peered past her.

Amber handed him the bulky letter. "I know you need to go."

"In a minute."

She thought he'd find the dreaded pen right then but he tucked the paper in his chest pocket and reached out his hand.

When she put hers there, he sandwiched it between his. He stared at her with sincere intensity. "It was truly an honor to meet you, too, Special Teacher Stanton. I won't soon forget you." Warmth emanated from his fingers and spread up her arms.

Soon forget? That meant he'd eventually forget, right? A weird panic seized her that she may never see him again. Her heart and mind raced. How could she make him know how much this meant to Bradley? Did Joel know what a rare and precious stone he was in this rocky world?

Aware the children had gone, Amber slipped her hand from his then reached up as far as she could without making frontal contact, and hugged him.

Bulky arms wound around her, pulling her close, reciprocating. My, she hadn't meant to get this close.

She marveled at how he could be strong and tender at the same time as he held her against a wall of security and warmth.

The guy was built like a tank. Thankfully he smelled of crisp air and soap instead of mortar and metal. She pulled back, instantly missing the comforting thud of his heart.

His eyes twinkled. "Wow. What was that for?"

"For giving him something to live for. A reason to hope. The will to fight." *For being one very special and sensitive human being that I suspect you are but try to hide.*

"Bradley's a real fighter. Hey, I should jet before they take off without me. Although, I could handle this all day." He grinned as if having a private joke with himself that she wasn't privy to.

"I understand." Even though she didn't understand what he could handle all day. The hug, or being with Bradley? She stepped aside so he could pass. His lip twitched as if to laugh. Her action took him by surprise, for sure. She turned to watch him board.

Every man hung out the chopper doors, gawking. Heat scorched her cheeks. Joel peered back over his shoulder, disabling her motor function with a bold wink and a disarming smile that made her pulse trip.

She quickly spun away, imagining he'd be relentlessly teased. Great. They probably didn't know her hug had only been out of thankfulness and nothing more.

Neither did her heart for that matter, for it beat over a hundred times per minute.

The choppers lifted off. Hurricane-like winds tousled leaves and bent limbs. Multicolored flowers and waxy green grass swayed as if a large invisible hand brushed back and forth across their tips.

Dust swirled in a cyclone, stinging Amber's skin. She shut her eyes and shielded her face. Once it died down, she waved her arm to clear air in front of her and caught sight of blue. She lowered her hand to study it, momentarily blipping on what caused it. Then she realized.

Ink had transferred to her fingers and palm from the paper Joel had handed her. She scrubbed. The impression only smeared, leaving imprints everywhere she touched.

"Stupid pen." She raked her hand along her jeans. It wouldn't erase. She laughed.

The pen was the soldier's problem now.

She peered around her.

Only charred cardboard remnants, firework soot and debris remained in the school yard.

On her trek to the entrance, Amber bent to retrieve a glass jar the bottle rockets shot from. A few more steps, and she picked up a flag from a stone bench near the garden. As she turned, something white caught her eye. Foreboding stopped her short but then the object in the middle of the fountain compelled her feet forward.

One of the toy parachutes thrust through the air with fireworks must have landed here. A bamboo plant clutched its tattered chute. Rocks wedged the plastic man. Water rolled over the side like a miniature flood, engulfing the toy.

Frozen, she studied the odd little scene.

Water. The Asian plant. A parachutist.

The flood. South India. Joel.

Amber snatched the little man from the water, hoping no one watched. It might be plastic, but she couldn't leave it trapped underwater by the fountain's rolling wave. She dried it on her jeans, folded up the parachute and tucked it inside her jacket.

Close to her heart.

From the Chinook, Joel watched the school until it became a tiny red dot in the distance.

"That was way cool," Manny said above the whipping wind.

"Yeah. I'll never forget those kids' faces when we landed. How long you figure that little guy's got?" Nolan's smile faded as he shifted to face Joel.

"His teacher says he won't make it to the end of the school year without a bone marrow transplant." Joel used the tip of his boot to push his newly folded parachute pack against the wall.

"He really bonded with you, man." Manny lifted his voice above the roar. "You ought to make it a point to get back there and see him."

You promised. Joel leaned sideways, resting on an elbow. "Depends on how long we're needed in Asia. I really liked him."

"And his teacher?" Nolan grinned and elbowed Chance. They both stared at Joel. "Because she sure seemed to like you."

Snickers erupted among Joel's Special Forces buddies.

Joel just shook his head.

"You get her number, Montgomery?" Manny asked.

"That's for me to know, Peña." Joel leaned his head back, intent on playing possum.

"Sounds like a challenge," Chance announced.

Next thing Joel knew, scuffling erupted. He vaulted to his feet but Nolan tackled him. SEAL Silas and PJ Chance restrained his arms.

The skirmish landed them all on the floor and garnered interesting looks from the new female pilot. Manny sat on his torso, and Nolan lunged for Joel's chest pocket.

Muscles tensed, Joel strained and cycled his legs, making contact with flesh. Someone groaned. Good, he got one. Others pretzeled his legs with grips of titanium. Crinkling sounded as Silas jerked the letter from his pocket. Something blue flew out when Silas flipped it open.

That pen. He knew she'd slipped it in there back at the school. He'd pretended not to notice.

"Don't rip that note or I'll—" Freed, Joel shot to his feet, lunging for the paper.

Arms grabbed him from everywhere, netting him in.

With a victorious shout and a fist shot to the air, Silas tossed Nolan the letter.

Joel took a deep breath, then laughed during exhale because they all looked as sweaty and disheveled as he felt. At least he'd put up a good fight. They needed to break a fun sweat now and then.

Nolan opened the blue polka-dot-splotched battle prize and flicked his forefinger at Amber's handwriting. "Told you, Peña."

Manny took the paper, looked, then handed it to Joel.

Joel picked up the pen and tucked it in his pocket with the letter before securing a comfortable seat against the wall.

Manny slumped beside him. "It figures. You got numbers, and I got nothin'."

Jack Chapman's dimples popped up, bracketing a teasing smirk. "Speaking of figures, nice from what I could tell with all those baggy clothes on. Joel could give us the stats since he got closer at her than any of us."

The other guys laughed good-naturedly.

Joel pinned them to the wall with a look, then closed his eyes and folded his arms across his chest, feigning sleep.

He'd never hear the end of it. Never.

The talk of women didn't usually bother him this

bad, even when some of the guys got raunchy. He'd simply walk away when the talk moved beyond PG-13. The thought of their minds tainting Amber's innocence over a hug made him feel defensive.

Not liking his shift in loyalty, Joel rubbed his chest, right where the attraction for Amber had stemmed from. He rubbed but it wouldn't go away. In fact, the more he thought of her, the greater it got. So he needed to stop thinking of her.

Shifting uncomfortably, he rested his other hand on his stomach, where concern had evolved into gut-deep compassion. It had been harder to leave Bradley than he'd anticipated. Still, he associated Bradley with Refuge. He wouldn't, couldn't go back there. *You promised.*

To keep his promise meant facing Refuge and his attraction to the teacher. Maybe he could just write Bradley. That would be good enough. Wouldn't it?

A distant echo of words swarmed his mind.

You promised. They grew loud to the point he couldn't hear anything else.

And you never break a promise, right? Whose voice whispered? Bradley? Or himself as a child pleading with an invisible mother, then for God to make her want to come home? He missed her so much it hurt beyond words. Then. Now.

Come back. You promised.

But she couldn't. Not now. Not ever. Death took her before she could keep her promise. He didn't want any child to go through that kind of loss. If he took the easy way out and avoided Refuge, Bradley was destined for disappointment.

Joel remembered how it felt to have childhood dreams ripped from his grasp like a favorite toy from the arms of a child in clutching need of its comfort. Every dream except one.

I want to be a PJ. Joel smiled at both the irony and the miracle. Joel's one realized dream packed potential to fertilize a little boy's last wish into fruition. He refused to let past hurts ruin the redemption of that child's hope.

He opened his eyes, imploring his men to hold him to the creed of courage and accountability that bonded them as a team. "I promised the kid I'd come back."

At his words, most of the men nodded. They settled in for the long flight, except Manny, who tugged something from his belt clip. "Ever seen one of these, Montgomery?"

Joel leaned forward and palmed the dark-colored handheld with a BlackBerry logo. "Not this brand. Thing looks pretty cool." He started to hand it back to Manny.

Manny pushed it back to Joel with a grin. "Try it out. Since you have her e-mail address and all."

Joel eyed the tiny keyboard and scratched his stubbled jaw. "Maybe I will. You know, to keep up with what's going on with Bradley."

After laughing, Manny leaned forward and showed

him how to make international calls and send e-mail. "Use it anytime you want. Even once we're there."

"This'll work all the way from India?"

"As long as we're in a secure location and keep the battery charged."

"It'll work right now?" Joel peered around the helicopter, and the sky that carried it. "Up here?"

"When those bars light up, that means you have a valid signal."

At least he and Amber could forge a friendship. Bradley's plight had already bonded them. He felt it, and suspected by her spontaneous hug that she had, too.

After intense concentration, Joel typed an e-mail to her. He gathered the nerve to hit the send command before constructing a second e-mail to the students.

Joel handed the gadget back to Manny, suddenly feeling unsure about this. Was there any way to retrieve those messages?

Manny tucked it back in his hip clip. "Don't look so scared, Montgomery."

Joel raked a hand around the back of his neck. "I'm not scared, Peña. It's just been a long time since I've…"

Just what was this? Joel clasped his hands on his knees. How could he define something he didn't know what to call?

Two bushy black eyebrows rose. "Since you *what?*"

"Pursued an interest," Joel said with honesty that

he knew would leave him an open target for relentless razzing.

"As I said, feel free to use it whenever the urge strikes you." Manny rested his head back, shutting his eyes.

Joel stretched his feet out before reclining his head back, as well. "Thanks, Peña. It will come in handy."

One of Manny's eyelids slid open. "For keeping up with what's going on with Bradley."

"Right." Joel slid his boot across the floor to kick his snickering friend into silence.

He'd never hear the end of it.

And maybe, for once, he didn't want to.

Chapter Four

Amber stepped into her apartment after bicycling from the grocery store Friday evening. Shoulders shrugged, her backpack clunked to the floor. Pouch unzipped, she tugged out two bulging sacks, evicting their contents on the countertop. At the rattle of plastic and clatter of cans, her cat bounded around the corner and hopped on the counter.

"Off there, Psych." She swept him to the edge with the back of her hand. His paws screeched until his giant fuzz ball of a body lost the battle with gravity. Amber transferred everything to the fridge except the Cornish hen for dinner. She'd save leftovers for Bradley to eat on Sunday.

She put nonperishables in her school satchel, since Bradley's foster mother couldn't seem to remember to pack him a lunch lately.

Amber preheated the oven before surfing Illinois

Foster Care online. While pages printed, she opened her e-mail.

Several new messages.

She replied to her dad's, noticing that folder held more saved messages than any other. She thought he'd stop once she moved here, but he still e-mailed daily. "He's trying, I'll give him that."

Amber groaned at the next message. "I hate those." She deleted the forward-this-or-have-bad-luck message from someone on her teachers' loop.

She clicked on the final message and nearly sent it there, too—then froze. Wait.

Sender: J.M.M. Subject line: Just Checking In.

Sender: J.M.M.... J.M.M.? Could it be *him*, and so soon? She dared to hope so. Her eyes scrolled to the bottom of the message.

Kind regards, Joel M. Montgomery, USAF

"Yes!" Unable to stifle a burst of eagerness, she glanced out the window. No neighbors watched. All clear, she allowed herself a few undignified jumps. The cat bobbed his head in sync with her motion, looking tense and prepared to flee.

"Psych! We have a cyber link to Mr. Gorgeous." She read the first line of text. "No-oo." Her forehead banged the pine desktop above the rollout keyboard shelf.

Her heart plunged with every word.

I hope this finds you all in good health and obeying your teachers. Please remember the people of India in your prayers. Thanks for having us at your school. The production was phenomenal. Each of my men felt honored and esteemed. Kind regards, Joel M. Montgomery, USAF.

"Ugh!" He didn't write her—he'd e-mailed her students. Amber chastised herself for her strong reaction.

She'd had no business hoping.

"False alarm, Psych. Story of my life." Had she imagined the fizz between them? In all her dreamy Cinderellaness, probably. "It's better that way anyhow, Psych. Bart shattered my glass slipper at the altar last year."

The cat padded over and raked against her ankle.

She scratched along Psych's ribs, then dusted orange-yellow hair off her hand. "What do you think, buddy? Is Joel just a player who flirts with all the gals?"

Amber stiffened against disappointment, and clicked through the remaining messages.

Another caught her eye. Her pulse revved at the name.

Sender: J.M.M. Subject line: Reporting For Duty, Ma'am.

She embraced the words with caution this time.

Hey, teach. Soldier Joel here. Making sure I got the right in-box. Reply if this is you.

Ignore if you're not you. Ha-Ha. How's our little playground prince? I'm sending a second e-mail shortly for you to share with your class. Let me know if you get these. Okay, signing off to compose the other message. Cordially, JMM—USAF

She scrolled to the first message, noting the time stamp. Sure enough. The message settings inverted the order received. She'd have Bradley fix it when he came over Sunday after church. Little tech whiz could do anything with a computer. She knew just enough to pose a danger to her sanity and her hard drive.

Amber arched a brow at her cat. "Are you the culprit who messed with my settings? I saw you enthroned on my keyboard terrorizing a moth."

Psychoticat meowed and curved his back under her fingers as she scratched. Amber suppressed the urge to sneeze. She had a feeling Psych's hair caused the allergies. But she couldn't bear to give him up since he'd been abandoned as a kitten.

Amber smiled in anticipation of the children's glee when she shared Joel's e-mail with them Monday. She hit Reply, then typed:

Last time I checked, I was me. Are you still you? Oven beep summons a hen basted in honey and oranges—a meal fit for a playground prince whose kingdom is Cloud 9 thanks to

G.I. Joel and his fearless friends. Will forward your other message to my students. Must go. Oven dirty. Particles burning and stinky. Fire alarm makes Psychoticat more neurotic than usual. Warmly, Amber M. Stanton

Twelve hours and two time zones later put Joel's team in Paris, France, the halfway mark to Mumbai where they would catch another flight to the Indian coastline near Cochin.

Manny plopped in one of the airport's lounge seats beside Joel and elbowed him.

Joel looked over. Manny shoved the BlackBerry back in Joel's hand. "Use it again. You know you want to."

"I think I'll wait until she e-mails me back. Thanks."

A grin overtook the squat and stout PJ's brown face. "Maybe she did."

Joel narrowed his gaze, looked at Manny then the device. "Gimme that Blueberry."

"BlackBerry. Don't worry. I didn't read it." Manny stretched the handheld out again. Joel reached for it.

Manny eased it back. "Unless you want me to…"

"Hey—" Joel stood, prepared to wrestle the thing from him if need be. Manny jerked it back a few more times as Joel grasped at it. Finally, Manny handed it over.

Joel took the teasing and the BlackBerry without preamble. He pulled up her message, trying not to show outwardly how much it meant to him that she'd responded.

"What did she say?" Manny scooted over and leaned in, straining to read the small text in the window.

Joel tilted the screen at an angle so his friend could see.

Manny nodded and tapped Joel's forearm with the stylus. "We're in Paris. You ought to go buy her something. That kid, too. Chicks like romance and flowers and stuff. Especially rare, exotic gifts from other countries."

Chapman tipped his cowboy hat. "Get her a beaded Indian sari."

PJ Vince Reardon smirked. "Nah. Save some cash. Bring her back a parasite instead. They're exotic."

Joel shook his head. "I'll hit the shops on the way back to the States since we're on standby for the next flight. We need to stick together. I don't want to get stuck in a checkout line."

Manny yawned. "You did good yesterday, Montgomery. I'm proud of you." He sprawled in a seat at the stainless steel aesthetic DeGaulle Airport. Other teams went by military craft, but since they'd deployed from Illinois, the government flew them domestic.

"It was harder than I'd anticipated. But it helped that I had the distraction of Bradley." A pretty teacher, too. "Only at one point did I feel myself slipping." He hoped it wouldn't hit him after the fact. He didn't need to be a train wreck heading into South Asia.

Manny leaned forward, clasping his hands in listen mode. "Yeah, when was that?"

"In the playground. You know I went to that school for a few years when I was a kid, right?"

Manny shook his head. "Ah, man. No, I didn't."

"Yeah, my mom—she used to take me there and swing me. That was the last thing we ever did together." Joel swallowed and cast a hard stare at the BlackBerry. He thought of Amber's determined quest to find Bradley's mom.

How many times had he prayed as a child for someone who wouldn't give up until they found his mother? How many nights had he cried himself to sleep missing her? Wishing he could at least have an answer? He'd prayed and prayed for God to bring her home but the only thing that came was news there had been a car accident. His mother had died but longing lived on for someone to tell his deepest fears and craziest dreams to. Someone to be real with.

Someone like Amber.

"Bradley's blessed to have her. She's good for him." Joel cleared his throat to rid himself of the emotion. He wouldn't let it crack him again. He'd lived broken as a child because he had no choice. As a man, he had a choice. He would avoid anything with potential to breach the dam walling his past from his present.

That included Refuge, and everything in it.

Joel coughed, but the elastic band wouldn't ease from his chest. He hadn't felt like this in fifteen years, and he hoped for another fifteen at least before he had to feel anything like it again. The pressure made it hard to breathe.

Manny eyed him with unwavering intent. "I think it'll be good for you to keep that promise. *She* could be good for you. You've never dealt with that junk with your mom and your uncle, dude. And you need to."

"I'll keep my promise to Bradley, Peña." *Don't expect more.*

"I know you will. And then some." Manny leaned back.

Joel tapped the keyboard to compose a message.

After sending it, Joel stared at the blank screen while Manny's mantra rang in the ears of his soul. *I know you will. And then some.* These guys held each other to the same stellar code of standards. Above and beyond, no matter what. On missions, in personal lives. When everyone looked, or no one.

Integrity. The creed didn't stop when the missions did.

They didn't make promises without intent to bulldoze mountains if that's what it took to keep them. Even Everest with a Barbie Jeep if that's what it required to maintain the pristine field of their word, and they'd all taken the creed together.

So Others Might Live.

He hoped he wasn't walking into a God trap. Surely He wouldn't expect Joel to confront the hurts of his past and the person responsible for them before he felt ready. Right?

Joel pressed thumbs to his temple, steeling himself against the insurgence of silence which advanced heavily on his mind. He listened for the question which carried a cavernous echo for an answer.

Truth was, he didn't know if he had courage enough to face it. His biggest fear had always been backing down from something.

Help me. I don't want to let him down, or You.

He'd keep his promise to Bradley. No matter what. *No matter what.*

A vague sensation wrapped around him that this promise would be severely tested. His job consisted of life-or-death danger. He didn't want to die before he fulfilled his promise to that fragile child who'd undoubtedly been placed in his path for a reason.

Joel settled in his seat and closed his eyes.

Don't let me run, no matter what comes.

Chapter Five

Saturday morning, Amber approached her computer with a glass of high-pulp orange juice, a wheat bagel and a tote brimming with foster care information. She sat in the cushy blue chair, pulling up her in-box. Two new messages. She felt doubly blessed. One from her dad. One from Joel. Proving to herself she could have self-control, she opened her dad's first.

Then opened Joel's, a smile going through her.

Greetings from Paris. We're halfway to our destination. Not sure how much opportunity I'll have to e-mail once we arrive but don't think I forgot about Bradley. Or my promise. Or you. I'm not sure when I'll be able to get away. I'll keep in touch as able. Tell Psychokitty to watch his back. I'm armed and dangerous. Ever been to France? Food's great. Really made my day to hear back from you. This e-mail stuff is amazing. Talk to you soon. JMM—USAF.

"Better watch out, Psych. He's armed and danger-ous." Her comment drew a blank stare from the cat. "More like charmed and dangerous." Amber sighed at her computer screen.

The cat scrambled across the kitchen, paw-skiing the smooth tile surface before skidding to a halt in front of the food dish. He looked from the bowl to Amber and flicked his tail.

"I know. I forgot to buy tuna yesterday. You'll have to settle for chicken." She got up and grabbed a can of soft cat food from the pantry. Fingernails lifting the tab, she peeled off the aluminum top expecting Psych to rush over and rub her ankle as usual. He did that when any can was opened, even green beans.

This time he only stared, and flicked. She tapped chicken into the bowl, then ran her finger around the can to get remnants out.

While Amber washed her hands, the cat hunched its shoulders and sniffed. He lifted his head, hissed at her, hissed at the food, then sashayed to the laundry room.

After glaring at the moody creature's back, she typed a reply to Joel:

Paris? Did you see the Notre Dame Cathedral or the Eiffel Tower? I've always wanted to.

You're probably world traveled. I've only lived two places—California and Illinois. Never been outside the U.S. Probably never will. I know you're short on time, so I'll sign off. Thanks for everything you did for Bradley. PS: You're nobody until you've been ignored by a bipolar cat. Kindly, AMS—

Amber drummed her fingers on the desk. USAF stood for U.S. Air Force. What could she put? She phoned Celia. "He e-mailed me." Amber held the phone back from Celia's loud kudos. "Now that you've blown out my eardrums, help me brainstorm a four-letter acronym to put behind my initials."

"Give him a riddle to figure out," Celia said.

Amber had it. "Apartment on Sonnet Drive." She added AOSD to her e-mail and then sent the message. Call ended, Amber gathered her keys and the tote of foster care stuff for her mom to help with, since Lela's profession involved legal paperwork.

Past the last stoplight out of town and nearing the guard towers flanking the government road leading to the nonmapped Eagle Point Military Base which Refuge secretly housed, Amber's cell rang. Celia's number popped up.

"Heard from him yet?"

Amber turned on the gravel road that would take her the half hour to her parents' place. "I doubt it. It's been what, a half hour?"

Celia clicked her tongue. "You mean you don't know if he e-mailed you back yet or not? Don't you check your e-mail?"

A deer darted across the road several yards ahead. Amber slowed. "Not while I'm in the car, and certainly not fifty times a day." Not that she'd admit.

"If I had someone that cute in possession of my e-mail address, I'd chain myself to the computer. You know there are cell phones with e-mail plans, right? You better tell me when he e-mails you again."

"*If* he e-mails me again."

"*When.*" Motorized gurgling. Then brutal clinking sounded, such as a spoon dying in the sink disposal. Silence. "And I want some serious details. In fact, forward the e-mails to me." More sink drain gurgling.

Amber laughed. "Not on your life." She approached a curve, scanned the tree-lined road for critters, then accelerated.

"He'll keep in touch."

"I don't know about that, but I hope he at least stays in touch with Bradley."

"When you get legal guardianship, that'll be convenient. How's that coming along?" Scraping sounds. Liquid sloshing.

"Mom's judge friend says there's not enough proof to get Bradley out of there."

Celia grumbled. "Her sending him to school every day with an empty lunch box isn't proof? Come on. She knows this school is bring-your-lunch-only while they're remodeling the kitchen. Even if we were serving hot lunches, I doubt she'd send him with money." Faucet thump. Water off.

"I know. It takes time. These are serious accusations. We have to keep documenting. In the meantime, pray for his well-being and safety. I hate the thought of him not getting decent meals. Also, Bradley's doctor pulled me aside at the market. He confided he has reason to suspect Foster Lady's not giving Bradley his meds. If he proves it, he can have her court-ordered to administer them."

The sound of liquid spraying in spurts. "That's horrible. He needs to gain weight and have both proper nutrition and the treatments in order to stay eligible for the transplant, right?"

"Right."

"Where is he in that process?"

"Moving up. Closer to finding a donor."

"I'd abduct him if I were you."

Amber laughed, knowing Celia kidded. Still, she was really glad the FBI didn't have a tap on her line.

"When Bradley's oncologist voiced his concerns, believe me, it tempted me. But I can't help him if I'm sitting in jail. He said if Bradley's levels don't rise, he'll have him admitted to be sure he stays medicated. We have to hurry up and wait. And pray."

"And pray." Water off, then on. Something metal plunked against stainless steel. A large splash.

"I better let you go before you drop the phone in

the water and electrocute yourself. Besides, I'm in a low-signal area. Cel? Hello?"

"Amb, you're cutting out. Anyway, I said if prayer doesn't work, I'll help you devise a plan to kidnap Bradley and—"

She lost the call in the deep country roads. No cell towers out here, just soybean fields and forests dense with poison ivy. She'd be able to reach Celia up ahead.

Once there, her phone rang as she went to flip it open. Amber switched it from speaker to earpiece and hit Talk. "Beat me to the draw. You better hope the FBI isn't listening in. They'll take us both to jail."

A heavy silence invaded the phone, then a huff of air and deep, masculine laughter. Amber nearly ran off the road.

"Do I want to know?" Joel asked.

"Hey! No. Sorry. I thought you were Celia."

"She's shorter than me."

Amber laughed, surprised how it pleased her to hear Joel's voice. He probably called for an update on Bradley.

"How's Bradley?"

She knew it. "He's doing great. You really made an impression. His caseworker phoned to tell me he hasn't stopped talking about you since Friday." *I haven't stopped thinking about you, either.*

Amber tapped a finger to her forehead to the beat of her CD. *Stop. Stop. Stop. Last thing you need is another heartache.*

"What about you?" Joel asked.

It took her a second to figure out the last thing she said. Her thoughts rang so loud, she sometimes couldn't remember if her mind or her mouth spoke last. "I'm fine."

"That you are."

Was he flirting? She fanned herself, hating the giddy factor. "How are you?"

"You tell me."

She refused to bite. Obviously he flirted with all girls or he wouldn't be so suave at it. A sick feeling roiled inside. Leave it to her to be attracted to a womanizer. Yet so much of what she'd glimpsed of his character spoke of the opposite. "I may lose you."

"Excuse me?"

"I'm getting into an area of low signal. Let me pull over."

"Just stay safe, Amber."

Amber. He'd called her Amber. Not Miss Stanton. "I'm not on the interstate. About the only thing that could get me out here is a raccoon."

"Out here?"

"I'm heading to my parents' fishing pond."

"Do you fish?"

"I love it."

"So do I. Don't get to as much as I'd like. I plan to retire in eight years. I hope to have more time then."

"Wow. Eight years? How old are you?"

"Thirty. That puts me in until I'm thirty-eight. I'll

have twenty years because they counted my ROTC in high school and college. My dream is to be a skydiving instructor for civilians and new recruits since I'll be old and decrepit."

"Thirty-eight is hardly decrepit."

"For a Special Forces soldier, thirty borders on geriatric. Forty's ancient. Fifty's antique. And sixty is not happening. They want the young pups in there who still feel invincible and whose knees don't creak when they sneak up on the enemy."

Amber laughed. "I hear rumors they have skydiving instructors at Eagle Point. You could come back to your old stomping ground."

Why had she blurted that mindless suggestion? "Not a chance."

A little ping of disappointment hit her with his rapid-fire response, which boldly shot down her idea with zero hesitation.

Wanting to keep things light, Amber's mind grasped for straws from her wit arsenal. "You could fish sooner than eight years, ya know."

"Is that right?"

Relief hit her that she could hear the smile in his voice again. "That's right. When you make it back to visit Bradley, you two can fish at the pond. Bradley loves it."

"Is the pond in Refuge?"

Her words had stripped all humor from his. Way to go, Stanton. Keep batting foul balls and run him right out of the park. But that's what she wanted, right?

Safe! Yeah, right. Maybe in baseball. The guy's smile was lethal alone.

"Refuge address, but out of town," she answered.

"That's good. That might work." His tone seemed thoughtful now. What an odd statement.

"You'd come with us, right?" he asked.

"Sure, if you want." Did he just ask her out? Or had he simply been polite and included her, since it happened to be her parents' place? And why did she dare even hope, after the heartache she stumbled out of last year? She wished she were more experienced with this sort of thing. According to her track record, she seemed destined for failure where relationships were concerned. "However, if you need some alone time with Bradley, I can just give you directions."

"No way. If I'm there, you're there. I'd love to see you again. Plus, I'll need a little moral support when I can get free to make it back. You know how I have that aversion to Refuge."

The hollow echo in his voice floated through her heart. His transparency caught her off guard. "I remember. So, how did you come to know about Bradley's letter?"

"I'm the PJ he mentioned who grew up there. That's why Dream Corps contacted me."

"I didn't know that. They kept the whole ordeal hidden from me beyond the note and phone call. Celia knew you guys were surprising Bradley and me, so she and the other staff put together the production to welcome you."

"It was awesome. My guys still talk about it. Celia, she's the Hispanic-looking teacher, right?"

"Yeah, the firecracker."

He laughed. "I wasn't gonna say it. She married?"

"Why, you interested?" Traitorous disappointment pinged her stomach again.

Another laugh. "No, but my buddy Manny might be."

"Celia is dead set against getting involved with men in dangerous jobs. She lost her husband in the line of duty as a cop. Her goal is to steer clear of guys packing heat, and go for ones packing calculators instead. She also wants to date a Christian."

"Then I won't encourage it. Manny is a backslider and running on the wild side right now."

If Joel was using Christian lingo, could he be a believer? She'd gotten the feeling at school that he was. Then again, so was Bart, and he still bashed her heart to pieces.

"What about you? What are your life goals, Amber?"

To have a baby. "Something that will never happen."

"Come on. Tell me. I told you mine."

"Maybe in time."

"Well, whatever you dream for, I hope it comes true."

"Thank you."

"Hey, I need sleep, and you need to escape the clutches of that rabid teacher-eating coon sneaking up behind you."

"Very funny."

His chuckle eased her tensions. "Did you look?"

She still was. "I'll never tell." Her eyes slipped away from her rearview mirror.

"Fair enough. I'll be in touch. Later, tater."

She smiled, touched that he'd remember her and Bradley's special exchange. "Later, gator."

The only thing Amber could think about as she drove the remaining miles was how pleasant Joel's voice sounded, and how Bart had never once called and e-mailed her on the same day.

It's just for Bradley, she told herself.

On her mom's patio five hours later, Amber eyed her watch. "I should go soon. Psychoticat is out of tuna and on a hunger strike. The market closes in two hours."

"Dad will be home in a few minutes. Can't you stay a bit?"

"Is he getting off early?"

"Yes." Lela's face flushed. "We're going out tonight."

Amber stared at her. "Like, on a date?"

"Yes. You should never stop dating your spouse." She tugged Amber close for a hug. "Thank you for sharing the day with me, and what that nice young man did for our little Bradley, giving him that beret and all."

"Mom, he's not *our* little Bradley. Things might not go through. If they do, it may be too l—"

Lela placed a gentle finger to Amber's lips. "It's never too late when God is in the equation. So does this soldier happen to be attractive?"

"You sound like Celia." Amber fanned herself with a stack of napkins and stood. "Yes. He's what I would consider attractive."

"Is he a Christian?" Lela motioned Amber down.

Amber sat. "His faith seems genuine."

"Are you interested?" Lela refilled Amber's tea.

Glass to her mouth, Amber let the sweet liquid linger on her tongue. No one made sun tea better than her mom. "In friendship."

"That's a good foundation." Lela smiled behind her glass.

"Don't count on it going anywhere." Amber swirled the ice in her glass. "Is this sugar?"

"Sweetener. Why just friendship if you were the only one at the school that day with whom he flirted?" Lela's eyes twinkled with wisdom and motherly mischief.

The glass in Amber's hand clunked down a smidgen too hard. "I'm going to throttle Celia."

"Oh, spare her life another day. She only told me a little. Plus, we have a Cupid conspiracy." Lela winked.

"Is nothing in my life private from you two?"

"Of course not, dear. What's the fun in that?"

Off the stool now, Amber placed her glass on the tray. "On that note, I'm out of here. Give Daddy hugs for me."

Lela stood, peering at her watch. "Why don't you

wait five minutes and he'll be home? I'm sure he'd love his hugs directly from you."

"I used to be the family peacemaker. Now it's you."

"I prefer the term moderator. Your dad regrets not being there for you all those years. If life provided second chances, his choices would be different. So would mine. We were young and kids don't come with instructions in the box."

Amber laughed.

"I regret putting you in the middle. You should have had a carefree childhood, not being a full-time ambassador working peace negotiations between the two people supposed to be taking care of you instead of arguing."

Amber shrugged. "You were like a single mom with Dad gone all the time. Which is precisely why I want my future adoptive children to have a dad with a stationary job."

She expected her mother to comment, but Lela stood silent. The kind of silent which usually meant she didn't agree with Amber, but wanted to let her figure it out on her own.

Her father pulled up. She met him ascending the porch steps.

"You leaving already?" He set his briefcase down.

"I have to get to the market before it closes. Psych's out of tuna and freaking out."

He laughed. After visiting several moments, he walked Amber to her car and opened the door for her.

He leaned in for a hug. Amber hated that she patted him awkwardly.

"Be careful. Deer are moving. Hunting weekend has them spooked," he said as she got in her car. He pushed her door closed. Then he rested his hand on the glass a moment, as though cupping her chin through the transparent barrier the way he used to when she was little before they'd drifted apart emotionally.

Halfway back to town, Amber rolled her window down.

"Deer aren't the only things wigging out, Lord. Not only am I learning how to relate to Dad, Cupid's henchmen are moving in for the kill where Joel's concerned. I don't know whether to flee or fling up a white flag. I'm glad You know what You're doing, because, though I'm not one to let feelings lead me around by a leash, I sure don't feel ready for this new season, whatever it brings."

Chapter Six

Amber stepped out of her car after returning from church. A cool breeze lifted hair from her face. Refreshing mist showered the air which smelled like fresh-cut grass.

She hadn't gotten used to the humidity here yet, so thick you could chew on it. She lifted supplies out of her trunk, enjoying the fragrance of impending rain as Celia drove up.

"What is that smell?" Celia waved a hand across her face while holding the door for Amber. She passed by the foyer with the piled-high milk crate.

Amber caught a whiff and almost gagged. "Maybe the roof is leaky."

"Tell your landlord. That smells moldy. You don't need that with your allergies."

Amber set the crate down and went to make lunch. "Yow!" She jerked her leg, half expecting to see a stinging scorpion attached to her ankle. Wait, Illinois didn't have those.

"Cat! What was that all about?" She rubbed red puncture holes with circular motions. Psych lunged, digging an arsenal of sharp claws and needle-tip fangs into her tender flesh.

"Hey! What is your problem today?" She tapped his paws and nose until he let go. The cat flipped around in an unnatural spine bend and skittered across the carpet, snagging Berber into tufts as he went. "Great. You're dying for me to lose the deposit on this apartment, aren't you? Of course, if you bite me like that again, only one of us will leave here."

"What's up with that crazy fur ball?" Celia pulled items from crates.

"He doesn't like anything except tuna-flavored cat food, and Mayberry Market is out. I put regular tuna in his bowl this morning, and you see how that went over."

"He'll eat when he's hungry enough." Celia's eyes tracked the cat to the computer. "Off topic here, but have you checked your e-mail today?"

Amber slathered mustard on rye and pretended not to hear.

"Fine, if you're not curious, I'll check. I might even e-mail him back on your behalf." Celia walked toward the computer. Amber dropped the lunch meat and sprinted ahead, scrambling for the keyboard. Psych skittered off the desk, tumbling the wireless mouse to the floor.

Celia snatched it. "Give me your password."

Amber laughed. "Over my dead body."

"Okay, I give." Celia surrendered the mouse and pointed to the monitor. "There. Who's that one from?"

"The president." Amber sat, rolling her chair closer.

"Ha-ha. Tell me who it really is."

"JMM." Amber couldn't keep from grinning.

"I figured. What does he say?" Celia draped herself over Amber's shoulder. Amber cupped hands over the screen, to aggravate her curious friend.

"I see how it is. You get e-mails from Soldier Cutie, and I get cold pastrami on rye." Celia wiggled away in her black, hip-length poncho over a classy white pantsuit, shimmying her shoulders in mock indignation.

Amber tracked her to the kitchen. "You look like a Latin penguin doing the Macarena."

"Ha-ha. Hey, you should set up an IM account and zap him an invite. I'll show you how after lunch."

"What does that do?" Amber rolled out the keyboard tray.

"You can talk back and forth in a little box in real time."

"He's busy. He might not have time."

"People make time for what's important to them. If he doesn't have time, he'll tell you. My guess is, he'll go without sleep if that means he gets to talk to you."

"I'm not sure, Celia." Amber replied to the area foster care coordinator's message, then scrolled for other important messages.

Celia aimed a butter knife at Amber from the kitchen counter. "Your broken engagement made you insecure that anyone could like you for the long haul. I know just the thing you need."

"What's that?" She printed out the e-mail list of Special Olympics coaches.

"One of my famous makeovers."

"Celia, you used to work in Vegas. I don't think I—"

"Hush, puppy. It's not like I'm going to tie you down and strap a headdress on you. You want provolone or cheddar?"

Amber snickered. "For my outfit?"

"Ha-ha. For your lunch. Cold or hot?"

"Provolone, and heat mine. Thanks."

As Celia put sandwiches together, Amber read.

Hey, teach. How are you? We made it to the hardest-hit coast. Things are pretty bad. It was great hearing your voice. What are your plans for today? Hearing it gives me a sense of normalcy. Catch any fish yesterday? Sorry to cut this short but I'm in a time crunch as we're about to land. The need is overwhelming every place we go. Pray for us as we triage. I hope Bradley knows I won't forget. JMM—USAF.

She hit Reply and typed:

I saw Bradley in church today. He says hello and thanks for the video game. Today Celia and I are preparing games for Special Olympics at the school in a few months. Psych is sulking. Federal emergency. Mayberry Market out of cat tuna. Backlash came in the form of a long scratch requiring Garfield Band-Aid. Please know you, your team and India's people are in our prayers.

Amber tapped the keyboard. What else should she say? Her gaze fell on the blue remnants across her hand. Faded some, thanks to soap and serious scrubbing, but remaining nonetheless.

If she never saw him again, he'd left an indelible mark on her by reaching out to Bradley. A deep and certain knowing hit her that Joel was a man of his word and he left deep impressions everywhere he went. Courage and determination defined him. If her instincts were on target, nothing short of death or deployment would deter him from keeping his promise.

Though her instincts had been wrong before.

She shoved away images of coming down the aisle to a groomless altar. She'd made vows that day, only not for marriage but against it. A vow that she'd never let a man hurt or humiliate her that way again. *Joel is not Bart.*

Forging ahead, she set her fingers to the keys for one last line.

PS: He knows you won't forget. AMS—AOSD.

She sent her message across the world with the plink of a button. Amber image-searched India. Once a map popped up, she brushed her hand down the screen, slowing to trace a finger along South India's triangular coastline. Chin resting on her other fist, she closed her eyes.

Please keep them safe. Grant strength to victims and humanitarian workers for the days ahead. Lead Joel and his teammates to those most in need of help and rescue.

Joel handed the olive-skinned baby to the orphanage worker, missing the feel of the fuzzy head resting against the crook of his arm. Weird. He'd never had a penchant for kids before.

Sitting in the orphanage, giving the crayons and paper to children, Joel formed another prayer of thankfulness in his mind that there were caring Indian women to take care of them. He prayed for more help for the women since the ratio of children to workers didn't always allot for much cuddle time. Women with a heart for little children.

Women like Amber. He suddenly wished she were here. For these precious little children.

For him.

Joel stiffened at the thought and shook it off. *Shut up, heart.* A military marriage and family hadn't worked for his parents, despite the fact they'd both claimed to be Christians. It wouldn't work for him, either.

Joel reminded himself that he'd made a vow to his heart and a commitment to his country—a vow with no room for competition of any sort. Even if she had the prettiest green eyes in Illinois. Joel tried to blink away vivid images of her that kept resurfacing like pop-up ads on the Internet.

Speaking of the Internet— "Hey, Peña. Let me borrow your BlackBerry a sec?"

Manny tugged the phone and text messenger from its clip and handed it over with a knowing grin. "Tell her hey, and that the rest of us feel left out because we didn't get to hug a teacher."

He scrolled down until AMS—AOSD came into view. He pondered what it stood for, and why it surprised him each time she replied back.

Joel kicked Manny for laughing at how much one paragraph from Amber made him grin. He resisted the urge to read it for the third time. Instead, he typed:

Yo, Psychoticat. I hear you're giving the lady trouble. Don't make me stop this chopper and come down there and confiscate your tuna. Treat her right, or I might move in for the kill. Tell her to give Bradley and the other kids hugs for me. It's hard here, so if they have time to write or send cards to the flood victims, or to the rest of my team, the address is attached. JMM—USAF.

Joel debated on deleting the sentence about moving in for the kill. It was pretty bold. That would drop a hint, so he could see how she responded. He didn't know if a relationship between them could be possible. Nor did he know if he could consider one should it be possible. He did know he couldn't dislodge her from his mind. He looked forward to her e-mails. He started to log out of the program when a message popped up. "Hey, Peña. What's this?"

Manny leaned over. "Cool! She's asking for your IM. Just hit the button that says Add. Next time she's online, this will blink, and you guys can open a little chat window."

"Do you get charged by the minute with this thing or what? I can reimburse you for the bill."

"Nah. It's unlimited, so chat to your heart's content. Here." Manny took the clip off his hip. "You use this more than I do. Go for it. I'm crashing, bro. If you need help, let me know, but you pretty much follow the prompts."

"Thanks." Joel pulled out the BlackBerry and followed the commands. He stared at the screen. Nothing happened. She must be off-line. He studied his watch and mentally converted to American time. No wonder. She'd be in the throes of his least-favorite school activity now.

Chapter Seven

Near the end of recess, Amber sneaked the sandwich, apple and juice box inside Bradley's lunch box, then replaced it on the hook by the others. Minutes later, she smiled at the steady stream of faces trickling back into the classroom. "Should we explain why the soldiers had to leave abruptly Friday?" she asked Celia.

Celia peeled sheets of paper from a rainbow-colored Bible memory verse book. "I think after they settle down from recess."

Bradley bounded up, face ablaze with joy. His pallor took Amber by storm. She tried not to stare, but she didn't remember him being so pale this morning. Maybe he'd played too hard at recess. He hated being indoors, though.

"Miss Stanton and Miss Muñez, Friday was the best school day ever!" Happiness glowed in his eyes. He presented a flag he must have found in the school yard. Concern multiplied in Amber when Bradley's fingers trembled around the straw-sized pole. "I already have one a these at my foster mom's house. Who wants this one?" Bradley waved it above his head.

In seconds, the room erupted in jubilee over it. Both teachers stood.

Amber eyed Celia. "Chaos in every corner. It's going to be an interesting day."

Celia scooted Bradley to his seat. "Especially since it's not even noon, and we've already lost control of the class."

Amber went to adjust the shades to reduce the glare on the whiteboard. She reached for the leveler twist and froze.

Had someone stepped on Bradley's flower? It lay nearly sideways. She leaned closer. The garden gate remained locked, and she hadn't heard children playing there.

Why would his flower be the only one not thriving? Hating the direction of her overactive imagination, she flipped the slats closed and turned her back on the window and the morbid thoughts. She marched to the whiteboard, intent to do battle with old ink.

As Bradley scuttled down the aisle, he laughed and bounced to his seat. For a moment, Amber could almost see the little energetic boy he probably used to be, and could be again if his leukemia would go into remission. *Lord, please.*

Concern flooded her as he wobbled and sat, breathing too fast for that little bit of exertion. Emotion hit her out of nowhere. Tears stung her eyes. She hardly ever cried, and never in front of the children. She blinked furiously and focused on drawing a huge smiley face on the whiteboard to draw the other children's attention away from Bradley's pallor and rasping. She'd gotten too attached to him, but what was the harm? Every child deserved someone to care about them.

Amber grabbed the whiteboard eraser. She wound her arm in rigid circles, rubbing away erasable ink, images of the wilting flower, Bradley's breathlessness and pallor engraved in her mind.

She wasn't going to be able to adopt him in time to fulfill his second wish.

The thought hit Amber like a kick to the chest, pulsing fear and dread forth. She fought for control.

Celia must have noticed her struggle with the tears because she moved to stand between Amber and the class. "How about making thank-you cards for the nice soldiers before lunch, huh?"

"Yeah!" A chorus of excited voices sounded all over the room. Amber retreated to the back and pulled craft bins out. She could not, would not lose it.

Celia knelt beside her. "You okay?" she whispered.

"I will be. I think I'm still dazed from all that's happened since Friday." Pops sounded as Amber removed bin lids.

"What part? Meeting Soldier Cutie who drooled

every time he looked at you, or the fact that he's wearing out phone and cyber lines to connect with you?"

Amber cast her friend a stern look, though she knew they were out of student earshot and that Celia purposefully provided a diversion from the emotional onslaught. "I was thinking more along the lines of a surprise production that a certain someone—" she jabbed Celia's ribs playfully "—knew about but didn't tell me."

"Yeah, Miss Five on the Richter. What else? There's more."

"Bradley's oncologist called to tell me his foster mother missed another appointment. I don't know why he called me, or what he thinks I can do about it. He said it's the third time she's been a no-show."

Celia tapped the bin. "I'll bet it's because you spend more time with Bradley when he's hospitalized than foster slug does."

Amber elbowed her. "The news pictures of the floods are downright depressing, yet I can't stop watching. All the orphans with no homes. Knowing Joel and his team are there makes me feel a shade better for them, but it's still sad." Amber wondered if India was open to international adoption. She'd take a truckload if she could.

Celia patted Amber's hand. "I know. It is awful. But it's a good opportunity to strengthen relations with India."

"True." Amber's eyes darted around the classroom. "Little ears are tuning in. Can you get the paint?"

Amber eyed the top shelf and the ladder. If she didn't have to go to the top rung, she might try it. The bottles sat high enough to file them in her panic zone.

"Since I don't want you to pass out, yeah." Celia climbed the ladder. Amber could barely watch. She hated heights since falling from a tree during an earthquake as a child. She'd climbed it to watch for her father to come home from a business trip. Spending the summer in a spica cast from a broken pelvis had been no fun, and that day had changed her life forever.

She took the paints from Celia who handed them down and folded the ladder. Amber ran her hand over her abdomen to smooth her shirt. An ancient twinge of sadness hit her that she'd never get to wear maternity shirts or feel the swell of a baby growing there. She shook it off and went to help Celia disperse papers and craft supplies to the children.

Her heart warmed as she and Celia observed crayon masterpieces being forged with little fingers, and childlike thankfulness flowing in creative motion.

At noon, attendants ushered children to the cafeteria.

"Want to eat in the lounge, or hang here?" Celia asked.

"Let's stay here and catch up. How's your son?"

"Javier's distant. Keep praying. Hopefully it's just normal teen stuff."

"I hope so. Keep me posted."

"Sure. Off subject, but Bradley seemed to bond with Joel."

"Big-time." Amber pulled her sandwich from the tiny dorm fridge. She propped herself on Celia's desk. "He promised Bradley he'd come back."

"Really? How great." Celia bit her pita sandwich.

"He has a hard time in Refuge. Think he'll keep it?" Amber asked several moments later.

Celia swallowed. "What, the promise?"

"Yes. Bradley doesn't need another broken thing." Amber brushed crumbs in the trash.

Celia slid off the desk and stared at her. "After what that guy went through to pull that thing off, there's no way he'll let Bradley down. That's not what he's made of. He went above and beyond." Celia crossed the room.

"What do you mean?" Amber rocked back on her heels.

Celia opened the supply closet doors and pulled out smocks. "I mean he planned this. He orchestrated it. He lined up the soldiers and thrashed like a human machete through mountains of red tape and tanked through brick walls of paperwork."

"I thought Dream Corps was responsible for all that." Amber grabbed handfuls of craft brushes.

"The person you spoke with at Dream Corps put the bulletin out. Someone who knows Joel recognized the name of the town and contacted him, then mailed Bradley's letter. Joel took the ball from there and ran like the good soldier he is." Celia cast her a pointed stare then spread out finger-paint paper, but the ends rolled up. "I'm telling you, this guy doesn't do things halfway. I don't get the feeling he backs away from or out of anything."

"Why do I get the feeling you're having matchmaking notions?" Amber smoothed her end down but it popped back up, too.

"Hey, I saw the way he looked at you." Celia flipped over the paper so it caught on the underside of the table. It bunched up in the middle and wouldn't stay flat no matter how many times she ran her palms across it.

"He's probably just a flirt." Amber stared at the paper, launching into problem-solving mode.

Crinkling sounded as Celia jerked the white, waxy sheet up, creased it and then spread it back down. It still curled. "I didn't see him follow anyone else around like a devoted puppy that day."

Amber ignored her and reached for a roll of tape.

A *thunk* echoed off the table as Celia set a heavy dictionary on the paper. It bubbled up on either side of the book. She glared at the obstinate sheet then eyed the tape in Amber's hand. "Hey, what are you planning to do with that, tape my mouth shut?"

Amber laughed. "Don't tempt me." She taped one side of the paper down on the table, then slid the tape across it to Celia.

Tape zipped from the roll. Celia tore a piece off. "Joel may be a flirt, but he's a flirt with moral substance. Some pretty spectacular muscle substance, too. You should know, from that hug you sprang on him."

"I'm done with this discussion." Amber left the table.

Hand on hip, Celia tracked her steps to the center of the room. "Well, I'm not. You need to get over what's his name, Barf."

"Bart." Amber tried to snatch the tape away from Celia.

Celia held it out of reach. "Oh sure, change the subject."

A laugh escaped Amber. She eyed the tape with deadly intent.

"Bart. Barf." Celia did wild, mutant karate chops with her arms. "Whatever. Same difference. Any guy who leaves a lady alone on an altar deserves his name raked across the coals."

"Shoved in your verbal blender and spun at meringue speed is more like it. Besides, I'm over him."

A smirk caused Celia's lips to pull an Elvis twitch. "Yeah, right. You might be over him but you're not over the hurt of what he did, nor that he left you with broken dreams and all the bills for a wedding that never happened."

Amber thought about Celia's words as her friend aimed a finger at the wall clock. "Hey, look what time it is. Our darlings will be tromping back in here with full tummies any second. We should let them know what happened."

They put their conversation on hold as children filed into class. Celia tapped the desk with the roll of tape to gain their attention. Amber prayed for the right words to speak about the tragedy across the world. "Can we please take our seats and quiet down? There's something important we need to talk to you about." Children settled in. Amber cleared her throat. "As you remember, the soldiers were called away early on Friday."

Little eyes ceased to blink, and quiet blanketed the room.

Celia projected an image of Asia on the wall screen. Amber flipped off the lights and pointed to India. "As your parents may have told you, a very powerful earthquake hit this part of the world. The soldiers went there to help those people. Miss Muñez and I would like our class to take a few moments today, and each day, to pray for those affected by this."

"Can we pray for the soldiers, too?" Bradley asked.

"That's a wonderful idea. Things may be very hard for them over the next few weeks," Amber said.

After the discussion, Bradley brought a globe up to the desk. "Can you show me where the soldiers are, Miss Stanton?"

Amber pointed to a random spot in India. "Somewhere here."

He leaned in, squinting. "Whoa. I never noticed that before. India is shaped like where we live."

She looked closely at Illinois on the globe, then spun it, peering at India. "You're right, Bradley. It appears so. It's almost directly on the other side of the world, too."

"What time would it be there?" another child asked.

"A half a day separates us. So if it's ten in the morning here, it would be about midnight there."

"If there's always a half day separating us, how will our letters ever make it there?" Bradley looked perplexed and the other child appeared a little more than distressed.

She reassured them with a smile. "It's the way the time zone system works. Most if not all of what we send will make it there." Amber opened her e-mail account, waving Celia over. "Shall we?"

"Yes. Miss Stanton has a surprise, so let's gather around the computer," Celia said.

The older children read Joel's letter aloud to the rest. Amber printed copies for each child. "Since we're learning typing skills and keyboard function, come one at a time, and I'll help you post a sentence to the soldiers."

"This will help you guys learn to navigate the Internet for research and learning, as well," Celia put in. "Pay attention. There's a lesson in everything we do here."

Once finished, Celia leaned in. "I see he e-mailed you personally. I'll handle bathroom breaks while you read it."

"You sure?"

"Of course. I have a vested interest. You're my best friend, so that gives me the right to be nosy." Celia winked, then lined up the kids.

As they marched out, Amber read the first line addressed to her cat and laughed aloud, drawing attention from students in the hall. She placed a hand over her mouth and read the rest. When she reached sentence four, her face heated ten degrees.

What did he mean by *move in for the kill?* Unless he planned to go AWOL to come execute her schizoid cat, that statement spoke boldly of romantic interest. Before Amber could ponder how she felt about that, Celia meandered over.

"Ready to do care packages?" Amber closed the inbox.

"You're not gonna let me read it, are ya?" Celia grinned.

"Not here." Amber spread out boxes and items to go in. She hoped the care packages the children put together from items she and Celia had brought in would touch the soldiers and flood victims, and teach the class to reach out to others.

At the bell, Amber rose from her desk. "Bring your cards up, and we'll be sure they get mailed."

Bradley beamed as he took the biggest card Amber had ever seen and leaned it against the desk. Amber had to stop herself from laughing. How in the world would she mail that thing? He hadn't used a standard piece of eight and a half by eleven construction paper like the other students. He'd used an entire poster board, folding it in half.

One way or another, Amber would get that card to Joel.

"Can we make the soldiers stuff every day?" he asked.

Celia looked at Amber, who shrugged. "I don't see why not. We could send care packages at least once a week and even get the entire school involved. Maybe send them gifts to give the children who lost things in the flood, and cheer everyone up."

Bradley ambushed the teachers' desk. He placed both hands on Amber's cheeks. "The day you came here and the Friday Joel came here are the happiest two days of my whole life."

Amber hugged him with all her strength.

And hoped with all her heart that he was wrong.

At mail call weeks later, Joel tore open the cardboard flap, popping bubble wrap in the rush. Nolan tugged several Ziploc freezer bags from the box, which smelled like oatmeal.

"Whoa. Check this out!" Joel tossed cases of granola bars around for his team to give to the village flood victims and orphanages later. There'd be enough left for his team, too.

His team helped him sort cards for the victims in a separate pile from cards to the soldiers. Amber and Celia and their class had been sending care packages every few days. By the sheer volume of that box, and the frequency the care packages arrived, they'd gotten the entire school involved.

Joel lifted out cases of crayons and reams of drawing paper, handing them to Nolan. "This is my favorite time of day."

Nolan put them in the pile to be taken to the orphanage. "Except when you're on the computer with Amber."

"Or whispering on the phone where we can't hear." Manny tensed his shoulder against the gentle fist Joel jabbed it with.

"No wonder he walks around yawning and grinning. Instant messaging her into the wee morning hours," Nolan said.

"Hey, I've cut back. Wait until you meet someone you really like. You'll see how it is." He'd run on fumes for sleep the first couple weeks he'd figured out the IM thing, so he'd had to be more disciplined with sleep time.

"Check this out." Manny held up an India-shaped conglomerate of elementary handprints, looked to have been stamped with finger paint in colors matching India's flag.

"That painting is awesome," Nolan said.

Joel admired it, but nothing topped that huge card Bradley sent him in the first shipment. Amber had mailed it in a large portfolio folder, in which Joel kept all his letters and cards. He also kept pictures Indian orphans made for him out of crayons and coloring pages American children sent. Joel couldn't bear to throw a single one away.

Memories assaulted Joel of drawings his father cast aside without a glance. *But I drew them for you, Daddy. Just for you.* Joel clenched his jaw against the little boy voice inside his head. He was being ridiculous to let it get to him after all these years. Something else hit him.

It had always been Uncle Dean digging the crumpled pictures out of the trash and smoothing them out in his wood shop between slabs of plywood. Dean's garage had practically been wallpapered in Joel's artwork.

Why? And why couldn't his own dad have made him feel that special? And why had his mother and his uncle caved to indiscretion and ruined everything he held dear and sacred?

He handed the India hand map back to Manny a little too harshly, and sifted through the remaining envelope pile, forcing from his mind questions and memories which seemed to come in warring waves these days. A result of going back to that town most likely. He didn't regret meeting Bradley and Amber, though.

"Here's the one you're lookin' for." Nolan swerved a letter in front of Joel's face and grinned.

Joel didn't bother to hide his own smile. He pounced, snatching the yellow missive from Nolan's fingers, and retreated across the property. Having just finished their "on" shift, Joel ducked into the marble-floored hotel, to one corner of the brass-adorned lobby where a teakwood sofa rested near a small lamp and Indian tea and coffee station.

He had to know what her letter said. Right now. The woman proved addictive. After his team headed up the spiral stairs to the sleeping quarters, Joel tore open the envelope and let his eyes devour her words.

Joel, here are more cards from students to soldiers and flood victims. We are praying. Please keep Bradley in prayer. Your letters are life to him. Warmly, AMS—AOSD

Joel read the letter through three times, then grabbed his pen. Something in the tone of her words shot slivers of concern through him regarding Bradley. They'd corresponded often enough for him to know something wasn't right. An urgency to pray settled in his chest. He put his pen to the linen Indian paper.

Hey, class, you're making a difference in the world of these children. I wish you could see their faces as they pull cards from what they've grown to call "Miss Amber and Miss Celia's Box." Mail time is the highlight of their day. Ours, too. The soldiers loved the packets of raincoats as it's monsoon season here. The children here like to make things, too, so the crayons and paper are cherished. They are making a special surprise for your classroom as a thanks. They're learning English as interpreters read your letters to them. They want to be pen pals after our mission is over in their village, so we're working on volunteers to help with that. Keep up the good work. I'm awed at the kindness of each and every one of you. Sincerely, Soldier Joel—USAF

He slid it in an unsealed envelope, then wrote a separate note to Amber, even though they'd talk before she received it:

I'm praying. I haven't forgotten my promise. Soon, JMM—USAF

Your letters were my sun during the dark early days in Asia, Joel thought but didn't add. He wasn't ready to reveal that yet, even though their letters had become longer, more frequent and increasingly personal the past weeks. He could tell she held back. He needed to be patient. Plus he hadn't thought of a viable solution for what he would do if things progressed romantically. He couldn't spend as much time in Refuge as a long-term relationship would require. Not with all the unresolved issues surrounding his parents and his uncle.

Not to mention his mother was buried there and he couldn't bring himself to visit her grave. He'd heard the argument between his father and his uncle about her wish to be cremated and cast into the air over a drop zone. Dean had accused Joel's father of trapping her body out of malice and grounding her for eternity. Joel wondered if that were true.

Despite it all, an unexplainable urge to return to Refuge gripped him, ambiguously jousting with his aversion. As much as he dreaded going back, the nudge grew persistent and unyielding. Amber would have phoned if Bradley had grown worse. Still, the feeling wouldn't release him.

You promised.

Joel radioed Commander Petrowski, who had informed him days ago that he had sixty days leave coming that he needed to use by the end of the year. Joel explained Bradley's situation. Petrowski put Nolan in charge of the team in Joel's absence, then assured Joel his team would manage without him.

He just hoped he'd manage fine in Refuge. If he didn't venture around Haven Street, there was little chance of running into his uncle. His allegiance to the promise he'd made to Bradley outweighed his hard feelings.

As long as he didn't come face-to-face with the man, he could handle one more visit to Refuge. That would release him from his promise. He could keep in touch by letters, phone and e-mail. As far as Amber went, he'd figure it out.

He put the second letter in the envelope and licked the seal, grinning. If everything worked out, he could beat the letter there and surprise them.

"Yow!" Joel pulled the paper flap back and dabbed a finger to his mouth which tasted of sweet sticky envelope gum and blood-borne minerals. His grin had garnered him a paper cut.

He sucked on the corner of his lip while taking the

stairs two at a time. At the top, he jogged left, stopping at the second door. He rapped his knuckles on the wood. "Hey, guys. Open up."

The door opened, releasing the smell of curry spice and coffee into the hallway. The group, lounging on furniture and the floor, turned from watching the cricket game on an Indian sports station to peer at Joel. He plunked down in a slightly musty bamboo chair that creaked with his weight.

"What's up with you looking all happy and scared at the same time? You proposing to her or something?" Manny asked.

Joel shook his head. "Very funny, Peña. Things aren't moving that fast. Besides, some guy broke her heart last year and that has her spooked."

"What's your deal, then? U.S. declare war on Asia or something? You looked all creeped out." Nolan eyed him.

"I'm thinking of heading back to Refuge for a week or so since things have slowed down here." Joel clamped his hands in front of his knees. "You guys okay with me leaving?"

Chapman rounded the corner. "Who's leaving?"

"I might be." Adrenaline-fueled excitement consumed him such as when he stood next up at the plane hatch threshold to lunge at a wall of air.

"Take that with you." Silas pointed to a large roll of burgundy-and-gold material against the wall.

"I didn't realize they'd finished it." Joel knelt,

untying three strings binding the Indian orphans' gift to the American children.

Nolan stepped over to help unroll it. "The orphanage director brought it by a little while ago."

"This is absolutely amazing." Joel eyed the Indian area rug which the flood orphans wove for Amber and Celia's classroom. "Look at the craftsmanship. Amber and Celia will love this." He ran hands along the ornate patterns and jewel tones.

"Good luck getting that thing on the plane," Nolan said.

"You guys are okay with me leaving?"

Chapman set Joel's rucksack at his feet. "Get outta here, Montgomery. Don't trip over that grin on the way out."

Silas tossed Joel's jump pack to him and smiled. "Stateside plane leaves in an hour."

Chance flashed Joel his famous lopsided grin. "What are you still standing here for?"

"Yeah. Hit the road," Manny said. "You got a teacher to see and a promise to keep."

Chapter Eight

Amber shrieked and tore from her sunflower-themed bathroom.

Heaving air, she snatched the cordless phone off its base and pushed Redial.

Please have your phone on, Cel.

"Hello?"

"Celia, something horrible has happened!"

"What's going on?"

"I dyed my hair," Amber wheezed.

Celia's sigh came through the phone like a cellular windstorm. "Oh, no. Don't tell me."

"I put the mixture on my hair but then Bradley's doctor called with some concerns. Then we had a conference call with his caseworker and I became so engrossed in jotting down the things they told me that I lost track of time." Amber turned the box over in her hands to be sure she hadn't misjudged. A sinking feeling hit the pit of her stomach. "Oh, Celia. I was a long thirty minutes late." Amber bit her thumb, cringing for the lecture. She felt bad enough already.

"Amber Marie Stanton! Thirty minutes? Thirty? Oh, goodness. Is it fried?"

"It's beyond fried. Try brittle and cracking. I blow a puff of air on it, and it crumbles like crackers."

Amber fought tears and held the phone away as high-pitched laughter stabbed her eardrum. A pause. Then, snorting and more laughter.

"It's not funny, Celia. What should I do?" Amber scoured the box for reversal instructions. Nothing. Panic set in.

"I'm sorry. I didn't realize you were so upset until I heard your voice quaver. Tell you what. I'll bring stuff to fix it after school. If that doesn't work, you may have to cut it. Can you wait until I drop Javier off at practice and hit the beauty supply store?"

"I can't go out and scare the public, so I guess I'll have to wait." Amber twirled feeble strands, hating how dead and dry it felt. But she'd been so concerned about Bradley that the doctor's words had been the only thing consuming her mind.

The chemo and radiation aren't working. He's not well enough for a bone marrow transplant. We're running out of time. We may need to think about veering our care more toward palliative treatment and hospice. Quality rather than quantity.

That meant Bradley was dying sooner rather than later.

No. She refused to believe it until he was in the grave. She'd begged the doctor to keep trying. He'd called the caseworker to see how they could speed the process up of her obtaining guardianship. His physician felt if he was in better surroundings where neglect didn't reside, Bradley may have a chance to thrive enough to undergo a transplant.

Just like the flowers. Amber sucked in a breath at the memory of Joel's words at the playground.

"Amber?"

"What?" How had she blitzed out another phone conversation? Her hair wasn't the only thing fried. It didn't help that she hadn't been sleeping well because of thinking of all the lonely orphans in the world and Bradley.

"I said, what possessed you to color your hair?"

"I wanted to look hip for Special Olympics."

"Good try, Miss Conservative. Now tell me the real reason."

Amber sighed. "Joel sent me a Webcam. He got one also for when we IM. I've been so consumed with pursuing my foster care license and fighting for Bradley's rights, I haven't kept up with hair and clothing styles. I began to feel self-conscious every time we'd chat." Amber couldn't pinpoint an exact moment she'd started to really care what Joel thought of her. If she'd been more aware of her feelings, stayed on guard, maybe this wouldn't have happened. Amber hated that she couldn't bring herself to enjoy Joel's courtship for fear he'd eventually reject her.

Truth be told, she'd taken the day off from school in order to meet with the foster care coordinator, who instructed her to start purchasing items she thought she might need if Bradley came to her on an emergent basis. She'd been picking up some Spider-Man shampoo when her eyes had lit on the hair dye kit. She'd have been better off if she'd passed it by. And maybe Joel, too, if her growing feelings were any indication of the trouble she was getting her heart into. Again.

Amber flipped the box over, glaring at the pretty blonde on the cover whose hair looked nothing like hers. "How'd my sub do today? She's a new teacher and the kids can be kind of wild."

"Kind of? She survived, so don't feel guilty for calling in sick, though you're out of the running for the perfect attendance prize now. I made tortilla soup. Want me to bring some when I drop the reversal kit by?"

"Sounds good. Ugh." Amber stared at the strand of crunchy hair that broke off with the twirling.

"What's wrong now?"

"Other than an epic disaster on my head and the fact that Bradley's running out of time? Nothing."

"We'll fix your hair. I promise."

That Celia didn't comment on her statement about Bradley gave Amber a sinking feeling. Celia had always reassured her before. Celia'd lost someone close to her, so maybe that made her cautious. All Amber could do was hope and pray. Bradley deserved that.

"Hey, I need to let you go. Just be sure and put a hat on before I get there," Celia said.

"Very funny."

"No, I'm serious. Put a hat on."

Amber clicked the phone off, wondering what a hat had to do with anything. On her way to get one, she stopped at the mirror. She'd only meant to highlight her red hair to look more stylish. Now she resembled a big-haired eighties throwback. She tilted sideways and caught sight of Psych behind her.

"Worse. I look like my cat stuck in a wall outlet." Amber groaned and flung herself across the soft bedspread. She rolled over, lit her pineapple candle and sniffed, enjoying the fragrance. Then she sneezed. Then again. So much for that. She blew it out.

A tickle fell across on her forehead. She brushed hair off it, then picked fallen strands from her bed. "Ugh!" She dusted black candlewick char from the coverlet but it streaked worse.

Edgy from allergy medication, she hauled herself out of bed, grabbed the wet hair towel from the sink and headed to the laundry room. The phone rang. Amber set the towel on the counter and picked up, glancing at caller ID.

"Hey, Mom." Amber stretched the cord so she could sit.

"We got your message to pray for Bradley. How are you?"

She spun the bar stool left and right with her foot. "Hanging in there."

"Do you need us to come back from our vacation to Grandma's early, Amber?"

"No. I'm just battling fear. You and Daddy stay and have a good time. I'll see you when you get back."

"Speaking of Dad, he wants to talk to you."

"Okay."

"Hey, baby girl."

"Hey, Dad."

"Playing hooky today, huh?"

Amber laughed. "Yeah. I guess you could say that."

He chuckled. "Anything special I can bring you back?"

Amber started to say no, but she felt he wanted her to still need him even though she wasn't little anymore.

She remembered their special activity before he got so busy. Before she grew out of it, really. Every business trip, he would always bring back a new puzzle to work with her. Maybe it hadn't only been him who'd pulled away.

"Actually, I could use a new puzzle…and someone to help me put it together."

A brief silence stretched across the phone line. "You bet."

Her eyes moistened at the gravelly emotion in her father's voice. Baby steps.

"I love you, Daddy."

"Love you, too, sweetheart. I'm really proud of you. I don't say it often, but I've always been proud of you. Goodbye."

"See you in a week. Have fun. Goodbye."

She clicked off, set the phone on the base and stretched.

Psychoticat stared at her with a bland expression.

"I'm bored, too, Psych. Let's play." Amber slipped her fuzzy yellow duck slippers on and wiggled them at the cat. He batted around at the bill with his claws, tugging them off her feet. Three seconds later, he skirted around her and darted under the bed, clearly done with the ducks.

"You're loads of fun." Amber stared at the mountain of dirty clothes mocking her from the living room. She groaned and shoved her toes back into the slippers.

She made a path to the sofa by kicking piles of rumpled clothes. She plunked down on the couch where the load of clean clothes sat.

She rummaged through, disgusted. "Nothing matches. Who cares? It's not like Celia's gonna care what I look like." She pulled out a bright pink T-shirt and hunter-green and mustard plaid pajama bottoms. Maybe she'd do laundry later. It would take her mind off worrying about Bradley.

"Beggars can't be choosers," she said to her only clean pair of pajama pants. Having had them since high school, the knees and rump were threadbare. She tugged them on, wishing she had a better sense of style. With twin jerks on frayed strings, she tied them at the waist and pulled on her purple chenille bathrobe.

Minutes later, she plopped in front of her computer, duck slippers quacking with every step. She set a cup of steaming peppermint tea down and stared at her reflection in the muted screen. "Face it. You've got the blues."

Why hadn't Joel e-mailed or called in a couple days?

She needed a distraction.

"Spider Solitaire or Free Cell?" Nah. She'd pull up e-mail once more. After all, it had been an hour since she'd last checked.

"What's up with you, Joel?"

She flashed an irritable glance at her e-mail. No use denying she hoped for the only other name besides her father's that she could count on always being there.

Only today it wasn't. Again.

"I hope everything's okay." She stared at her new USAF screen saver, afraid to ponder just how dangerous his job could get at times. She ran her finger along the screen, trailing the line of white parachutes mushroomed along the air behind some kind of military aircraft. "Protect him." Her voice echoed through the empty house which suddenly felt even more so.

When had she come to take for granted his presence in her in-box and his soothing baritone on her voice mail? Maybe he'd become really busy. Too busy to contact her. Or maybe not. After all, she'd been dumped before. Yet nothing had been verbalized between them as far as commitment, just hinted at. She'd been too afraid of rejection to come right out and ask him if they were still friends, or if he considered them more.

She was probably a fool to harbor even a glimmer of hope. She'd be better off to put her guard back up. Things were better that way. Safer. It provided a barrier to hope because hope led to hurt, at least where she and relationships were concerned.

Besides, if the idea of being a father didn't appeal to Joel, he and Amber had no future together. If she was honest with her heart, she'd admit he'd been hinting at dating. But she couldn't risk dating someone she wouldn't consider marrying.

Her deepest desire encompassed being a mother and though Joel had seemed to bond with Bradley, he'd made it clear children were not in his future. He'd probably flee hard and fast the other way if he knew of her intent to try and adopt Bradley. A sick feeling rolled through her that she'd eventually have to make her intentions known.

Amber dreaded that day because it would probably mean goodbye.

Convincing herself the tension binding her shoulders couldn't be disappointment, she switched positions. Hands to keyboard, she settled into surfing news sites about the progress of humanitarian efforts in South Asia.

A while later, Amber bit her lip at flood footage as the doorbell rang. She checked her watch. How had she spent two hours vegging at the computer? She hoped for her hair's sake Celia'd arrived.

Amber reached for the door as it opened. "Hey, Celia."

Her friend bounced in, then stopped short when her eyes lit on Amber. Her mouth froze in a horrified O as she stared. She clamped a hand to her head as her gaze skittered down Amber's attire.

"I didn't hear from him again today." Amber flapped her hand at the computer screen.

Celia dashed to Amber, shaking her head.

Not wanting to infect her if she had a cold brewing instead of allergies, Amber moved away. "And you'll be glad to know I'm very disappointed." There. She'd finally admitted her feelings.

Celia moved close and flailed her free arm. Her friend mouthed something, twitching her head backward seizure-style.

"Did you swallow a pound of Mexican jumping beans on the way or what?" Amber coughed to clear the wheeze in her chest.

"No wonder you're dressed this way. You're obviously ill. Have you been tested for asthma? Because my CPR card expired two days ago, just so you know."

"Too bad 'Soldier Cutie' isn't here if I go into respiratory failure." Amber tugged the DVD from Celia's grip, eyeing the title. "I'm sure Joel knows CPR."

Chocolate, almond-shaped eyes widened. Celia tapped a red taper-tipped fingernail to her lips and performed another not-so-subtle head twitch.

"You've gone loco, señorita." Amber made circle motions with her finger around her ear. "Is that my soup behind your back?"

Too bad Bradley couldn't be here to share the soup with them. Foster Lady forbade him to come, saying he had to clean the yard. Amber had seen that yard. Making Bradley clean it bordered on dangerous. Especially since he seemed to be going downhill. Maybe she should call his caseworker about—

Celia brought her other arm forward.

Amber stared at the bouquet of flowers Celia presented as if they'd plunked to earth from another galaxy. No wonder Celia'd had one of her hands tucked away.

"What's this?" Amber leaned forward, breathing in the fragrance of roses and yellow wildflowers.

"What's it look like?" A satisfied grin took over Celia's mouth.

"I know it's a bouquet. Who from?" Who'd send her young widow friend flowers?

Celia's grin widened.

"Come on, tell me. You look like the hungry shark from *Nemo*. What's his name?" Amber wiggled her eyebrows.

Confusion twisted Celia's face. "The shark?"

"No. The totally romantic guy who sent you these flowers."

"They're not for me. They came to the school today." Gum in Celia's mouth crackled. "For you."

"Me?" Amber blinked, recalling if today was teacher's day or what. Her mental calendar came up blank. "From who?"

If Celia's smile got any larger, her face would crack horizontally and her chin would fall off. "From right here." Celia stepped aside.

A tall figure moved from the hall into the frame of her doorway, filling it.

Breath flew from Amber's mouth. The DVD clattered to the floor. "Joel!" She lunged toward him, then stopped. Just friends? She wasn't sure.

Their correspondence had gotten pretty personal. Joel had mentioned his buddies had started referring to her as his girl. But is that how Joel saw her? He had started the last few phone conversations with, "How's my girl?" She stared at the flowers, catching sight of her own attire.

An inward cringe gripped Amber at the sorry state of her hair and outfit. She'd been so busy plowing through the legal motions to secure a decent future for Bradley, she had taken no time for herself. Now would be a good time for the Rapture.

"Now that I've led him here, I'll leave my soup and go. Here." Celia thrust a box in Amber's hand. "Wash your hair in this, according to the directions. That should fix it."

Amber could only nod. She remembered Celia's

hat comment. She must have known earlier that Joel wanted to come over.

Joel nodded at Celia, who edged out the door. "Thanks. I owe you one."

Celia shimmied back inside. "In that case, I'll collect now. I'd like you to autograph something for my son. He wants to be a PJ someday, thanks to Bradley going on about you."

"Really? That's great. What's his name again?"

"Javier." Celia spelled it out.

Joel scribbled words on the paper she presented. Celia took it, handed the pot to Joel, shot a conspiratorial wink Amber's way and then fled the scene humming "Love is in the Air."

Amber's face grew so hot she knew it must be nearing purple. Celia was dead meat. Joel stood two feet across from her, still holding the pot. A tender grin tugged at one side of his mouth. *Ask him in, dufus.*

"Here, let me take that soup." Amber lunged forward at the same time Joel stepped inside.

They collided on the spot, jarring the lid. Soup sloshed onto his turquoise polo. "Oh!" Amber darted around and snatched a towel off the counter. She dabbed madly at the splotch of broth on his shirt. "I am so sorry!"

Through her allergy-swollen nose, he reeked of jalapeño and tortillas and something else she couldn't decipher. As he set the pot on the counter, she continued to dab, blush and cringe.

He placed his hand over hers. "Hey, no big deal. It's just a shirt." His grip stayed gentle, and his eyes projected mercy. The twinkle hinted that he might be quite entertained by all this.

She slipped her hand from his. After a lingering second, he let it go. Self-consciousness jolted through her as she remembered she hadn't even had a shower today. The urge to laugh at the absurdity seized her. What else could she do?

She ran her hand through her tangled mess of overcooked ringlets. "You must think I'm a slob." She shifted her weight. Both feet quacked. She cringed. Her face heated several degrees. She refused to look down.

He didn't. His mouth spread into a full grin as he stared at her duck slippers. His gaze moved up in a bemused manner.

She could not bring herself to look. If she did, he'd see her dreadfully red face. Why hadn't God asked her opinion before giving her red hair and freckles, and the uncontrollable tendency to blush at the drop of a hat?

Uh-oh. What was he doing now?

One of his feet stepped forward. Then the other. So close his toe bumped noses with the bill of her duck slippers.

A heady scent of masculine cologne floated around her. Ninety-eight-degree humidity wafted off him. He wore cologne here? And why wasn't he saying anything? His nearness and scent threatened to sedate her. *Careful. Don't risk your heart again. Don't fall. Don't fall.* Her mind whispered the mantra to her heart. *Obey.*

"That's not what I think at all—Blondie." He ran his fingers along strands of hair, tugged one curl, then let go. It sprung back against her forehead.

She held tufts of hair out either side of her face. "Yeah. I, uh, had a little mishap with the, uh—"

His knuckle moved her bangs aside. She froze. Why did he lean so close? If he kissed her, what would she do?

The idea warmed Amber's face. The warmth spread as it occurred to her that he might sense her thoughts. Ugh. The only thing she needed right now was to let a daydream carry her off into a cave.

She started to take a step back.

He placed a hand on her shoulder. "It's great to see you again, Amber." His voice rang deep and tender.

She cleared something gargantuan from her throat. "I missed you."

"It's nice to be missed." He leaned down and brushed a featherlight kiss on her cheek.

Okay, okay. That wasn't so bad. Could have been a friendship gesture. She chanced a peek. His eyes shimmered with tenderness as his gaze roved her face, stopping to rest on her mouth a second too long before connecting with her eyes.

How badly she wanted to rush forward and hold him. A good-sized tornado could have blown through

the room and Amber still would have waxed cata-
tonic. She never would have dreamed a connection
this strong could have formed through e-mails, phone
calls and letters.

He held her gaze, lifted the pot cover, raising one
eyebrow. "Ducky hungry?" A full grin splayed
across his face.

Tension in Amber sprang, and she burst out laughing.

He probably thought her a terrible housekeeper.
Normally she kept things spotless. Why, of all weeks,
had she neglected to wash her laundry, her face, her
dishes?

Oh, man, even her teeth? She ran her tongue across
them, wishing she had a breath mint.

When she looked up to find his gaze firmly fixed on
her mouth again, she stepped back. Friends didn't stare
at friends that way. "I—I'll find something to dip soup
with." Where could her ladle be? Had she even
unpacked it? For all she knew, it could still be in storage.

The longer it took her to find it, the longer he'd
stare. She knew he did because she saw from the
corner of her eye.

At a loss and floundering in a state of mortification,
she flung a drawer open. No ladle. She did find a
basting syringe. She untwisted the bulb and did the
only thing she knew to.

Chapter Nine

"If you were a ladle, where would you hide?" Amber whirled, her eyes beseeching and serious.

The big pink bulb on the end of her nose caused a sharp inhale that lodged gum in his airway. He bent at the waist, coughing out the glob.

He could see headlines now: *Her sense of humor killed him*.

Airway patent, he rose laughing and drank in the welcome sight of her. She had wit to defuse any situation. The girl was undiluted fun. "I'd hide in your pocket so I could be with you wherever you go," he answered. "Lucky ladle."

"Do you talk to all the ladles that way?"

He fostered a serious expression. "No. I never flirt, actually. This is new to me. I've never met a—ladle—who brought that kind of vulnerability out in me," he answered honestly.

"Oh." She spun. "Well, speaking of ladles, it may

be in a box. We might have to dip our bowls in the pot."

"That's how they do it in third world countries." Joel thought of the orphans. He'd been thinking of them a lot actually. He leaned against the counter with his arms braced behind him. Amber's rapid-fire chatter and incessant darting reminded him of a goldfish with a net in hot pursuit.

And he only chased her with his gaze.

He smiled. She could act aloof all she wanted. He wasn't fooled. "Don't cook often?"

"I'm domestically challenged when it comes to kitchen organization." She swooshed across the tiles to a different drawer. A quack sounded with every step. Her cheeks went beyond pink.

He took in her outfit, deciding not to comment. He'd embarrassed her enough. He didn't regret dropping in unannounced, though.

He'd missed her and couldn't remember being more amused.

"Bradley's caseworker might be able to bring him by if you want to see him." She zoomed to the drawer by the oven.

He rotated his neck. She'd give him whiplash if he didn't quit staring. "I spent the morning with Bradley."

She pivoted. Surprise washed over her face. "You visited my classroom?"

"Yeah, but you were playing hooky."

"You sound like my dad." She peered over a

fuzzy purple shoulder. "The two of you have things in common."

"Is that good or bad?" He crossed his ankles.

"I'm not sure yet."

"I'd like to meet your family." He plucked the bulb off her nose, squeezing it in his palm, wondering about her dad.

"They want to meet you, too."

Her words sent warmth through him. That she wanted him to meet her family had to be a good thing, right? He moved out of her path as she quacked her way behind him. "How many junk drawers do you have?"

She snickered, rummaging in frenzy. "Too many. I got tired of digging through boxes, so I started tossing stuff in drawers. My parents always buy me cooking gizmos. I don't have a clue what half of them are or do. I have two food processors and three choppers, but I use one knife for everything. I don't want to hurt their feelings by getting rid of things."

He enjoyed the chatter and being in the kitchen with her. He could get used to this. "We don't have to use a ladle. A serving spoon should do it."

She froze, looking momentarily panicked.

"A large tablespoon?" He chuckled.

A victorious pointer finger pierced the air. "That, I have. And believe it or not, I know right where it is." She performed a silly duck waddle to the sink, causing him to laugh.

"You're the perfect kind of person to work with kids, Amber."

"Thanks. I think." Either she'd given up her quest for a ladle, or gotten distracted multitasking because her arms came down from the counter with two glass plates.

Joel took them from her and set them on the table. "I admire anyone who can. I don't have it in me."

Amber turned slowly. "Work with kids?"

"That, and raise them. You know I can't have kids, right?" They'd touched on it briefly the first day they met but he felt they were at that crucial point in their relationship where they needed to determine whether to move forward or not. He hoped they could work out their differences, but if not, he wanted to find out now, while their friendship could still be salvaged before any serious romantic commitments were made. He'd hinted around at dating her and how he felt about her but she never seemed to voice how she felt.

She looked at him funny. Almost seemed relieved. "Huh. That's weird, because neither can I."

Her admission jarred him. He wanted to know details but resisted asking sensitive stuff. He'd wait to see if she volunteered it.

"I fractured my pelvis as a youngster. They were unable to stop internal bleeding. I lost my uterus." She shrugged.

"I'm sorry." He approached her.

"There's always adoption. What about you?"

He felt like a heel. He slid his hand along the

counter until his fingers rested on hers. "I shouldn't have put it the way I did. Unlike you, I can't because I choose not to. I made the decision long ago. It doesn't fit my lifestyle, and I'd be no good at it."

For the first time since childhood, Joel wished things were different. He hated being so jaded by his upbringing. But if he risked fatherhood and it didn't work, a child would be hurt and he couldn't be responsible for that. He wanted to commit to Amber, but doing so would require him to rethink his future. He didn't know if he could. Even for her.

Her face fell. "I think you'd be great working with kids." Her voice softened, shoulders deflated. She slipped from his grasp and opened the fridge.

He politely averted his gaze when she stooped. Those pants could use a few more threads across where she sat. Thankfully the purple robe provided sufficient cover when she stood straight. She handed him a plastic pitcher. He lifted the hard lid and stuck his nose close, inhaling. Very sweet tea wafted up, just how he liked it.

"I think you'd be a great dad, too." She glanced at him.

"I might work with kids." He put the lid back on too hard, though he had no idea why. "But I'll never be a dad."

That stopped her. Confusion flashed across her face. He wondered if it were his actions or words that caught her off guard. He hadn't meant to sound so grumpy about it but truth was, his feelings were scaring him to death. Nothing had challenged his no-children vow ever. Until now.

"Excuse me." She brushed by him with a pan of something syrupy-smelling. She went from the table to the sink. Quiet, she pulled a large spoon out, dripped an overdose of suds on it, washed, rinsed, dried it and then went to hand it to him.

She stopped mid-step. Her eyes widened as they scanned his chest. The spoon clattered to the tile. "Oh, no! Oh, Joel—your shirt." She pointed.

Joel looked down. White splotched his blue-green polo. He held a section up to his nose, sniffed, then shot a suspicious glance toward the soup. "Bleach?"

Amber stepped forward. "I'm so sorry. I'll buy you a new one." She grabbed the towel she'd dabbed soup off his shirt with earlier, then pointed to her hair. "I must have—"

He studied the towel, then things registered. The look of remorse on Amber's face was priceless. He smiled. Did she have any inkling how adorable he found her?

"You're good for me." He glanced at her slippers, pleased when she blushed again.

"I'm glad you didn't parastorm out and miss soup."

Sensing by her enflamed cheeks she was certifiably embarrassed despite her humor, he eased up. "I'd never storm out. Terrorists and tyrants are about the only things that anger me easily. Besides, I can't let you eat all this by yourself." He leaned over the pot.

She laughed, but something vacant lay in it. Maybe he could fill the uncomfortable gap with small talk.

"Bradley's lost more weight and hair." What a drastic change in subject, but he couldn't retrieve the words. Their correspondence the past weeks had deepened and strengthened their bond. He felt totally at ease talking with her in person.

She turned a stove burner on. "He had another round of treatments. It makes him nauseated so he has trouble eating. His classmates said Bradley's concerned he'll go bald and look different. He doesn't want to stand out. They asked if he'd lose all his hair."

Joel set the pot on the burner then gave her his full attention. "And?"

"I told them I imagined so if they continued treatments." She tightened her eyes.

Joel had the insane urge to breach the polite space between them and hold her. "Why wouldn't they continue treatments?"

Fierce determination settled in her face as she glanced at a stack of envelopes on the counter. "Because Foster Lady didn't want them continued."

He stared at them. Government address. "Lady?"

Amber pressed fingers in her bangs. "Sorry. Celia calls her Foster Lady."

"Why wouldn't Foster Lady continue his treatments?"

"Claims they're too expensive and he'll die anyway. She refused to sign consent."

He shifted foot to foot. "Can she do that?"

"Not anymore. I filed a grievance and took her to court. His caseworker and I are in a legal battle with her and the snail of a system. We secured a motion for treatment in the meantime."

"That's good."

"Anyway, the class asked how we could make him feel better if he lost his hair. I devised an idea I thought would help him not feel out of place should it happen."

"What's that?" Obviously she didn't want to discuss the legal battle or foster mother further. He'd let it go. For now.

"Cut my hair." She laughed. "Guess I have nothing to lose now. They asked their parents if they could cut theirs, as well."

"Great group of kids." He carried two bowls of soup to the table. She gestured to a chair that looked as if it belonged in a playhouse. He dwarfed the seat, hoping it wouldn't splinter. The room boasted a garden theme. Her furnishings splashed a bright white room with sunshine yellows. Her bouncy personality added to the cheery decor.

His chair scraped the floor as he scooted forward. "So, this haircut. How short are we talking?" He scooped a spoonful of soup.

Amber chewed her lip. "Short like yours."

The spoon halted near his lips. "You're buzzing your head?"

She peeked over her glass rim. "Uh-huh."

Joel regarded her a second, trying to imagine her bald. "You'd look beautiful with a tree frog on your head, so it wouldn't matter."

Cup to the table, her hand splayed beneath her neck.

"Choking?" he asked.

She shook her head. Tears sprouted from the corner of her eye and a stifled cough slipped out.

He recalled the conversation he'd overheard between her and Celia at the door. He simply could not resist. "Need CPR or something?" He stood. Blood rushed to her face. She shook her head faster, embarking on a sputter episode.

Joel sat, pleased at her state of fluster. "Wonder why I'm here?" Joel asked after her coughing subsided.

Amber dabbed her lips with a napkin, lifting her head. Something akin to terror caused her unblinking eyes to stretch wide.

"I hoped to take you on a date tomorrow if you feel up to it."

Quack. Quack. Qua—

The sound ceased when he dipped his head to peer under the table.

"The doctor thinks it's only dander allergies. The people who lived here before me had a dozen cats. In fact, they abandoned Psych as a runt. He nearly starved to death under the porch before weak meows led me to him."

"Not a good mouser?" Where this conversation was

headed, he had no clue. He supposed nervousness over the mention of a date caused the abrupt change in subject.

"The worst." Amber moved the pot to the table on a trivet.

Joel dipped another bowl for himself then tilted a heaping spoonful to her bowl. "More?"

She shook her head. "I nursed him to health, wormed him, chauffeured him to the vet, adorned him in fancy flea collars and introduced him to tuna and fine living. The rest is history."

Her nervous chatter made him smile. "You have a heart for abandoned things, don't you?"

Her spoon swirled around in her bowl. "Yeah."

"I bet you'd take a giraffe in if it showed up at your door."

She laughed. "My landlord would take issue with that. He's having a coronary over Bradley as it is."

Joel folded his arms across his chest. "Bradley?"

"Yeah, you know." She held her hand horizontal at waist high. "Skinny little kid who adores you."

"You're taking him in?"

"I'm trying. He wants a family. I'm doing my best to give him one." She averted her eyes.

"As in find someone to adopt him?" Joel leaned on his elbows.

"You could say that." She stretched. "Anyway, it would be good to get out. I mean, as friends. I nearly died of boredom today."

"Friends don't let friends die of boredom." Her "as friends" statement surprised Joel. From all the time they'd spent on the phone and online, he'd felt that they were more. They obviously needed to talk openly and decide exactly how to define what they were. Time to stop skirting around the issue.

He pushed his empty bowl across the linen tablecloth, then reached for the saucer holding the pastry she put in front of him. His mouth watered when he sank his teeth into a crescent of layered sweetness.

"These are good." He pointed a fork to the pan. "May I?"

"Please. The more you eat, the less I have to jog off."

His gaze skittered over her. "You look fine how you are." *Very fine.* "It wouldn't hurt you to eat a couple of those."

She flushed, grinning. "Eat all you want for sure now."

"Uh, that would be the whole pan." He sliced the side of his fork into another moon-shaped delicacy. "What are these?"

"Mountain Dew apple dumplings."

"My team would love them. We hardly get home-cooked meals or baked goods."

Her hand propped her chin. "Doesn't anyone cook for you when you come home?"

He fought to keep his face neutral. "Home's where my team is."

Remorse cloaked her expression. "I'm sorry. I remember now you spoke of your mother in the past tense. When did she pass away?"

He crinkled his napkin. "No idea. She left when I was seven. I learned when I was ten that she died in a car crash coming back to Refuge. The only memories I have of her are cradled in clouds. My team's my family now." He finished off the second dumpling. He could tell by her lip chewing she wanted to delve but probably didn't want to come across as prying.

He didn't blame her for the questions. He had plenty of his own. Like, what had happened to his mother in those three years, and was she coming back for him or not?

She slid the pan to him. "Here. Eat another."

"One more." Amber spooned another onto his plate and put the soup in the fridge. He stood. "Let me help clean up."

She waved him down. He kept the last bite on his tongue as long as he could without violating a personal code of manners. Resisting the urge to lick his fingers, he leaned back to pick up the box Celia had left. "Want help with this?"

"Would you?"

He nodded, reading directions. "I'd love to." He lowered the box and grinned. "If it doesn't work, I have a razor in my rucksack."

"Ha-ha." She pulled a towel from a hall closet and

went to the kitchen sink, moving dishes to one side. "Shall we?"

He joined her. She put her hands beneath the water stream while he pulled detailed directions from the box.

Water specks landed on his cheeks when she flicked her finger. The second time it happened he knew it wasn't an accident.

"Hey!" He nudged her with his hip, knocking her off center. He cupped his hands under the water.

Her hands flew to her face. "Don't you—"

His hands volleyed, dousing her.

"Dare." She yelped and grabbed a bowl. He wrestled it from her, enjoying the sound of her laughter with his.

"Oh! Oh! Wait. Oh, no!" She held the soppy directions.

"It's all right. I memorized them already."

Her gaze widened as she stared at the two-sided paper with microscopic type and very little white space. "The whole thing?"

"It's part of my training."

"Then let's do battle with this army of frizz, soldier."

Amber dipped her head under the warm spray. He brushed his hands down from her scalp to the ends until it was all damp. While she put on a towel turban-style, he pulled a chair up by the sink. "Sit."

Gloves donned, Joel opened stinky purple stuff that

made his eyes water and stood behind her. Seated, she patted excess water from her hair and lay the towel aside. He snickered and squirted a happy face design atop her head. With his fingers, he massaged the goop all around while watching the clock.

Her head lolled with his motion. "Going to sleep?"

"Maybe," she murmured. "This is my favorite part."

"What?"

"This scalp massage. If you were my beautician, I'd get my hair done every day."

Her languid tone and half-lidded eyes sent his thoughts haywire. He closed his eyes, intent not to go there. This hadn't been the smartest thing he'd ever done. *Just friends. Just friends.* Right. They were both kidding themselves.

"Maybe you should finish this." He marched to the bathroom trash to rid himself of the gloves and the zinging sensation of her hair tangled in his fingers.

Amber followed him. "Are the fumes bothering you?"

Joel laughed. "Not really." Although chemicals had something to do with it, they didn't come out of that hair treatment box. A few more minutes of massage and melting, and he'd have kissed her.

What would she have done? Responded to his kiss? Or slapped sense into him? Maybe that would be better. Easier to deal with.

Tenderness and hope for a future with her swarmed him. He refused to ruin this by acting on impulse. She'd become way too important to him. Amazing that could happen through letters, phone conversations and e-mail. It gave him hope and respect for other military relationships.

Too bad they didn't have this sort of stuff when he was young. Maybe his mom and dad would have had a better chance.

He'd assumed Amber had been unaffected, until she unfolded the towel from her shoulders. Hives covered her neck.

Unless she had a skin reaction to the chemicals, the scalp massage had gotten under her skin, too. "Let me rinse it out and we'll watch that movie," she said.

He cleared the table and washed her dishes while she dried her hair in the bathroom. When she came out, her face glowed with a hint of makeup, a light fragrance followed her, and her hair was healthy and shiny.

She'd gone and gussied up. Now he'd have a really hard time not staring. She'd even changed her clothes.

Just friends, huh?

"Did you have something particular in mind for tomorrow? Or did you just want to pal around?" She walked back from the living room where she'd put the DVD in the player.

He flashed a challenging look and what he hoped to be an irresistible grin. "What I had in mind for tomorrow, I'm not sure you'd be up for."

She studied him a second. "Something tells me this isn't a normal date we're talking about." She lifted her tea to sip.

He pulled his bottom lip through his teeth, and grinned. "Exactly how afraid of heights are you?"

She set down her glass and blanched. "H-how… h-high…are we talking?"

Chapter Ten

"Why would anyone jump from a perfectly functioning aircraft?" Amber yelled above the jet engine's roar the next day as the earth scrolled below.

Joel snickered and tightened Amber's goggles. The pilot had signaled they'd reached seven thousand feet. Ten would be high enough for her first tandem jump.

"Sure you're up for this?" he asked, noting her trembling hands as she smoothed her hair back under the safety helmet.

"That depends. Are you sure that parachute is going to open?" She eyed it with an arched brow.

"If it doesn't, the second one, the reserve, should."

"Should? Should? *Should* makes me nervous. I don't like *should.* Can't you say *will? Will* open?" The words wobbled out on a breathless tremor. "Is this where we jump from?" Her face lost color.

Joel checked altitude. "Yes. In about ninety seconds."

She stared out the gaping hatch and gasped as if an angry flock of bloodthirsty pterodactyls swarmed in the air outside.

"Trust me. It's a tandem jump. You'll be attached to me the entire way down. I've done this thousands of times."

She visibly tensed. "What if I pass out?"

He stifled a laugh. "I promise not to tell anyone."

"What if the second one… What'd you call it?"

"The reserve." He attached four tandem clips on the back of her harness to the front of his.

"Yeah. What if that one doesn't open?"

"They'll give us a refund."

She laughed out loud. "We'll be dead."

"Yeah. Probably so. But what a way to go."

"You're crazy."

He lowered his head, putting his mouth an inch from her ear. "About you."

She smacked at him. "Stop teasing. I need to concentrate. So do you." She took in a fortifying breath and tilted her face where he stood inches behind her.

"You okay? You seem dizzy." He adjusted her harness.

"Not dizzy, just…nervous. I'll be fine."

He spread his arms, placing palms on both sides of the hatch, and grinned. "You ready?"

"No. But let's do this before I lose my nerve."

"There's still time to back out." He winked in challenge.

She lifted her chin and put her face to the wind. "Never."

"That's my girl." Joel positioned himself closer to her. Close enough to feel her trembling through her jumpsuit. Hands to her waist, he nudged her forward.

She tensed, starting to back up. "Wait. Wait. Wait. How many years have you been doing this?"

"Long enough." He inched forward.

She pushed back. "Be serious."

He inched forward. "I did my first tandem at age five."

She looked at him like he'd grown three heads. "What kind of crazy person would let a five-year-old skydive?"

"My mother." He eyed the clouds, and gauged wind velocity. "By the time I was twelve, I entered the sport and had over eleven hundred logged jumps. That didn't include tandems, or the two years I got lazy with logging." Joel inched them to the door.

Judging by the rapid, shallow rise and fall of her chest, if they didn't jump soon, she'd hyperventilate. Out of respect, he maintained as much airspace between his front and her back as the harnesses and clips would allow. It wasn't much, and the intimate proximity wreaked havoc with his senses.

He jerked his focus to the jump.

"Ready?" He tapped the front of his left boot to the heel of hers, inching it forward. He repeated with the right foot.

She nodded, but when they stepped another foot

forward, putting the ground in view, she slammed back against him, clawing his forearms as he imagined Psych did on a vet's table. Her feet backtracked. Heels stepped over the top of his boots. "Wait! Joel, on second thought, I don't—"

Now or never.

In one swift, powerful, calculated motion, Joel propelled them into a pool of blue sky with island clouds. He'd never heard such sounds fly out of a teacher's mouth.

"You pushed meee-eeee!" rose above the cold wind slamming into them as they free-fell. She screamed and flailed her arms for the first forty seconds. Shrieks and garbled words vibrated through her back into his chest. The wind wavered on deafening and he still heard her above it.

He laughed. He couldn't help it. She'd need a throat lozenge once they touched ground, and he'd need hearing aids.

"You're doing fine." Besides screaming and flailing.

"No! Can't! Breathe!" She flung her face sideways, guppy gulping, ear pressed into shoulder. Teeth gritted, eyes clenched, cheeks puffed out. It wasn't that she couldn't breathe; she held her breath.

"Take me back!" she yelled.

Like he could.

He laughed again then lifted her protective ear gear and put his mouth there. "Amber, you're okay. This is normal."

"No! Not normal! Crazy! Only crazy people do this on purpose! I'm going to die, and all you can do is laugh!"

He tried not to laugh again. "You won't die, but you're killing me." He'd give anything for a video camera right now.

He put his mouth to her ear and said firmly, "Arms out."

"Is that…a direct…order, sir?"

Joel smiled, glad her humor remained intact. He feared she'd disemboweled it back on the plane. He thought she would flail again, but she inched her arms out like a baby bird stretching wings for its first time in true flight.

"Open your eyes," he coaxed, once her form held steady the way they'd practiced before the jump.

She jerked her head side to side. "I don't, I can't." She gulped air. "I hate this!"

"C'mon. Eyes open. I don't want you to miss this. Please?"

She peeked. Her entire body relaxed. "Oh! Oh! I love this!"

"Yeah. Beautiful, isn't it?" He still had to outyell the wind. She didn't have to know he wasn't looking at the air and groundscape, but at her profile. At long eyelashes brushing the inner lens of her goggles. And how fingers of wind razored its breeze through hair at the side of her temples. He envied it.

Beautiful. Everything about her, from the inside out.

She tilted her face to the ground and he could no longer see her face. He let gravity pull them through the thrill of it, and spoke no further. He let her senses take in every detail of the experience. He loved it up here. Sharing it with her caused peace-induced warmth to flood somewhere deep inside him. He could ride the winds of forever with her.

Basking in contentment, he peered down, enthralled at the brown, black, green and pale yellow blocks of earth that fit together like a farmland patchwork quilt. It amazed him how they got the fields so perfectly square.

Boats bobbed in a lake like pepper floating in Celia's soup. Cars, like multicolored ants, crawled in lines down asphalt roads. Frigid air up here but somehow refreshing. Purging even.

Planes dotted a light-lined lot near metal-domed hangars. They looked like toys. Roofs of buildings spiraled in a geographic kaleidoscope, rendering the sensation of them being still while the ground rotated beneath.

Sensing their altitude, he warned her and pulled the chute cord. With a sudden jolt, the sensation of free-falling halted with an upward jerk. Amber's hands flew, grasping air. He placed his hand atop hers and squeezed, assuring her she hadn't disconnected from him. Her feet had also flown up and out, then back against his. He quickly disentangled them.

Their downward momentum slowed to a gentle float. He surmised her neck felt okay when giggles bubbled out of her as the ground drifted up to meet them. The rush and roar of wind and glide of flying ceased. But his heart still soared.

Closer to the ground, she tensed.

"Remember what I told you about landing?"

"No!" Her hoarse voice blasted his eardrums. A gust of wind veered them sideways. Though not dangerously, she must have thought so. "We're crashing—" Feet writhed, tangling in his.

"We're not crashing. Bend your knees." He tugged his feet but hers scrambled, relocking his in a vise. Her legs were strong. He wondered what she bench-pressed. Jogging and panic didn't build that kind of muscle.

If they landed off-kilter, one of them could end up with a fractured ankle. He didn't want to force her feet from his boot, but he had to do something. Fast.

"Amber!" He gave a mighty jerk, finally freeing his feet to land properly for both of them. She drew her knees up. Too far.

"Amber, not so—"

Thunk.

Too late. Joel landed square but Amber tumbled knees down, face-first in the dust. Her momentum plus gravity tugged him forward. His hands flew out to stop an awkward situation.

"Oomph!" That had to have knocked the wind out of her.

He'd spread his feet to avoid landing on her but wasn't very successful since her knees were bent up under her. A rainbow of primary colors floated down over them turning the drop zone into a miniature circus tent.

He scrambled to pull himself up, and the chute off.

Her arms flailed like a pair of hostile windmills as she attacked the material.

"Whoa. Hold on. Let me help before you get tangled." He tugged the chute off her, folding at mach speed as he went.

She groaned, and pushed herself to a sitting position.

He assessed her—no blood, no bones sticking out. Not bad for that landing. "You all right?"

She flung her goggles off and away, then dropped her head to her knees. "That depends." Her chest heaved a cough.

He brushed her hair back. "On?"

"Whether we're getting our money back," she mumbled.

He bit his lip from laughing. "No refund, since the reserve opened."

Wild eyes and hair snapped up. "The reserve? You mean—"

He held a palm up. "Kidding. The main chute did deploy and made it to the ground intact."

"We did, too, so I guess that's good, right?" She rolled sideways, grabbed the goggles and blew dust off them.

"Right." He grasped both of her hands and helped her to a sitting position. "Slowly, now. Dizzy?"

"Dead, I think." She patted the ground. "Wow. If it

hurts that bad to land with a chute open, I hate to think what it feels like when one doesn't."

"Trust me, you wouldn't feel a thing. If you did, you wouldn't remember."

"Don't remind me. Can I go home now?" Her hands trembled as they brushed hair from her face.

He helped her to stand. He'd hoped she would have enjoyed it. As she walked the drop zone floor, every muscle twitched, probably from adrenaline. Reminded him of a windup toy jittering across a tabletop.

"You didn't like it, did you?" Hand to her elbow, he veered her to the building.

"Don't know. Ask me next time."

He paused mid-step. "You're willing to go again?"

"Of course. But not today. I think I should not plan to eat Celia's tortilla and bean soup before the next jump, though. That chute's not the only thing that deployed up there."

Joel laughed out loud, glad color had returned to her face. "You did great." He squeezed her shoulder.

She cast him a tentative glance. "For my first time."

"No. You did fine," he lied with all his heart. The girl was windblown cute. He snapped the chute cover closed.

"Until the landing."

He grinned, tilting his hand side to side. "The landing was a bit touch and go, but seriously, you're a natural."

"Gee, I hope not. We'd both go deaf." For the first time since landing, a smile peeked through.

At the DZ office, he held the door for her, then they obtained the key to the locker they'd shared.

He put a possessive hand to Amber's back as they passed the female employee who'd given him the eye earlier. She'd turned the heat up in Amber's absence despite the fact that Joel rudely ignored her. She wasn't the kind of girl who interested him.

"You're beautiful. You know that?" Joel blurted.

Her face flushed that endearing shade of red. "Me?"

"Yeah. You." He lifted her bag from the locker, then tugged things out. Something smelled rank. She waved a hand across her face so she must have smelled it, too.

"I think there's a dead mouse in the wall."

He laughed. "Me, too." They turned in the key and descended the steps to the parking area. Amber wasn't moving as fast.

"Do you hurt anywhere?" He thought of her ankles.

"Just my throat. I may not be able to talk for a week."

"That's all right, because for the same reason, I won't be able to hear you for a week."

They shared a chuckle as they approached her car.

"Hey, mind if I drive?" He eyed the Mustang.

"I've always wanted a cute chauffeur—be my guest." She planted the keys in his hand. The spot her fingers made contact with tingled. She slipped into the seat and Joel closed her door and got in.

"Bradley goes to church with you?" He pulled onto the road.

"Yes. I pay his foster mother gas money to drop him off."

"Why doesn't she let you pick him up?"

"I have my suspicions, but I'd rather not say until they're proven. I hope I'm wrong. Anyway, why are you asking?"

"I'd like to spend time with him before I get called back. Maybe I'll go to church with you guys Sunday."

"That would be great. Want me to pick you up?"

"Yeah. I'm staying at the Refuge Bed-and-Breakfast. I'd like us to hang with Bradley during the day if we can borrow him for a few hours. Then you and I can do something that evening."

"I'll arrange it with his caseworker. Next time you come into town, you can stay at my parents' house. They have plenty of space, and you wouldn't have to spring for a room."

He scrubbed the back of his neck, wondering how to break this to her. "Amber, I won't be coming back."

She stared at him. "Won't they give you leave if Bradley gets bad?"

"In that case, I'd come. It's not that they won't give leave. It took every ounce of strength to come here for a few days. I don't like this place. Being here slams me back to a past I've spent a lifetime getting free from."

He'd had no idea she lived on the corner of Haven and Sonnet either until Celia dropped him off. He'd steer clear of her apartment since it sat blocks away from his uncle's house.

"Okay."

He could see from her face it wasn't. He hated this pull of cowardice, but knew his limitations. Hard memories lived here. He could deal with it only because he knew there was a way out and an end in sight. He'd spend quality time with Bradley because he'd pledged allegiance to his promise.

This visit would be his last.

"How big are the fish in your parents' pond?" He steered her car onto the road leading to the bed-and-breakfast where he was staying.

"Big enough to need a net to drag one in. Want to try your hand tomorrow?"

"Yeah. I would. I can meet your parents, too."

A catlike grin tugged her mouth up. "Then you'll just have to come back to Refuge. They're out of town for another week."

He smiled and exited the car, now at the B and B parking lot. "Nice try." Did she want him to come back for Bradley's sake only? He didn't want to push if they weren't ready. If things progressed, he'd figure out how to see Amber, sans Refuge.

"I'm wiped out from jet lag. Let's call it a night and get an early start. See you in the morning, sunshine." He leaned in the open car window and tousled her hair. The flash of uncertainty in her face gave her away.

She'd thought he'd been about to kiss her. He grinned. Great idea.

Bad timing.

They needed to talk first. Establish and define their relationship. Be strategic about this.

He pushed away from the window before he could change his mind.

Chapter Eleven

One of these times he'd turn and catch her staring like a stalker. Last night when she'd given him a ride back to the B and B from her apartment, she'd found a perfect angle to back her car up and watch him ascend the steps.

Soldier of compassion.

Joel, with his disarming grin and guileless spirit.

She sighed to herself. "I actually tried something dangerous." She reminisced the exhilarating skydive. She loved friends who refused to let her veg in her comfort zones.

Celia was like that. Now she had Joel, too.

Only one problem—she saw her and Joel as friends, and thought they were on the same page with that. Until he'd flipped the book upside down at the drop zone.

Right before going to the plane, she'd observed his aloof nature toward the lithe DZ employee who'd sidled next to him as he waited for Amber to use the restroom.

Neither of them had heard her come out, but Amber had seen Joel give her the cold shoulder. He hadn't flirted an ounce, though she was built like a super-model and dressed to kill. Amber had stopped to compose herself before turning the corner, set at an angle where they were visible to her but not her to them. She'd darted back with one word.

Girlfriend.

The girl had asked Joel if he skydived often.

"Yes," he'd answered. "But this time is special since it's my girlfriend's first jump."

Amber wasn't sure if he'd said that to fend off the DZ girl's advances or because he actually thought of Amber as his girlfriend. Regardless, those words had landed right in her heart.

Back to present, Amber waited for a car to pass. "What you see is what you get. I hope you're the real deal," she whispered to his reflection in her mirror as he leaned over the B and B banister.

He waved as she pulled onto the highway leading home.

Each lonely mile back to her apartment magni-fied the silence inside her car where his voice had earlier filled the space. Masculine cologne still lingered on her seat cushion, and baritone laughter still rang in her heart.

Every grin replayed in her mind, every remem-brance of gentle shoulder squeezes, the discovery that she might potentially be the only girl on earth privy to his flirting…even the way his black hair stood up on top without a drop of gel.

When she arrived home a little past eight, Amber changed into her jogging shoes and went for her evening run. Halfway through, she tied her jacket around her waist. A whiff of something skunk-like followed her. She glanced over her shoulder to be sure Pepé Le Pew wasn't stalking her.

She laughed so hard she nearly tripped. She ran faster, pushed her legs harder, wanting to get home to bed sooner so morning would come and she could see her soldier again.

Amber slowed, wondering when she'd started thinking of him as hers. She groaned and ran on. Hopefully morning light would shine sanity back on her perspective of things.

It's the lonely night. Nothing else.

Morning light would clear her muddled mind.

Morning light brought a killer headache. The sun crested the horizon of her chipped windowsill, dazzling her with spots before her eyes. She glared at the clock and willed time to pass. She'd only been able to fall asleep a couple hours ago because anticipation over the day wouldn't let her sleep.

Nor would her confusing emotions regarding Joel. Last night had her ready to jump. Today she wanted to chase the plane down and strap it to the hangar. It didn't help that she'd remembered that today hailed the one-year anniversary of her canceled wedding.

When 7:00 a.m. finally showed its ugly face, she dialed Bradley's caseworker, left a voice mail then headed to shower. Once out, her answering machine beeped. Amber ran to grab the cordless.

Dead.

Amber groaned and slogged to the kitchen to get the stationery. She jerked up the receiver but the line tangled, pulling the entire unit down. She dived, caught it an inch from the floor. She jostled the black spiral cord free as a beep sounded.

A voice came through. Not Miss Harker. Her pulse galloped.

"Morning, sunshine. When you wake up, call me at the—"

Perked up, Amber snatched the receiver and jammed it to her chin. "Hello?" Fatigue fled and her sour mood dissipated.

"Hey. Did I wake you?" Joel asked.

"No. I've been awake for…a while." She couldn't fess up since he was the cause of her sleep deprivation.

Her call-waiting tone sounded. "Can you hold on a second? That's Bradley's caseworker."

"No problem."

Amber clicked over. "Hey, Miss Harker."

"Hello, Amber. I got home to your message about Bradley's soldier being in town at midnight. This is Camp Hope week."

"That's right. I forgot."

"Bradley returns noon Sunday. When is the soldier leaving?"

"In a few days. He'd like to see him Sunday."

"Would you like me to call camp and ask Bradley if he'd like to leave early to see Mr. Montgomery?"

"I think it would do him as much good to be with other children who know what he's going through."

"Okay, Amber. If you change your mind, call me back. I'll keep him at my house until I hear from you Sunday."

"I'll ask Joel what he thinks. If you don't hear back from me, then he wanted Bradley to go to camp. He may stay an extra day since he came all the way from India to see Bradley." Amber yawned. Lack of sleep caught up to her.

"A little birdie told me they think he came back to see you as much as Bradley," Miss Harker said in a singsong voice.

Amber only knew of one mutual acquaintance they had besides Bradley. "A little birdie, huh? Well, next time you see the squawking Celia, tell her I'm pinching her beak inside out."

The next twenty minutes seemed to pass in an hour for Joel as he watched the window for anything yellow. He hoped Bradley wouldn't be disappointed, but Camp Hope seemed right up Bradley's alley. Joel fled his cabin like it had caught fire when the Mustang pulled into the bed-and-breakfast lot.

Bells jingled over the doors as he reached the main room. Amber's smile lit the lobby when she waltzed in.

"What's the plan since it's just you and me?" she asked.

He stood closer, taking in a berry scent, and gestured to the dining room. "Let's grab breakfast here, then go for a walk. I have an appointment at eleven."

"Appointment? Are you ill?" She looked him up and down.

He adopted a serious expression. "I'm short of breath."

Her pace slowed. "Really? That can't be good."

"I made an appointment at the health center for you."

She stopped, dipping her chin. "Me?"

"Yeah. Thought you might want to get your CPR card updated."

"Very funny." She smacked his arm, flushed red and faced forward. "Are you really feeling bad?" she asked after regaining her composure.

"No. I feel great." He let out a dramatic sigh and drooped his shoulders. "Unfortunately."

Her mouth opened then clamped shut as she swooped past him to a corner breakfast nook.

He scooted in beside her instead of across. She peered over her shoulder at him. "There's ten feet of bench space on this thing, so I think we can use more than two."

His elbow pressed into hers. "What's the fun in that? I like to be close to you."

She eyed the other patrons, then the empty bench across from them. "Well, be close over there. This is a small town. People talk."

"What would they say?"

"No telling."

He tugged a strand of her hair. "Could be fun to see what kind of rumors we can start up about ourselves. I can hear it over the Faith Elementary intercom now. Joel and Miss Stanton sitting in a tree. K-I-S—"

"Shh! I'm serious. People are looking."

He scooted off her side of the wooden booth and slid in across from her, growing suddenly serious. He took her hands in his across the table. "We need to talk."

She blushed and flung the menu in front of her face. "I know."

He put a finger to the top of it and pushed down until he'd lowered it enough to see the green of her eyes. "Careful. You'll melt the plastic on this if you get it close to your cheeks."

Her forehead crinkled like an accordion, so he decided to let up with the teasing. "Seriously, Amber. Let's talk about us."

"Us. So is there definitely an us?" She drew in a breath.

Joel couldn't decipher whether it was relief or panic. "Don't you think there is?"

She finally let out the breath. "I was afraid to think so."

He wondered what she meant by that. He wished he understood the way women thought. Had his mother been in his life longer, maybe he'd be better at this sort of thing.

"So, we're not talking about friendship?" She tilted her head, lifting her shoulders as if afraid of his answer. He had concerns, too, like how they'd work out their obstacles. Sometimes you had to throw fear to the wind and trust God to work stuff out.

"I've never seen friends who act like us." He sat back, chuckling as he lifted his own menu. She jabbed his ankle with the toe of her shoe. Hard.

The hostess bustled to the table. "Can I help you?"

"Yeah, you can help me. This lady across from me keeps trying to play footsies with me—ow!" Joel reached down, rubbing his shin. "See? There she goes again."

"Orange juice, coffee, and kicks under the table are free to guests, but anything else will have to be added to your tab. So, what can I get for you besides a shin pad?" She poised pen above paper.

"What's the appointment?" Amber asked after returning from the buffet.

"A surprise." Joel peppered his eggs.

She froze, her eyes growing wide.

At the paranoia taking her face hostage, he swallowed juice before speaking again. "Don't worry.

We're not shopping for rings yet if that's what's got you petrified."

She reached for the canning jar. "I wasn't thinking anything like that." She jabbed a knife in the jelly and slathered it over her plate. The wrong plate.

"Grape jelly on your omelets convinces me otherwise."

Amber stared down at the purple smearing her eggs, then to her plain toast. She looked up. "I eat jelly on my omelet all the time." As if proving a point, she took a bite.

He laughed. "What do you put on your toast then?"

"Salt, pepper and hot sauce, of course."

After sharing half his omelet with her, and fending off her interrogation to unravel the mystery of the eleven o'clock appointment, he dropped payment and a tip and stood. "Let's go walk some of this food off and talk some more. This brochure says there are hiking and nature trails behind the bed-and-breakfast."

She set her napkin down and stepped from the booth. "Sounds great. I love to hike."

"Good, let's walk and talk."

On the third trail, near a rocky waterfall, they approached a steep ledge. Amber's foot slipped on a wet, mossy rock. Joel reached to steady her.

She sat. "Let's go a different way."

He studied the map. "The only way is back down and around a few miles or along this ledge to the top. Let's go to the top and see the waterfall." He pocketed the map.

Fear suffused her face.

He sat beside her. "What's going on?" The question meant more than just the fear. She'd avoided his direct questions since their feet hit the trail.

"I can't walk along the edge." The words tumbled out.

"Is it the heights?"

She nodded. "I jumped from a plane so it doesn't make sense." She shoved fingers through her bangs. "I hate this. Only two things rattle me. Three, actually. Heights and earthquakes."

"What's the third thing?" He reached for her hand.

"Broken hearts."

Bull's-eye. Now they were getting somewhere. "I'll lead you. You don't have to look. Trust me." *I'd never break your heart.*

"But I'll know I'm walking on the edge. I'm afraid I'll be nervous and my footing won't be sure. I don't want to tumble us down the cliff. Go on without me. I'll wait here."

"It won't be the same without you. Please let me help you conquer this. I rescue people from scary places all the time."

"You're too charming for your own good. Or mine." She stood, taking the hand he offered. Closer to the edge, she trembled.

He kept her on his left side, the edge on his right. "How long have you been a teacher?"

"That doesn't work." Her words puffed out in short gasps.

So much for diversionary tactics. He had an idea, but it might get him slapped. He grinned. Either way, it would be worth the risk. Arm already around her shoulder, he tilted her chin up, held firm with his hand, dipped his face and planted a firm and lasting kiss on her lips.

She wiggled and mumbled protest then jerked back and stomped off, glaring at him. She flung tree limb after tree limb aside…all the way past the ledge.

Once there she stopped, turning slowly, narrowing her eyelids. "You did that on purpose."

He didn't suppress his grin. "Worked, didn't it?"

She stared at the edge, then at him. "I suppose, but I'm not sure which one of you is more dangerous." Brisk steps carried her down the stone-dotted trail.

The tone of her voice caught him up in a hurry. "Amber, wait. I didn't want our first kiss to be like that. I'm sorry." Just as he reached for her shoulder, she climbed over a damp river rock, out of his grasp. She slipped a few feet, landing in a dry creek bed.

"Don't be mad at me." He tugged her up, then helped her scale the jagged rock. Once over, he let go of one hand but not the other.

Holding it felt right as they walked more stable terrain. Pine needles cushioned their feet. Juniper and elm sap aromas swirled with wild onions and cottonwood in the air. Yellows, browns, reds and a few greens canopied their heads.

"I'm not mad at you, Joel. I'm mad at me."

Had she changed her mind already about dating him? Had he moved too soon out of the friendship realm?

A distant arrowhead of southbound geese penetrated the sky, flying in formation similar to the air force fighter jets which had been Joel's world for a decade.

Amber grew unusually quiet, and her hand turned to granite beneath his. He sat and tugged her down to a rock in front of him, reluctantly letting go. "Okay, what gives?"

She stared at the ground, the trees, the rocks, the waterfall. Everywhere but him. "I'm not sure I'm ready for a serious relationship."

"My gut tells me that's not it, or at least not all of it."

"I care about you, but I'm afraid to care about you more. Maybe we should rethink this, and pray about staying friends."

"I get it. You're the type of person who has to have everything figured out before you take a step, aren't you?"

She eyed him carefully. "I never thought about it, but I guess I am. And you're the type of person who is okay with figuring things out as he goes along, aren't you?"

"On some things. Okay, look. I know there are things that could become major barriers if this relationship progresses. So let's talk about those things now, before we get in too deep. If we can't come up with viable solutions over Refuge and the kids thing, we'll sever ties and cut our losses. No matter what, I still want to be your friend."

"Yeah, that's what Barf said, too," she muttered.

"Barf?"

She looked at her watch, appearing suddenly disgruntled. "It's fifteen after ten. If your appointment in town is at eleven, we should head back."

Clearly she didn't want to discuss it. One day and already they were running up against a communication wall. But he wanted this too badly to give up so easily. He saw something special in her. Felt inexplicably drawn to her. He'd assumed God was drawing them together. If that was indeed the case, God would work things out.

If not, and his radar had gotten jammed, someone was likely to get hurt. He'd rather it be him than her.

I need wisdom and direction, Lord. I want Your good and perfect will, and know she does, too.

He stood, careful to hold her elbow to assist her over the more dangerous terrain and not her hand. He put plenty of space between them so she wouldn't feel uncomfortable, but not so much that she could think him mad or upset. He fell into step beside her, wondering where the fire was. At the rate she walked, they'd make it down the trail in minutes.

Her face stayed flushed, leaving him to wonder if she fought within herself over her decision. He hoped so. Having given the discussion a rest, but unable to let this lie, he moved to stand in front of her, forcing her to look in his face.

"What?"

"Exactly," he said, noting her scowl. "Why don't you take a chance, let this progress naturally where it's meant to? Friendship is the best foundation for a solid romantic relationship. We're past friendship. So that's why this time is awkward. We are learning each other on a romantic level for the first time. Where's your sense of adventure?"

She elbowed past him. "I lost it in San Francisco."

He caught up to her. "What happened in California, Amber?"

"I don't want to talk about it."

"If you can't talk to me, then maybe we don't have what it takes." Though he didn't believe it for a minute.

That stopped her. She turned with eyes so wide, he wished he could take back his words. Someone must have really wounded her in the past. He wanted to throttle the guy.

Joel reached for her. "I'm sorry. I didn't mean it like that." He stepped closer and held her arms in his.

"It's not that I don't want to talk to you. I'm scared what I have to tell you will change your mind about us." She pulled from his grasp and started down the trail with her back to him. "I will understand if you'd rather be fif-furr-ends." Her steps wavered with the word.

He moved closer in case she stumbled. A laugh escaped him. Then another.

Her head whipped around. "What's so funny?"

"Nothing." He laughed again, not meaning to but

she looked so miffed, he couldn't open his mouth without one slipping out.

She halted, face drawn, fists clapped against her legs. "Tell me."

"Friends isn't a three-syllable word, Miss Stanton."

Her hands shot palms out. "Don't read into it. I'm just thirsty so my tongue couldn't spit it out in one syllable."

He jostled the end of her ponytail. "Friends might not be a three-syllable word…but persistence is."

She shook her head, laughter deepened the lines in her face. "You're impossible, you know that? Do you ever give up?"

"Only when I'm convinced my mission is truly over."

She put hands to her hips. "I'm a mission?"

"Me getting you to talk to me is a personal mission, yes."

She poked her finger at him. "Even if I talk about it, that doesn't mean our differences will be easy to fix. It's going to take work."

He tugged a pinecone off a tree, tossing it in the air. "And honesty and transparency. Who hurt you, Amber?"

She watched the cone go up and down. "Where's your appointment?"

"You're changing the subject. My appointment is at Refuge Cellular. I ordered a surprise for us. Even if we go backward, friends keep in touch, right?" He put a healthy amount of sarcasm on the word then tugged another pinecone off. He bent to get a third from the trail.

"I wish our goals weren't different." Her volume lowered.

He put a hand to her shoulder, tone serious. "Hey, I didn't mean to upset you. We can work it out."

"But that's it. I'm not so sure. I'm floored someone as special as you would be interested in simple, small-town me."

"You are far from simple." *Interested* barely hit the tip of the iceberg. "But I do have a sense of dignity. So, if you're waiting for me to fling myself at your feet and beg, it's not happening. But I am interested in this progressing to something long-term. So yeah, I know we need to be up-front with each other about important issues that could make or break us as a couple."

He juggled the cones while walking and wondered if she'd ever want to leave Refuge. If not, that would present a monster hurdle. Then there was the kid issue. And he got the idea she wasn't telling him something. He wondered if it had to do with whoever hurt her. Or something else?

"I didn't know you could juggle."

"I can do up to six."

"But for how long?"

He knew from her tone she wasn't talking pine-cones. "Is that what you're afraid of? That my feelings will change? That my interest will wane?"

"Partly. Feelings always change."

"They might. And so might yours. My feelings and emotions do not rule me. My commitments and my creed and my vows do. If I make a commitment, I will not break it, no matter how I feel, or how my feelings change. You're the first person who I felt would approach the storms of life that way."

"What about the no-children vow?"

He held branches off her face. "There's a valid reason for it."

"Like there's a reason for my reluctance for romance."

"Point taken. Maybe it's time for goal reevaluation. We're clashing. Commitment doesn't work without compromise."

"Ditto, Joel. The road of compromise runs two lanes."

She was right. It had to go both ways. The implications of that rattled him, and nothing much rattled him. Except Refuge.

He couldn't very well expect her to rethink her life goals and not be willing to himself. How selfish would that be?

Suddenly needing to put space between them, he grabbed two bottles of water from the ice-filled washtub outside the B and B while she hoofed it to the car.

His heart had already locked in tandem and leaped. Now he had them falling without a reserve or a net. Something had to give, or they were in for a crash. There had to be a way to salvage this jump.

She was too timid to hold on to what they had and he was too stubborn to let go. So he'd hold on for both of them and glide with the wind of God wherever it took them.

Regardless, he knew they were in each other's lives for a reason. He just hoped that reason was for more than a season. They'd become irrevocably bonded through phone calls, e-mail and letters despite the fact that they'd not had that much face time.

He felt ready for a lifetime love. Was she ready? And if so, would she surrender her fears to God and let Him work out the details and differences?

Let Your good and perfect will be done. Help us to surrender to it, even if it's not what we want to hear.

Chapter Twelve

❧

"Can I help you, sir?" the Refuge Cellular clerk asked.

Joel propped an elbow on the chest-high counter. "I'm Joel Montgomery. I have an eleven o'clock appointment."

"Yes, sir. For service setup. Just a moment. The store owner wanted to see you."

The employee tapped on an office door and exchanged words with someone inside before turning back to Joel. "He'll be right with you."

"No problem." Joel watched Amber browse.

Seconds later, an African-American gentleman in a charcoal suit stepped out, extending one hand beneath the counter and the other across to Joel. "I'm Mr. Johannson. Nice to meet you, Mr. Montgomery."

"You, too." Joel shook his hand.

He pulled out two cardboard boxes. "We have your order here. If you'll step down to the second booth, we'll get this service set up for you and the missus."

Joel grinned and moved where the man indicated.

"My children attend Faith Elementary. I was there the day the Dream Corps choppers dropped you down. My little girl's the one who sang." The man's dark face beamed. "She thinks she's gonna be the next American Idol."

Joel chuckled. "She might be. I get chills remembering her voice. That was really special, what those kids did for us."

"That was really special, what you did for Bradley and those kids. It floored me they all kept it secret from Bradley and Miss Stanton an entire two weeks. That's a miracle in itself." He chuckled. "Listen, I have to run an errand, but my associate can assist with all your needs. Pleasure meeting you. I hope to see you around more."

Joel motioned Amber over. She approached the booth.

"Have a seat. We'll get you fixed up," the associate said.

She looked to Joel with a teasing gleam. "Fixed up?"

The man stretched a handheld to her. She eyed it. "For me?"

Joel nodded. "They're like Manny's BlackBerry, but they do a little more. It's a phone, e-mail companion, text messenger, Webcam. It does GPS, all sorts of other stuff."

"You'll never lose touch with that thing." The clerk

handed Joel a form that looked like a receipt. "Service is paid on both phones for two years. Unlimited use. No roaming charges, no long distance. No hidden fees. You should be all set."

Joel handed the form back. "There's a mistake. I haven't paid yet. I just filled out what I wanted. I'm paying today."

"The phones and two years of service are paid up, compliments of the owner." The clerk tapped a note on a red, white and blue linen postcard. Joel picked it up, reading:

Freedom costs so these phones do not. Please accept our gift as appreciation for your dedication and sacrifice to our country. May God grant time with your loved ones, and bless you as you serve and protect this nation. We know freedom comes with a price which most of the free will never know about. So this is the least we can do. Stay the course. Show you care. Stay in touch. Sincerely, Refuge Cellular Staff.

Joel looked up. "This is incredible. These phones are top-of-the-line."

"The owner has a policy to do that for all military personnel. It's his way of giving back. Let me box these up."

"I can't believe you planned these. They had to have cost a fortune," Amber whispered as she stared at the handheld.

"It's nothing compared to the frustration I felt those two days my phone went on the fritz. This gift is for me as much as for you. God will honor this business owner. I would have paid triple to have a link to you."

She wrapped her arms around his neck and squeezed with a hug that lingered. He never expected the gesture. No complaints, though. He grinned. If she always thanked with hugs, he might have to buy her stuff every few hours.

He enjoyed the affection to the last drop. He hadn't realized how much he missed human touch. He lived, ate and breathed with his team for the last decade. And if he tried to hug one of them, he was liable to get a scorpion in his sleeping bag, exploding pants from a well-placed flash-bang grenade, or nice and slugged.

"Thank you," she said. The clerk set them up with passwords and voice mail and a gazillion other things. By the time they rose from the booth, the clock ticked one o'clock.

Standing side by side, Joel picked his phone up and dialed her number. She answered it, looking at him funny.

"What now?" he said into his phone.

She giggled. "I don't know. What do you want to do?" she said into her phone as they walked out of the cell phone store into the mall. "I'm hungry," she added.

"Me, too," he said into his mouthpiece, looking at her.

"How does Chinese sound?" she said into her phone.

"Gross," Joel said back.

She tossed her head back, laughing. Joel enjoyed the way her ponytail galloped at the top of her crown.

Patrons and mall walkers cast curious glances their way.

Feathery hair tips stroked the back of her neck like a watercolor brush when she looked around. "People are beginning to stare because we're walking inches apart and conversing by phone," she said, passing vendor booths and store marquee.

He grinned. "So what? Let them stare. We're just checking out our new toys." He eyed the food court. "How about Italian?"

"I hate pasta," she said, still talking into her phone.

"There's a shoe store." He gestured to a side shop.

She looked over, laughing. "Leather isn't part of my diet."

"No, but I have holes in my soles. Hang a left." He clicked his phone shut and veered into the store but stopped when Amber inhaled sharply.

"Hello, Amber."

Joel looked up to find a man a few feet away. Amber paled by shades. The tall blonde clinging to the guy's arm eyed her up and down. Amber didn't speak, just swallowed. Joel moved close to her. His motion seemed to snap her out of whatever funk she'd slipped into.

Amber brushed a ringlet out of her eyes, avoiding

the blonde's gaze but meeting the man's head-on. "Bart. I didn't know you were in town." Amber's expression as it darted to the woman seemed to say she didn't realize a lot of things.

Sensing the tension between Amber and the man called Bart, Joel put his hand to her lower back. "If you'll excuse us, we're late for lunch."

Though minute, Joel noticed tremors in Amber's fingers as she tucked a prodigal ringlet behind her ear. He reached to clasp her hand. She gripped it firmly and his hand seemed to steady whatever emotions had bumped her off center.

"I was going to suggest eating in the mall food court, but how about we go somewhere outside the mall instead?" He hadn't wanted to run the risk of seeing his uncle out and about. But he'd chance it in order to protect Amber from having another jarring mall confrontation with this stuffy-looking guy and his cling-on blonde.

"We could stop by the market on Mayberry, grab steaks to grill at the pond." Her words tumbled out as fast as her feet did toward the mall exit.

Joel wondered about the man, and why it bothered Amber to see him. Obviously, by the way the guy shifted foot to foot, Amber was an old flame. By Amber's reaction, Joel wondered if her end of the flame had ever completely died.

He remembered back to the hike and how she seemed to be dancing around something. Joel hoped her reservations toward their relationship didn't have to do with lingering feelings for an old boyfriend. He hadn't considered that.

Obviously the guy had moved on. Had Amber?

"Joel?" She eyed him carefully.

He realized he never answered her. "Grilling at the pond sounds great if your parents won't mind us trespassing while they're gone. Hey, hang another left." Joel veered her into a toy and gaming store. "I want to get something for Bradley."

Amber walked along the aisles while Joel perused rows of games and toys. Something must have caught her eye on the end cap, because she moved toward it. "Joel, look."

He stepped over to view the box in her hand. "That's absolutely perfect." Joel turned the box over. "A paratrooper costume equipped with a canteen, radio and goggles."

"Even a maroon beret." Amber pointed to it.

Joel studied her. "You knew that?"

She blushed. "I know the difference between a PJ and a Green Beret. I've been studying up."

That touched Joel to the core. "I'm glad you found this," Joel said as the checkout clerk rang them up. At the total, he shook his head. "That's not right. You're undercharging me."

"It's ringing up nine dollars and thirty cents."

"Sure there's not a recall on it or something? The ticket on the box says thirty bucks. The sign says twenty-five."

"I'm sure. Our manager is a stickler for things like that. We got two shipments. Maybe they're trying to run through them."

Joel paid the money feeling out of sorts. Nine-thirty. When the numbers popped up, a twinge went through him of longing, of sadness. September thirtieth—the last day he'd seen his mom. Nine-thirty was also the address of his uncle's house on Haven Street. *What are you trying to tell me, Lord?*

"You okay, Joel?" Amber asked as they exited the store.

"Yeah. No. Actually, no. But let's talk about what's bothering us over dinner." He eyed her to see what her reaction would be to that.

She squeezed his hand. "Okay. I'll try."

It pleased Joel that she held his hand all the way to the car. He let go reluctantly to open her door, closing it before going around to the other side and getting in himself.

Miles later, Joel hit the signal and changed lanes on the main road that ran through Refuge. "Are we market-bound?"

"Yep. I'm ready for takeoff." She stuck the skydiving goggles on.

He laughed, glad her humor had resurfaced. "Speaking of, do you not fly due to heights?"

"Yes. The second rung of a ladder is sketchy, and the third is certain death."

"I'm really proud of you for facing your fears,

Amber." He hoped she knew he didn't only mean heights. He squeezed her hand for emphasis.

Down the road she pointed ahead. "Turn left at the light."

"I thought so. Place hasn't changed much." Joel chuckled when the passenger in the car next to them looked oddly at Amber, who still had the flight goggles on.

"How old were you when you moved away?" She tugged the goggles off and patted her wild ringlets down. They boomeranged back to partially curtain her eyes.

"When I joined the air force after college. My dad sent me to military schools on and off for part of those years."

"What did you major in?" she asked.

"Majored in art. Minored in phys. ed with an ROTC track."

Two green eyes grew luminous. "Art?"

"Yes, and that's all I'm saying about that."

What a multifaceted man, Amber thought.

Pangs of guilt hit her because he'd been so open with her, and she still kept secrets.

Namely one big secret that when revealed, would determine their future together.

God, please give me courage to tell him I'm actively pursuing adopting Bradley.

"After we hit the market, I need to check on my cat. He goes schizoid when left alone."

His smile wilted. "At your apartment?"

"No, at the zoo."

"Very funny. Tell you what. I'll shop while you check on Psychokitty, then swing back by and pick me up."

He pulled into the only available parking spot, near the back. "Portabello, Monterey and Vidalia?"

She tilted her head. "You remember?" They'd discussed favorite foods during early IM conversations.

Joel brushed hair from her forehead. "I remember every single thing you tell me." He leaned in and pressed warm lips where his fingers had touched.

Amber thrust a fifty between their noses, creating a barrier, probably to hide the blush his words brought to the surface.

He pushed the bill aside, running a thumb along her hand. "Put your money away, Chief Redcheeks. My treat."

Joel enjoyed her deepening flush as she scrambled to the driver's seat, trying to act unaffected.

He chuckled all the way to the entrance.

The girl's mouth could have kept saying "just friends" all it wanted, but the girl's cheeks always gave her away.

At least she'd finally admitted it.

They were no longer just friends. He couldn't go back if he wanted to.

Chapter Thirteen

My boyfriend. Boyfriend. My. Boyfriend.

As much as Amber hadn't wanted to hope that's what they were, her heart had betrayed her sensibilities and leaped at the word. At the very idea this valiant soldier, this compassionate warrior could be called her very own.

He didn't want to date other people, he'd said. That meant he was hers and she his.

But where would that lead? To happiness?

Or eventual heartache?

Not wanting to be found confused in the parking lot when he came back, she ceased staring at his fluid stride and turned the ignition. The transmission screeched in a spine-cringing whine. Her neck heated.

Joel paused at the market door, turned around, brows AWOL.

She shrugged, laughing. He'd never shut the

engine down. Why did his nearness always cause her to geek out?

Embarrassment dropped her head to the steering wheel.

Honk.

She groaned as Joel turned around a second time, heading back to the car. She waved him on. He came anyway. Her face grew hotter with every step closer.

He leaned in the window. "Everything all right?"

"Fine." She fought the urge to snicker.

"Then why'd you bimp at me?"

An undignified laugh escaped her despite how poised she tried to be. "Bimp?"

"Trucks have real horns. They honk. Cars only bimp." He flashed a maddeningly potent grin. The one that made her pulse do weird things. Things that would probably make nurses come running and a cardiac monitor go berserk if she were hooked up to one.

Amber rubbed the dash of her Mustang. "Hear that, Miss Mussy? He's making fun of you."

"Miss Mussy?" He eyed the car. "Nah. I'd call her Stang." He ran his hand along the hood, then pivoted toward the store entrance. His broad shoulders lifted with a rhythm she knew to be laughter.

She flipped the air on high. En route to her apartment, her mind grappled with the mystery. He seemed okay with the market, but not her apartment. He'd go down Sonnet Drive but never Haven Street. If it were a matter of temptation, he wouldn't be gung ho about going to her parents', knowing they were gone.

"What's the deal with Joel and Haven Street?"

Her cell rang as she backed out of her drive minutes later. Caller ID said private. "Hello?"

"Hey, sunshine. Bring Psych along if you want. Does he travel okay?"

"I have a pet carrier, though it's five times too big because it's for a dog. He does okay in it. I'll run back and get him then be there."

"No hurry. I'll be outside on the bench. They had cat tuna so I picked up a few cans. See you in a few."

He bought food for her cat? Amber put Psych in the colossal carrier. "Let's go to the market and pick up some steak, a sweet soldier and your stinky tuna."

When she pulled into the lot, Joel lounged on a wooden bench reading a newspaper. Something in her chest fluttered at the sight of him. His crisp white T-shirt contrasted with dark skin. India's sun had deepened his tan. Jeans stretched across muscular legs.

She admired how both of them—Joel and the jeans—stayed in shape. His job would require top physical conditioning, and she imagined his jeans stayed in shape by hanging in his closet when his camos went to combat. If the man weren't so tall, dark and charming, it wouldn't be so easy to wish she wasn't scared.

Not *of* him—falling for him. Putting her heart in a position to be trampled. Or in this case, marched across with lethal-looking jump boots. She should have been content with friendship. Everyone needed a close friend, right? Then what would happen when one of them became involved romantically with someone else?

Oh, who was she kidding? She wasn't too keen on the idea of him being someone else's boyfriend. *Please protect me from ambivalence. I'm scared to want this. But I do. I didn't want to care. But I do.*

When he walked close enough to potentially see her eyes beneath the visor, she dropped her stare.

"Hey, Psych," he said to the carrier as he placed cardboard boxes and sacks in the seat.

Amber stared at the cases of cat tuna, then at Joel. "A few?"

He winked, then pushed the cart back to the front entrance. Amber crawled over the hump to the passenger seat.

Celia was right. This guy didn't do things halfway.

Upon returning to the car, his face broke forth in a grin that caused that flutter thing again. She took a deep breath, but it didn't go away. The man posed a real danger to her heart.

Amber sifted through CDs. "At the last stoplight in town, go straight. Turn right at the bait shop."

Once past that point and on the country road, Joel turned the music down. "How long have you lived in the apartment?"

"Since a week before school started last year.

Fourteen months now. A position opened up at the last minute. I took it to live closer to my parents. They moved to Refuge five years ago."

"What brought them here?"

"My dad got a new job, and they transferred him—"

Joel braked, his arm shot out to keep the cat carrier from flying forward.

Amber looked up, seeing why he stopped. "Oh no!"

A doe lay in the middle of the road. A fawn knelt beside her, sniffing and pawing at her. Joel stopped the car several yards back. Amber unlocked her seat belt when he did. He put his hand out to her. "Why don't you wait here?"

"I've seen dead deer before," she protested, wanting to help the baby.

"She's not dead. I see her breathing from here. She's hurt, and I don't want her thrashing you."

"Let me come with you. Please?"

He sighed. "Fine. But stay back and be prepared to run."

She stayed close behind him as they approached the deer cautiously. "Why didn't the person who hit her stop?" Amber whispered, seeing the mother's abdomen heaving.

Her voice must have startled the deer because the doe lifted her head, snorting and flailing her hooves. The fawn quaked. Fear seeped from their skin in the form of sweat. Desperate sadness in their eyes made Amber feel like sobbing.

She blocked it, not wanting to frighten them again. Joel moved so catlike, they didn't even seem aware of his presence. She tiptoed away, wishing she'd listened and stayed in the car.

Joel came to her side in an instant, hand on her shoulder. "Hey, come here." He pulled her close.

"I'm sorry. I didn't mean to scare them. Is it a newborn?"

Chin resting on her head, he nodded.

"Will it die without her?"

He shook his head. "I don't think so. They're born with survival instincts."

"You're not a very good liar," Amber whispered.

A rustle and snort brought their attention back to the deer. Amber couldn't stand it another second. "Is there anything we can do? I don't want her to suffer. Can you put her out of her misery?" Tears streamed out despite her best efforts to contain them. Seeing animals or children suffer tore at her heart in treacherous ways.

Joel swallowed as the doe writhed in the road. Puffs of gravel dust blew in front of her nose as she huffed.

Amber turned her face, grasping handfuls of Joel's shirt. "She's so scared and hurt. Please do something." Amber couldn't help it, she looked back. The baby sniffed and licked its mother, who wobbled her head to face the fawn, huffing air in its face, blinking, before dropping her head back to the road.

"Please, Joel," Amber whispered. "What can we do?"

"I'm thinking." Joel looked at the deer a second then set Amber aside gently. "Stay put." He walked around the mother several times, eyeing her inch by inch. "I don't have a firearm to put her out. I have other means but I don't want to do that in front of the fawn, or you."

He looked closer. "Besides that, I don't think she's mortally wounded. I hate to take the mother from the fawn." He knelt by the doe's head, staying out of her line of sight. The fawn tracked his movements, and trembled all over.

"You're not ready to be without her, are you, little one?" Unbridled compassion in his words jerked Amber's heartstrings.

She knelt, resting a hand on his forearm, thinking of him and his mother. "I'm sorry, Joel. Let's go. God will work this out."

He shook his head. "Just gimme a second to figure it out. You know anyone with a truck?"

"My dad, but it's full of wood. He has an empty trailer."

"You know how to hitch it up?"

"Yes. I can drive, too, but backing up is tricky."

"I'll wait here to direct any vehicles that happen by. Bring back the trailer, a tarp or blanket and some rope."

Since the deer were only five minutes from the pond, Amber had the trailer hooked up, taillights connected, and on the road within minutes. When she made it back, her heart sank. Joel knelt over the doe. Since she wasn't flailing, Amber figured she'd perished. As Amber got out, he stood, capping a syringe.

"What's that?" Amber eyed a blue pack lying in the road beside the duffel thing that he carried with him everywhere. The fawn remained in the same spot. Amber supposed his Special Forces training had enabled him to manage all that without scaring the baby off.

"I sedated her to load her on the trailer."

Amber dragged rope out. "What should we do first?"

"Get them out of the road. If you think your parents would be okay with it, we'll take her to the pond so I can treat her."

"I'm sure they would."

"I don't think she has internal injuries, but this knee is shattered. If I can bandage it, and keep her sedated until the game warden can come for her, I think she'll be okay."

"I hope so." Amber pulled tarp out.

"As soon as you left, she nearly mauled me when I tried to move her fawn. She's still got a lot of fight left in her. I think she was mostly dazed when we pulled up, so whoever hit her must have been right up ahead of us."

"Thank you." Amber leaned forward and hugged Joel.

He hugged back, eyeing the fawn. "Will Psych ride in your lap?"

"Yes. Will the fawn fit in the carrier?"

"Yeah, but it'll be tight. I'll have to catch and sedate it in order to get it in there. I'll need your help."

She donned gloves Joel handed her. He put on some sort of surgical splash suit and chased the spotted fawn down. He gathered it in his arms, hindering its legs from kicking.

Joel jutted his chin at her.

Amber took the syringe from his teeth. "Where do I put it?"

"Deep in the left hip up to a millimeter from the hub. Hold the syringe steady. Pull the plunger back, make sure you don't get blood. Then push the plunger until all the liquid is in."

She jabbed as he described, pulled back, then pressed. The deer wiggled. Joel strained, tightening his arms around it.

Amber yanked out the needle. "Some is leaking back out."

"That's normal. Hold a cloth on it."

She grabbed gauze from his pack and pressed it against the injection site.

Fifteen minutes later, the fawn stopped kicking. Joel relaxed his hold. Heavy lids eclipsed luminous brown eyes. The rise and fall of its chest deepened and slowed.

"That took the fight out of her. How do you know how much to give them? Never mind. You're a combat paramedic."

His eyes twinkled. "You know that?"

"I've been studying up on PJs with Bradley." Her face heated with the admission. She clicked the carrier door shut after Joel laid the fawn in it.

"You'll need to disinfect this thoroughly after we let the fawn go." He put a new pair of gloves on and rolled the mother onto the tarp. Amber helped him lift her onto the trailer. He put the carrier beside the doe and secured everything with bungee cables.

"Did you get hold of anyone?" Joel asked as Amber navigated him through country roads to the pond.

"The wardens will meet us there in about ten minutes they said. They're taking the doe and fawn until she's well, or until the fawn can survive on its own."

"Good."

Once they got to the pond, Joel bandaged the deer and medicated her. Amber rounded up grass and food for the fawn. Joel pulled the tarp off and placed it inside a fenced area. He let the fawn out near the doe. "I think she'll stay right with her, but if she runs off, there's not much we can do."

"Sorry I freaked out back there. It bothered me to see her suffer."

"It bothered me, too. I'm just better at hiding it." He ruffled Amber's hair, then left his arm around her shoulder as they watched the fawn snuggle beside the doe. Joel's strength and warmth eased her worry about them.

A vet came with the wardens. Once the deer were loaded and taken, Amber unlocked her parents' house so they could wash up. She borrowed one of her father's old work shirts for Joel and tossed his in the washer. He showered while she went to the pole barn to gather fishing supplies and disinfect the carrier.

Psych pranced on an open bag of potting soil in the wheelbarrow.

"Still want to fish?" Amber asked, after they'd checked for ticks and given each other the all clear.

"Yeah, but let's grill first. I'm hungry." He placed a hand on her shoulder as he passed by, stopping to squeeze it before continuing on. Relief and emptiness vied for her emotions at his distance. She missed the contact and wished she didn't. His nearness challenged her resolve to keep her heart firmly planted on the ground until she could be certain their differences could be worked out.

No free-falling allowed.

"What's wrong? Catch sight of a rabid coon?" Joel's voice behind her ear made her jump.

She placed a hand to her chest. "I didn't hear you come up." She eyed the plate of grilled food but his eyes bored into hers.

"What's with the cloud cover, sunshine?"

Amber met his gaze. The depth of care in his eyes touched her until she remembered. "That's the same way Bart looked at me before he pledged lifelong love and proposed. He dumped me by phone minutes before our wedding a year later." The memories made her want to go home and stick her head under the covers.

Joel set the plate of food on the picnic table and pulled her into his arms. "Is Bart the mall guy?"

"Yes. And the girl stuck to his arm was my next-door neighbor. I met Bart in San Francisco. That means he got to know her while we were engaged. I had suspicions something was going on between them but they weren't confirmed until today. I just never thought I'd have to come face-to-face with him again. I don't know if he's moving here, or just visiting her or what."

"Are you over him?" Joel tightened his hold on her, hoping to hear she was.

She turned her face up and met his gaze. "Yes, Joel, or I wouldn't be here."

"Are you sure there's nothing left there for him?"

"I'm sure. Anger maybe, but how he ended things, and how he treated me before washed away any attraction or love I had. I do think I'm still dealing with the hurt of what he did, though. That's why I'm leery of us, especially since we know there are differences between our goals going into this."

"Amber, I'm not Bart. I'm nothing like him. I don't go back on my commitments."

She pulled away. "But you committed to never have children. What about that?"

His expression remained unfazed, and he tightened his grip on her hand. "Let's trust God to work things like that out."

"Things like that, Joel, are why a lot of people get divorced." As soon as the word left her lips remorse hit her.

He swallowed hard and let her go. "I think we should eat."

Amber closed her eyes, hating that she'd hurt him. She'd grown familiar enough with his voice to pick out the woundedness, though she doubted he realized it was evident. She'd dreamed of his voice night after night after talking to him on the phone. Countless conversations while he'd been in Asia. She hadn't suffered the pain of divorce as he had. She'd had no right to blurt that out. Obviously he had unhealed wounds from it or he never would have made the vow.

Please help him surrender to what You want for his life instead of what he wants. Thank You that You know us better than we know ourselves.

After chowing down on steak and mushrooms smothered in grilled onions and cheese, they packed a cooler with water and soda and headed to the dock. Relief flowed over Amber when he reached for her hand with his empty one.

The sunset stretched silvery-pink hues on the water. They cast their lines and sat side by side enjoying the sounds of crickets, owls and impending night. Psych chased moths on the banks. She needed to get up the nerve to tell Joel about Bradley. But after the last conversation didn't go so well, her courage faltered.

"When did you first want to be a PJ?" Amber asked after an hour of watching her bobber do absolutely nothing in the water.

Joel looked up after tossing back his third bigmouth bass. "As long as I can remember. Three or four. I heard about paratroopers in Vietnam from Dad."

Amber stretched. "Same branch?"

"Dad?"

She nodded and stood.

"No. Army. High ranking. Often a bodyguard for ambassadors and diplomats. Gone a lot." He peered at her. "You getting tired?"

"No. Just stretching my legs. I run every evening at six. I haven't missed a day since track in high school. If it's any consolation, my dad was gone a lot, too."

He stood then, reeling in his line. "Tough growing up like that, but I guess I didn't know any different until we started living off base and I met kids whose dads were around a lot."

"When was that?" She eyed Psych's wheelbarrow frolic.

Joel looked at her, then back out onto the water. "When we moved to Refuge." He reeled her line in, too. Disappointment hit her at the thought of the evening ending.

"Are you ready to leave?" She peered around, locating Psych on the deck near the house. He'd obviously grown tired of dancing in the wheelbarrow.

Joel stretched one leg then the other, did a heel bounce and smiled. "Nope. I'm ready to run."

"We're jogging?" She stretched, too.

"I don't want to break your record. Besides, I want to see how fast you can go. Ready?"

Loving the challenge, she pretended to stretch, but took off instead, looking back at him. "Set! Go!"

She faced forward, pounding the balls of her feet hard into the ground. As she sensed him gaining, she screamed and pushed to an all-out sprint. Within seconds, he streaked past.

"No fair! You went to boot camp!"

"Twenty years ago." He cast a grin over his shoulder that challenged her footing. He slowed his pace until she joined him at a leisurely jog.

She lost all sense of time, and stopped keeping track of how many laps they jogged around the pond. Descending darkness made it hard to keep from tripping over unseen tree roots.

"Ready to quit?" he asked for the tenth time.

"Are you?" She'd swiped enough sweat from her brow to flood the pond.

"Nope," he said, barely breathless.

"Neither am I." She prayed for a second wind.

"I'm not going to be able to move in the morning." She pushed the words out between huffs a while later.

"You're not giving up until I quit, are you?"

She shook her head. "Not until you quit or I drop dead. Whichever comes first. I'm thinking the latter."

He slowed to a cool-down trot. "I like having you around, so that's enough for today."

She eyed him. Though a fine sheen of moisture glazed his forearms and neck, he hardly seemed winded. "It's going to take a bottle of Motrin and a crane to get me out of bed in the morning, and you could probably run the rest of the night without breaking a sweat." They slowed to a walk.

He grinned, lifting his shirt to swipe beneath his eye. He held the damp spot out. "I'm sweating. See?"

She rolled her eyes and dropped to the grass. "One spot."

He sat beside her and plucked a green blade off her pant leg near the hem, rolling it between his thumb and finger.

"I'm curious," she said once her breathing rate enabled her to complete sentences. "What made you want to be a PJ?"

Joel's face hardened. For a moment she didn't think he'd answer. He drew up his knees, clasping them. "Tragedy struck my family."

"I'm sorry. If it's too hard to talk about—"

"I'll let you know."

She reclined on the grassy knoll.

He stared across the water. "When I graduated kindergarten, my paternal grandparents asked to do something special for me. With Dad deployed, Mom arranged a trip to an air force museum in Chicago for the weekend. A night fire gutted our hotel. There weren't enough rescuers to get everyone out in time, including my grandmother, who used a walker at the time but couldn't find it or her way through the dark and the smoke."

She could hardly believe one life could endure such calamity. That he'd stumbled out of it with his faith intact made her admire him all the more.

"I stood blocks away and heat still chafed my face. Hours after the fire trucks left, Mom let me stay because I was convinced she'd still walk out of the ashes. We both cried enough that day to have put the fire out. Dad blamed Mom for his mother's death, which added to the growing rift between my parents."

A distant whistle of a whip-poor-will punctuated his pause.

"The tragedy burned in my heart the need for rescuers. I loved skydiving and the air force. Being a PJ became my dream. I've never regretted my decision. I believe I'm doing what I was created for. That sense of destiny came out of grief's ashes."

Eager to comfort, she leaned closer. "Where are your other grandparents?"

His arm hair brushed hers as he plucked grass and sifted it through his fingers. "My maternal grandmother died before I was born. My mom never knew who her father was because he left when my grandmother got pregnant. My paternal grandfather is in a retirement home. He has dementia and hardly remembers my dad, much less me. He's missing an entire generation, memory-wise." The lawn around the pond bank would be bald soon. It didn't matter. She stayed silent, sensing he wanted to tell her more.

After several moments of nothing but crickets and the tearing of grass, he shifted. "My parents fought all the time. Mom sought a position as a skydiving instructor at Refuge after they married. Dad's brother lived here. Dad encouraged the move because he thought my uncle would look out for her, and me when I came along."

"He didn't?" She bent her knee and rested her chin there.

"He did. He got too close to Mom, in fact." Sarcasm dripped from his words, filling in the blanks.

"I'm sorry," she whispered. His glance skittered to her a second before returning to his grass excavation.

Amber reached for a green tuft. "Have you thought of reconciling with your uncle?"

He stood so fast it startled her. He started walking. She followed, heart longing to reach out. "Joel?"

"I haven't spoken to him since she died. I don't intend to."

"Joel, I'm concerned you have bitterness against your uncle. It can't be good to leave it festering." She followed him onto the dock.

He bent and gathered the poles. "I don't think they're biting anymore. Let's call it a night."

Cold tingled from Amber's fingertips through her body from the ice in his tone. She felt horrible for asking. The need to find answers for him branded her. But she couldn't go behind his back to ask Dean. He and Dean would have to work that out on their own with God.

A whiff of something akin to stink bait assaulted Amber as she pulled on her jacket. Joel stepped left as she did, tilting the dock. She struggled to keep balance on legs spent from the run. Joel's hand shot out, but she tripped over the cooler. Before she could fall, he moved like a dart, righting her, his arm scooping her close.

"Thank you. I don't see well at night."

He didn't loosen his grip, didn't answer, didn't blink. Moonlight sparkled off his eyes as they roamed her face.

She scrambled back, scared at the emotion in his.

He tightened his hold, hindering escape. "What's this?"

She blinked. "What?"

He patted her rib cage. "Something sharp, right here in your pocket. It jabbed me."

Her mind raced, then screeched the instant she remembered she'd put the little parachute man from the school fountain in there. *That's* what smelled. The chute must have mildewed.

He tugged it out, turned it over, then lifted it to eye level. The plastic man dangled in the air between them. Joel's gaze shifted to her face. His mouth twitched a couple times before birthing a grin. "Someone you know?"

Her cheeks sweltered. She wanted to bang her head on the wooden dock post for not remembering to take the dumb thing out. "I, um, rescued him—it—out of the school fountain." She looked everywhere but at Joel.

"I'm not sure if I should be touched or jealous." He spun the miniature soldier around by the parachute.

Her tongue turned to sandpaper. "Be touched."

"I am." His soothing voice held deep sincerity. God had given him a perfect kind of voice for a rescuer. Afraid of nothing—tough yet soothing tender. She bet it calmed victims and hostages in even the most terrifying or uncertain situations.

Speaking of uncertain…

Whiffs of masculine soap renewed her awareness of still being in his arms. Her senses zinged. Her mind whirled.

She stared at the pond, giggling away the acute discomfort his nearness caused.

He didn't laugh. He stared intently at her. Sounds muted except for his breathing, and hers. Silence plus heat wafting off his skin made her feel both comforted and nervous.

"It's dark and I think we should be heading back since there are no street signs along the road and I don't want us to hit a deer," she blurted.

"That what you really think, Miss Amber?" His throat sounded like he needed to clear it. "Because I'd love nothing more than to kiss you properly this time. I'm asking your permission. Ma'am, may I kiss you?"

The gentlemanly query and tender depth of his voice calmed her.

Attraction sparked like remnants of a welding arc. Yet she glimpsed a vulnerability there that she doubted he granted many access to. It drew her and he felt safe. She leaned in. The sensation of bulky arms tightening around her filled her senses. When his gaze swept her lips, then her eyes in another gentle query, her brain blipped. Time slowed.

After all that protesting, they were going to kiss. Right now. Right here. Surrounded by tree frogs and bait.

Amber closed her eyes and froze, not sure whether she should flee or tilt her face upward. It had been so long since she'd kissed someone. She hoped she remembered how. Feathery breath tickled her forehead, her nose, cheeks, lips, and then—

It didn't happen.

Her eyelids fluttered open.

He clenched his eyes and teeth. How he still muttered through them she'd never know. Something about tossing his Southern manners right into the lake.

Yet he didn't release his hold. He brought her to his chest and nearly squeezed the life from her lungs.

He placed a quick but gentle kiss on top of her head. "You're right. We should get going." He bent to pick up the cooler then cast a disarming grin at her as he rose. *"Pal."*

Amber skidded to a halt on the dock, narrowing her gaze. "You were testing me. That was a trick."

He tossed his head back and laughed. "If I wanted to test you, I would have gone ahead and kissed you.

I'm trying to honor what I would think to be a father's wishes for his daughter." A bold gaze riveted her. "Even though I really did want that kiss."

His honest admission kept her skin flushed until they pulled up at the B and B. He popped the trunk to get his bag.

He kept a polite distance between them. "Let's meet for breakfast here before church, though I didn't bring dress clothes."

"Jeans are fine. We're casual." She scooted into the car.

"See you in the morning, sunshine. Bye, Psych." He wiggled fingers at the cat, then closed Amber's car door.

She watched until he made it through the stained-oak door, then put a hand to her chest as if pledging allegiance and stared at Psych. "Let's hold on to our hearts, okay? There are a lot of bugs to work out of this program if it's headed for the hard drive. Don't get your hopes up, you hear?"

Psych purred beneath her fingers, lifting his chin so she scratched deeper.

Amber eyed her reflection in the mirror. "And don't you get yours up, either." She pulled onto the tree-lined road.

Once home, she felt the need for a couple more laps to clear her mind. She liked to meditate and pray while she ran, and hadn't been able to concentrate when running with Joel. The man proved to be a distraction in many ways.

She knelt and laced her new shoes. Several blocks had her laughing as she thought of the plastic man and his rotting chute. All this time she thought a skunk had taken up residence in her coat closet. While a toy parachutist rotted in her pocket, a real one rooted in her heart.

Just as the wall of air that had slammed into her and stolen her breath the second they'd exited the plane at ten thousand feet, Amber felt powerless to stop her feelings. No going back, no reaching for the safety of the plane and sure footing because they'd already leaped.

Free fall or nothing.

Just like she'd had to trust Joel to get her safely through the uncertain season of the jump until her feet touched solid ground, she'd have to trust God to get her through this because she was falling hard and fast and blind.

If you stay in this plane and never jump you'll always wonder what it could have been like. If you jump, you risk breaking your heart if you crash. But if you jump, and this love is strong enough to carry you through the winds of adversity, you'll have the most exhilarating ride of your life.

Amber veered over a curb, slowed her pace to walking, then sat on a bench log near the edge of Refuge City Park to catch her breath. She put her forehead in her hands, then lifted her face to the sky, past stars to the One who suspended them.

"Oh, God. I'm already out of the plane, aren't I?"

After shaking off her stunned emotions, she stood, hoping her trembling legs and cautious feet would carry her home.

"God, if You're piloting this, I'd rather crash with bravery intact and a shattered heart to the ground than stand back in the shadows of cowardice and watch it scroll by. Spare me the regret of wondering what it would have been like had I only summoned courage to jump."

Chapter Fourteen

"Is it tangerine or pineapple?" Joel asked over Sunday breakfast.

Amber looked from her waffle to her fruit bowl. "Mandarin orange slices."

He poked a fork in his French toast. "I wasn't talking about in the bowl. I meant the scent you wear. I like it."

"Oh. It's grapefruit, and some type of flower garden scent, I think."

She peered at the clock. "It's time to head to church. You ready?"

Joel walked her down the steps, hand at her elbow. "You look nice in that dress. Your hair turned out great, too." He opened the car door for her, eyeing approaching storm clouds.

She lowered herself in, determined not to blush. "Thanks. The famous hair fry is one mistake I hope never to repeat."

A chime sounded from the floorboard as they pulled into traffic. "Oh, that's my voice mail. I must have dropped my phone out of my purse." Several missed calls, three from Celia. She dialed.

"Amber Marie! Where are you?" Streams of rapid-fire Spanish followed the question.

Celia's tone sent alarm coursing through Amber. She turned the radio down. "I'm on my way to church with Joel."

"Is he driving?"

"Yes."

"Give him the phone." Celia sounded out of breath.

Amber studied Joel's face as Celia spoke to him, but it revealed nothing about the content of the conversation. The fact that Joel did a U-turn in a restricted area alerted her that something was wrong.

"We'll be there right away. Call if anything changes before we arrive." Joel pulled the car over and faced her, his cheeks ashen. He put his hand over hers and held tight.

"They tried to reach you. Bradley, he's—" Joel swallowed hard.

No! I don't want to hear.

"Sunshine, he's really bad." Joel squeezed the bones together in her hand. "It doesn't look good."

"Wh-what? How bad? No, Joel, I just talked to him yesterday." She got out of the car. He followed her.

She paced beside it. She didn't even know why she got out, she just needed to walk. No, she needed to run. "He can't die. He never got to have a family." Sobs rose and she couldn't keep them down. "I'm not ready for him to go yet. We just needed a little more time."

Joel pressed his hands against her shoulders and veered her back toward the open car door. "Come on. We'll pray on the way to the hospital." He lowered her to the car and knelt in to help buckle her seat belt.

"He must have taken a turn for the worse." Amber felt utterly numb. *Don't take him yet. Please let him have a family first. I'll give up Joel if I have to for Bradley's dream to come true.* "What happened to plunge him downhill so fast?"

"I don't know. Celia just said his doctor and case-worker have been trying to reach you all morning."

They sped the rest of the way, Amber in silence, Joel making small talk, asking about her family, her other students.

About anything but Bradley.

She appreciated what he was trying to do, but all she wanted was to get to Bradley and hold him.

At the hospital, they sprinted across the lot and down the main corridor. Dr. Riviera's nurse met them coming off the elevator. "I'm glad you came right away. They're calling in family. Bradley asked for you. We have to wait until the doctor comes out."

A half wail of a prayer heaved from Amber's gut despite how hard she tried to contain it. "Please don't take him today."

Joel pulled her close.

She buried her face in his chest. "I didn't buy Peter Pan peanut butter, Joel. I bought what was on sale. I can't forgive myself if he—I just wanted to have enough money for his transplant. Why didn't I get the stupid Peter Pan? It was only two dollars more—"

"Amber, don't torture yourself. You loved him. That's what he needed most."

"I don't want to have loved him. I don't want him to have needed me. I don't want to have to think of him in the past tense!"

"Neither do I. Let's pray—"

The phone trill broke into his words. He answered the call, pulling her head against his chest.

He practically hefted her to the edge of the hall, for which Amber was glad. She wondered how many people those capable shoulders carried from frightening situations. How many tears had been cried on his collar?

Joel emitted a huff. His arm tensed against her cheek as he switched ears. "They can't do this without me, Petrowski?"

Amber froze, listening.

"This couldn't have happened at a worse time. The little guy is pretty bad off... A half hour ago... I'd appreciate that."

"You have to go, Joel?" Amber fought to keep her voice calm. She could tell Joel already felt bad enough.

"I might. Petrowski's gonna see what he can do.

They were already running a skeleton team as it is because half my guys joined part of a SEAL team on some other mission. Now there's another high-profile mission and I may not be able to get out of going. I may have to leave in five minutes, five hours or five days depending on the next set of intel received."

"I understand." But it hit her with brute force that this is what life with Joel would be like. Could she handle it? Could she handle being with a man who may not be able to be there when his family needed him most? Family? Amber felt betrayed by her own thoughts. But of course she wouldn't date someone she wouldn't consider marrying.

Amber pulled away from the sheltering embrace of his arms. The last thing she needed was to start depending on him.

"Miss Stanton?" The nurse waved them toward a set of double doors painted with the words Pediatric ICU beneath a rainbow.

Amber's throat clogged when she caught sight of Bradley. Hooked to various machines, he looked frail and dwarfed by the bed. Blue-mauve rings surrounded his eyes and mouth like circles of death. Skin translucent, and flour pale, eyes closed.

IV tubes hung from bony wrists, making him look like a marionette.

A machine beside his bed flashed red and alarmed. Amber's breath hitched until Joel squeezed her shoulder. "It's okay. Just a loose lead." He leaned over Bradley and smoothed each round sticker below his collarbone until the beeping stopped. Bradley didn't stir.

"Thanks." A nurse scurried in and poked a button on the machine. "Are you a medical professional?"

Joel nodded. "Paramedic."

"Then you might want to stay when Dr. Riviera talks with Miss Stanton in case she has questions. Sometimes when you're understandably upset, it helps to have another person listening in case we need to make a hard decision in the next few days."

Joel shifted. "What kind of hard decision?"

"Right now Bradley is on oxygen because his body isn't compensating. He could end up on a ventilator. Because of his lowered immunity, he developed an infection in his bloodstream. That can be fatal if not treated early. We're not sure we caught it in time. The doctor suspects meningitis on top of sepsis. Patients rarely survive septic shock so—"

Joel held a palm up. "We get the picture. Let's wait for the doctor and the lab results before making assumptions or decisions."

The nurse blinked several times, tapping her pen to the clipboard as if not sure whether to be annoyed or not. "Also, Bradley's caseworker left a message for you stating she's expediting the adoption paperwork."

"Adoption paperwork?" Joel looked from the nurse to Amber.

The nurse flipped through papers. "You are the family planning to adopt him, correct?"

Amber cast Joel a remorseful look. "We're not married. I—I plan to adopt Bradley."

Joel's eyes hit the floor and his brows collided. She hadn't wanted him to find out this way. She should have told him sooner. She knew Joel wouldn't discuss it in front of Bradley. They needed to talk privately but she didn't want to leave Bradley's side for a second.

It hit her like thunder that she might lose them both today.

"What's th' c'mmotion?" Bradley's feeble voice wafted across the room.

Amber went to him. Joel stepped to the opposite side of the bed. Each clasped one of Bradley's hands. He didn't seem to have strength to lift his arms.

"Hey, buddy," Joel said.

"You came back for me?" Bradley tried to lift his head but it fell back.

"Of course. PJs never break a promise, right?" Joel's voice cracked in the middle.

"I'm sorry, Joel." Bradley coughed. "I tried to fight as hard as I could. But I don't know anymore. I'm tired."

Amber dipped her head from the tears springing forth.

Joel knelt, placing one hand on Bradley's forehead. He pulled his other hand, which still clasped Bradley's, to his chest. "I know, buddy. I know. But I need you, okay?"

Bradley slid his eyelids half-open. "You do?"

Tears glittered in Joel's eyes. "Yeah. I sure do. You remind me how to be brave. You remind me to never take a second for granted. You remind me how to be the best bullet dodger and rescuer in the world. So you have to fight harder, okay?"

Bradley's eyes closed but he nodded. "'Kay. I'll try. For you. I'll try my best." His voice faded off with the last word.

"He needs to rest now. Why don't you step out in the hall while we administer another dose of anti-biotics? Hopefully it will do the trick." Dr. Riviera eyed them with compassion. Amber wasn't sure when he'd returned. She felt glad it was him instead of Nurse Tactless.

Once in the hall, Joel headed in the opposite direction.

"Joel, please wait."

He stopped but didn't turn around.

"I'm sorry."

He pivoted, jaw clicking. "When were you going to tell me?"

She suddenly felt the need to vomit. He looked so angry and hurt. "I'm sorry. Soon. I planned to tell you soon." She stepped toward him. He stepped back and shook his head. She stopped, respecting his space but needing his closeness.

She'd ruined everything. Everything.

"I'll be back." He turned, his shoes squeaking with the motion.

"Where are you going?" Panic hit that Bradley could die while he was gone.

"To the store across the street. Need anything?"

She scooped hair behind her ear. "No, thank you." Not unless he could buy her something to rewind time.

She'd really messed up.

Please, God, work this out. I'm sorry.

She watched Joel's retreat until Dr. Riviera emerged from Bradley's room. "Where did the soldier go?"

"He'll be right back."

Dr. Riviera nodded. "Don't lose hope, Amber. He needs us to be strong when he can't."

"I know. I'm trying. It's just, he looks so sick."

"He's very sick. But he's not dead yet. Until he is, we'll keep hoping and praying. He may pull through and outlive us all. We'll know more in a few hours whether we got to the infection in time. Until then, you may stay at Bradley's side since his foster mother apparently had more important things to do."

"She's not even here?"

"I had her boyfriend take her home. She was extremely inebriated and sounded close to coughing up a lung. I thought it best if she didn't expose Bradley to her sickness."

"What did I miss?" Joel walked up, cradling a brown paper sack in one arm and three sodas in another.

"I will let Amber update you. I received a page from the E.R. that I need to see about. The two of you may sit with Bradley as long as you like. When a patient is this ill, we bend the visiting policy."

After Dr. Riviera left, Amber updated Joel then they returned to Bradley's side.

Joel handed her a soda and set the second one on the bedside table then rolled the tray of it over Bradley's bed. The creaking sound awakened him.

"Doc ain't gonna let me drink that." Bradley's voice sounded like something between the croak of a frog and Psych when Amber accidentally stepped on his tail.

Joel grinned at Bradley. "I know. But we're giving you two more good reasons to hurry up and get better." Joel lifted the brown paper sack and pulled out the biggest container of Peter Pan peanut butter Amber had ever seen. He placed it beside the soda, in Bradley's direct line of sight. Those were what would greet him every time he opened his eyes. Amber smiled, blinking back an onslaught of tears at Joel's creative thoughtfulness.

She mouthed Joel a thank-you when Bradley closed his eyes again. Joel nodded and winked. Was he still mad? He wouldn't have gotten over it that fast. Probably he didn't want Bradley to detect something amiss between them. For that, she was grateful. She sat in the recliner, holding Bradley's hand. After a long period of praying silently, she laid her head back to rest her eyes a moment.

"Amber. Let's get some coffee." Joel stood above her. When she remembered her surroundings and realized she'd fallen asleep she surged up. He put a finger to his lips and held her steady.

Bradley slept peacefully. Gone were the blue circles around his eyes and his skin looked pinker.

"He's doing better?"

Joel nodded. "Yeah, but he had a rough night. So did I. Let's get coffee." He tugged her up and grabbed his jacket which slid off her lap. She hadn't even known he'd covered her with it. Tears erupted at his kind gestures despite her keeping that secret from him.

"I'm sorry, Joel."

"Let's talk about it after we've both had a decent night's sleep."

She nodded, glad he spoke to her at all. "Have you heard back from your commander?"

"Yeah. I'm still on standby."

"Okay." She whispered a prayer of thanks that God had allowed him to be here through one of the hardest nights of her life. With Bradley's illness, she could have a lot of these nights. It didn't matter. She loved Bradley and wanted to be there for him, with Joel, or without him. But, oh, how she prayed God could work things out so they would all three be together. At this point, it seemed impossible, though she knew all things were possible with God.

Since she couldn't control the outcome, she knew this to be a perfect situation for God to work in. Whether that manifested as Him infusing strength in her to get through it if she and Joel parted ways, or whether He softened Joel's heart toward the idea of children, and healing the trust she'd shattered.

Lord, work this out. Not my will, but Yours be done. This is a hard prayer to pray, so help me mean it. Even if things don't work out the way I want.

Chapter Fifteen

Two weeks later, Amber hung up from speaking with Dr. Riviera. Bradley had been home five days and seemed nearly back to normal, something the doctor had termed a miraculous turnaround. A week into Bradley's hospitalization, they'd found a donor match for his transplant.

"What did he say?" Joel asked at the B and B breakfast table on Sunday. Though Bradley'd improved, Joel was glad Petrowski had okayed another couple weeks' leave Joel needed to use or lose by year's end.

"He said if his blood counts stay the same and he stays fever free for another two weeks, they'll do the transplant."

"What did he say about us taking him somewhere?"

"He said he could return to normal activities as long as you're there to monitor his vital signs. He wants him to be able to live like other kids. He'll just have to be careful about infection and rest more often until the transplant."

"That's good news. Why don't we try to make church this morning? Then we need to talk."

"Sure." A lump lodged in Amber's throat as she walked through the door Joel held for her. He kept saying he wasn't ready to talk about the adoption, or the fact that she'd kept things from him since the day it happened. Amber wasn't even sure where they stood in their relationship.

She'd find out today, though, and it ate at her insides. She was glad to be able to go to church first. Maybe worship would calm her fears and soothe her frazzled nerves. It seemed every time they'd tried to make it to church the past couple weeks, something had hindered them.

At the church, Joel shut her door after lending her a hand out. The weight of stares settled on them, especially from young ladies as they walked across the lot. Her heart soared at the thought of them thinking he was hers. Only after today, he may no longer be. At least she'd finally found courage to jump. She never thought she would after Bart. If God got her through that, He'd get her through losing Joel, too.

Hopefully she wouldn't have to.

Don't get your hopes up.

She lassoed in her imagination. "We can get coffee before the service, if you like."

"Sounds good. Although Indian coffee spoiled me.

It's thick and sugary and they always heat the milk, even for cereal."

"Our church has a microwave and a sugar bowl."

He smiled and put a hand to her lower back as they entered the church's coffeehouse.

Just inside the door Joel's steps slowed, causing Amber to look up. By now he had completely stopped. His face turned ashen and he stared across the room as if detecting a suicide bomber in the crowd. She tried to track his gaze but couldn't tell what or who he looked at.

She placed a gentle hand on his arm. "Joel? What is it?"

He blinked, glanced at her a split second before pressing his gaze to the far wall where people lined up at the coffee bar. "Unbelievable." He turned and hiked toward the door. His tone had dripped sarcasm, and any faster would put his feet in a record-breaking sprint.

Amber had to run to keep up. "Joel, wait up. Joel!"

She approached him in the parking lot. He paced back and forth until she stood in his path. "What's wrong?"

He swerved to go around her, but she moved. He spun the other way, then turned back to face her. "I can't believe you didn't tell me. How can you expect me to trust you now, after Bradley *and* this?"

"This?" She had no idea what he meant. Then it dawned on her. "Did you see Dean in there? Joel, I didn't even think about it. He hasn't been coming very

long. I didn't keep it from you intentionally. I forgot."
How would he ever believe her? But it was true. She
loathed herself for not remembering Joel's uncle
attended her church. How could something so important have slipped her mind? She'd been consumed with
Bradley, but still. She should have thought of Joel.

"I don't believe this." Joel shook his head and went
toward the car.

She jogged to keep up. "Please believe me. I would
have told you had I remembered. Why can't we talk
about this rationally?"

"I need you to take me to the airport. Please don't
ask questions."

But they screamed in her head. "Right now?"

"Right now." He darted a finger to the earth and
paced again, raking hands through hair that wasn't
there.

This wasn't typical Joel. She doubted he'd ever
acted like this in his entire life. That probably irked
him more than anything. She had a feeling God
pressed a deliberate finger down on him, and wouldn't
relieve the pressure until Joel stopped fighting against
what God wanted to do.

"Do you have a ticket?" she asked calmly.

"I don't need a ticket. I just—I need to get out of
here." He placed an imploring look on her. For a second,
he reminded her of the student who once tried to
convince her a monster lived in the school's craft closet.
The monster wasn't real, but the child's fear was.

Though Joel's request seemed illogical, the wrenching plea in his eyes reflected a monstrous turmoil.

"Okay. The car's this way. You have the keys," she said.

The pacing settled. "Okay. Okay."

He probably would jog to the airport if he had to.

"I put my purse on a hook in the foyer. I'll be right back." She turned to go, but he grabbed her wrist. Not harshly, but she doubted he realized how firmly he gripped.

"Don't talk to him. Please don't even mention my name."

"All right. I won't." She proceeded on.

By the time she returned to the car, he occupied the passenger seat.

She settled in and started the ignition. "Should we drop by the B and B to get your stuff before I take you to the airport?"

He shook his head. "Since Bradley couldn't come to church, take me by to see him."

"To say goodbye?" Tires crunched over gravel as she exited the lot.

His jaw tensed. "Amber, please don't."

She squeezed the steering wheel. "I can't help it. I don't understand why you're running."

He turned to peer at her, then out the side glass. He expelled a breath. "I wanted to forget he ever existed. I can't imagine why he's at your church."

Amber braked for a stop sign. "Maybe he's

changed. If your last name is Montgomery, why is his DuPaul?"

"He and my dad had different fathers."

"Would you at least pray and ask God if He wants you to reconcile?"

"Dean ruined my family, Amber. You have no idea the hurt he caused when he cheated with his own brother's wife. I've forgiven him and my mother both, but that doesn't mean I am required to have anything more to do with him."

Her heart fell because she couldn't imagine the man ever being cruel enough to rip a family apart. Now wasn't the time to tell Joel, though. "It will only take a moment to get your stuff."

"I'd rather spend time with Bradley. My rucksack's in your trunk because it goes everywhere with me. That's all I need."

"Do you even know if you can get a flight?"

"I can always get a flight."

Amber dropped Joel off at Miss Harker's house and then drove to the B and B and asked for his key. She stuffed all his clothes and toiletries into his duffel bag. At least this would give him and Bradley some one-on-one time.

En route, she called Celia and asked her to pray for Joel, and for wisdom on how to deal with this. Though things seemed to be out of control, Amber sensed God was completely in control.

When she returned, Joel and Bradley sat on the

steps of the caseworker's house. Neither one looked particularly sad, so she doubted Joel had broken the news to Bradley yet about leaving.

At her approach, Bradley jumped up to greet her. Joel smiled in a shy manner. Since the guy definitely wasn't shy, he must be embarrassed.

"What's going on, guys?"

Joel scooted over. She sat beside them.

Bradley grinned. "We're going to play a paintball game."

Amber looked from Bradley to Joel. "You are?"

"You, too," Bradley informed her.

Amber looked at Joel.

He fiddled with her purse strap. "Yeah. You up for that?"

"Sure. Although I've never played."

"It's easy. You just point a gun and shoot like crazy," Bradley said, making the motion with his hands as if using an invisible air rifle.

"Gun?"

"Paint gun," Joel clarified. "Which shoots tiny balls of colored paint. Hence the name."

"Paintball. I get it. Sounds like a blast."

Joel stood, running the wrinkles out of his slacks with his hands. "I noticed a paintball field on the way into town. His caseworker said she'd clear him to go with us for the evening. I figure we can play until he gets tired, even if it's five minutes, then grab something to eat."

Then what? Leave for good?

Joel tapped Bradley on his shoulder. "You have play clothes here? The paint is water soluble, but you're liable to get mud and grass stains on you."

"Yeah. I'll go get them on." Bradley hopped to his feet and sped into the house. It amazed her that his health had improved so much so fast. He must have had that infection brewing awhile.

Joel faced Amber. "Sorry about back there."

She nodded, knowing he'd talk to her when ready, and that fewer questions were probably better. She'd just go with the flow and roll with the changes. Amber looked down. "I'm not exactly dressed for mud. I do have running shoes in the car."

Miss Harker descended the steps. "What size are you?"

Joel cast lifted brows at the rail-thin woman. "Even I know you're not supposed to ask a lady the two taboos."

"Two taboos?" Miss Harker looked from Amber to Joel.

Joel winked at Amber. "Age and weight."

"I'd add height to that," Amber said.

"Come in a second. We'll find you some clothes, Amber." She paused at the door. "Mr. Montgomery, would you like to come inside?"

"Sure. If you'll point me to your bathroom, I'll change." He dug a hand in his duffel, pulling out camo fatigues, heading where Miss Harker motioned down one hall. She motioned Amber down another. Amber followed Miss Harker like a lamb to its shearer. No way would she fit in Miss Harker's clothes. There had to be four sizes separating them. This would be embarrassing on all fronts.

Amber caught up to her. "I wear a size eight on a good day. I can squeeze into a six if I lie on the bed and suck it in. You can't be more than a size two, and I can't breathe in anything less than a four," she whispered.

"Don't worry. I have maternity clothes that'll fit."

"I didn't realize you had children."

"I did. Not anymore."

She badly wanted to know details. Miss Harker looked to be Amber's age or younger. If Amber opened up, maybe Miss Harker would, too. Sometimes vulnerability proved contagious.

Amber took a ponytail holder from her purse. "It may be the only time I ever get to wear them."

Miss Harker paused in the hall. "Maternity clothes?"

Amber nodded, pulling her hair into a bundle, then took the band from her teeth and bound it at the nape of her neck. "An accident left me unable to bear children."

"I gave my baby up for adoption as a teen. Maybe we can meet for coffee sometime and talk. Today, you should spend time with those cuties outside. Here you go." She handed Amber a stylish hip-length button-down shirt.

If she hadn't told her, Amber wouldn't have known they were maternity. Miss Harker handed her a pair of low-rise jeans next. "These are regular jeans, size six. When I got close to term with my pregnancy, I wore maternity tops over them and no one ever knew my baby rode over the belt loops."

"These are name brand. You won't mind if they stain?" Amber wondered if the clothing had a sentimental element to them.

"They were packed and ready to head to the Crisis Pregnancy Center. I got them at a consignment shop."

Amber looked forward to forging a friendship with this woman Celia thought so highly of.

"Thank you. A dress isn't exactly paintball garb." Amber changed into the ensemble and they stepped outside.

"Told you my size twos would fit you, Amber," she said in Joel's presence.

Cheeks hot, Amber hoisted her purse over her shoulder as she faced Joel. "Shall we go?"

She didn't want to rush this day, especially since it might be her last with Joel. She also wanted Bradley to have as much time with him as possible.

At the playing field, Joel rented three paintball rifles.

Amber eyed Joel's gun. "Hey, yours looks more potent."

Bradley squished his nose. "Yeah, how come you get the big gun and we get these dorky little ones? Might as well use a water pistol."

"Because it's going to be two against one. I'm making special rules of engagement. You guys can do whatever you want, but I can only run backward and on my knees."

For the next hour, Amber watched in amazement as Joel held back on all levels to give them the advantage. She'd never heard the guys laugh so much. He'd set Bradley in charge of guarding the flag so he didn't have to run a single step the entire game. But Bradley got to shoot plenty, and Joel couldn't seem to stay out of his path. Amber figured Joel planned that on purpose. He also seemed to keep shooting anyone who'd try to shoot her.

Each time adrenaline and laughter carried her away, remembrance of Joel's imminent departure propelled her behind the nearest barricade to fend off a fusillade of tears and paint. By the time they'd obtained Joel's last flag, they'd laughed and yelped and dodged themselves silly.

Multicolored paint covered Joel head to toe. Bradley had four or five splotches. Amber had only one, which she'd given herself by accident, a brag which she touted shamelessly.

As she leaned in to put the chamois towels she kept in her trunk on the seat so paint wouldn't transfer to her upholstery, a barrage of sharp stings hit her.

She whipped up and around, hands to hips.

Two grinning guys pointed at the other.

Her gaze narrowed as she studied the red and blue paint. During the game, Joel had used red balls and

Bradley blue. Both raised hands in surrender and shot twin grins that warmed her all the way to her paint-splotched shoes.

After washing and changing in the men's locker room at the paintball facility, Joel led a squeaky-clean Bradley to meet Amber at her car. "Where do you guys want to go eat?"

Bradley jumped. "Cone Zone! Cone Zone!"

"It's a popular new youth hangout which serves pizza and ice cream. It has a game room and pool tables," Amber explained.

"Sounds like my kinda place. Cone Zone it is," Joel said.

After eating and gaming to their hearts' and stomachs' content, the threesome wound their way to the yellow Mustang.

Joel tensed his shoulders against the weight of sadness. He should be relieved since he'd made the decision to go. He could finally be rid of Refuge. Goodbye would be hard, but freedom would be worth it. Wouldn't it?

Not two miles down the road, Amber tapped Joel on the shoulder. "Look."

Joel peered at Bradley in the backseat. His head rested against the side of the car, his mouth hung open, and his chest rose and fell in deep sleep beneath the seat belt.

"Still leaving today?" Amber whispered.

"I needed to leave in a few days anyway."

"Thanks for spending this time with him today. With us."

Joel swallowed hard. She knew how to cut straight to the heart, didn't she? "I know you're not trying to make it hard for me to leave on purpose. But I can't stay here. Too much has happened, too many bad memories."

"Maybe I can help you work them out."

"Look, I'm overwhelmed. I'm torn. I'm not making rash decisions. I've made vows that I can't break."

"Not even for Bradley?"

"Especially not for him. He's better off in the long run. If he gets too attached to me and I can't be there for him, it's better to pull the rug out from under him now than a whole houseful of carpet later. Dr. Riviera says with his kind of leukemia, he has an excellent prognosis if he gets the bone marrow transplant."

"Speaking of rugs, I have a thank-you letter from our class for the one you brought from India that the Dalit widows and orphans made. Celia and I agree it's beautiful. The class did story and Bible time on it the day you brought it in." He'd hung out at the hospital with Bradley while Amber worked at the school once it became apparent Bradley's infection had been nuked by the powerful antibiotics they bombed him with. That kid was resilient.

Joel eyed the backseat, thankful that God had

brought Bradley through. He couldn't remember a more precious sight than when Bradley had gotten well enough to drink that soda and OD on peanut butter. "He still like his cricket bat?"

"Loves it. He looked up the rules online. We're adding a cricket game to our Special Olympics in a few months."

"Sounds like fun. During downtime, the Indian Air Force soldiers taught our team how to play. They didn't know Chapman grew up in India. We gave them tough competition. I really like playing."

"We could use a Special Olympics coach."

He reached for her hand. "You know I can't stay."

"Can't? Or won't?" Her words rang gently.

"Both. You don't understand what a hold this place has on me."

She squeezed his hand. "Then I say, stay and deal with it."

"Not right now." Joel pulled into Miss Harker's drive. He carried a drowsy Bradley inside and laid him on the daybed where the caseworker directed. Joel knelt. "Listen, buddy. I'm leaving now."

"When will you be back?" Bradley asked, rubbing his eyes.

A pause ensued as Joel swallowed several times, debating how to answer. "I'm not sure."

Bradley sat up, fists clutching Joel's shirt. "I wish you didn't gotta go. Can't you stay? Please?"

"Bradley," Miss Harker warned.

Bradley let Joel's shirt slip from his hands. He reached them around Joel's neck and held tight. "Thank you. I actually felt like I had a dad today."

Amber dipped her head, but not before Joel saw tears. He held Bradley tighter. Moisture soaked his shirt. Every sniff, and every tear hitting Miss Harker's carpet from her and Amber, pushed his heart through a meat slicer.

He never dreamed goodbye would be this hard.

"I wish I knew you'd be back." Bradley kept his face down.

Joel tilted Bradley's face. "Chin up, bud. We'll be in touch."

Bradley nodded. "Okay," came from his mouth, but his eyes and tone said, *It's not the same.* He fiddled with his faux PJ watch, then eyed Joel's. "Thanks very much for the toy. I always wanted to be a hero."

"Bradley, you are. The way you fight this cancer, you're my hero."

"That's cool, 'cause you're mine, too. Since I'm trying to be a man of integrinary, I—I hafta tell ya. At camp, I did two things good and one thing bad."

Joel sat cross-legged on the carpet. "What did you do, buddy?"

Bradley swiped his nose. "My bad thing was I pretended I was being adopted. Only I did it out loud so everybody could hear. But when they had alterations, I went up and put my fibs in Nevereverland."

Miss Harker brought a cartoon blanket to Bradley.

Joel noticed another child's name embroidered on one corner. "Alterations is an altar call at camp. Nevereverland is what the kids call it when God casts your sin as far as east is to west." She fluffed Bradley's pillow.

Bradley lay back. "Yeah. You're forgiven, and He never ever remembers your sin. When God says something three times in the Bible, it's very important. So we call it Nevereverland. When you tell Jesus you want Him in your heart to be your God, He never ever stops loving you. Never ever leaves you. Never ever remembers what the heck you're talking about when you talk about your sin."

"Don't say heck, Bradley," Joel whispered.

"I didn't say heck, Bradley, I just said heck. Miss Harker said since Jesus got my heart, my mouth will follow. She says it's because I lived in a dugout."

"Drug house," Miss Harker amended.

Joel tousled Bradley's hair. "That decision to follow Jesus, and to confess took courage. We all need alterations, and pretty often. Some minor, some major. God's got a pretty big sewing kit with my name on it that could fill one corner of Heaven I think. I'm proud of you."

"Thanks." At a thunderclap, Bradley tugged his blankets up high and slid down in the bed, staring wide at the ceiling. "Guess that would be the sewing machines starting up."

Lightning streaked the sky, illuminating the bay window.

Bradley shot up. "I—I think an angel just got lec-
trocootied. Lectercutie. Shocked. That happened on
TV once. A lady author spilled soda on her laptop
cable and zap. That's all she wrote."

Joel laughed. "You come up with some good
ones, Bradley."

He grinned wide and goofy. "I know. Thanks."

Joel's heart melted to butter at this precious child.
"You're welcome. I'm sorry we didn't have more
time." Joel's voice had a raw element to it that he
couldn't shake.

Bradley didn't protest. By his downtrodden look,
Joel knew he sensed this was goodbye, and nothing
else in his life ever worked out, so why wish for Joel
to stay? He'd seen the look at the orphanage. In the
faces of children who'd suffered the most tragic blows
life offered. After a while, their capability to hope
succumbed to despondency.

Joel didn't want that to happen to any child. Especially not this one. Bradley had hobbled into his heart
and taken up residence. "I love you, Bradley."

Amber looked up and Bradley's face erupted in a
grin. "I love you, too, but don't go all sappy on me.
That sorta ruins the tough-guy image."

Joel laughed. "You're my hero, Bradley. I've never
met anyone more courageous."

Bradley's grin saddled his cheeks as he lay back,
yawning.

"Go back to sleep, buddy. We wore you out today." Joel stood.

"Bradley, I'll call you later," Amber said and hugged him. Before they got across the room, Bradley had fallen asleep.

After leaving, they drove in silence to the local airport.

Joel put the car in Park and shut the ignition off. Seconds clicked by with no words. He reached his hand across to her. "I don't want this to be goodbye."

She squeezed his hand but didn't speak. He shifted in his seat, facing her. She stared at a solitary raindrop that made an uneven trail down the windshield. It built momentum, growing larger the farther it fell, picking up stagnant drops.

It also raced the tear convoy moving down her cheek.

"Say something, Amber. Anything." Joel grasped her hands.

She met his gaze. "Stay?"

Chapter Sixteen

A cool drizzle leaked from melancholy clouds drooping from gray sky above the Refuge airport as Joel exited the car.

Amber met him in the middle of her back bumper. She clicked her trunk open. He tugged out his bag.

"Please? For Bradley? For me?"

Joel set his bag on the asphalt and pulled her close. Green eyes implored. "Just try to face this?"

He planted a kiss on her head and hugged her one last time. He relinquished his hold, fighting anguish. He didn't have to say the words. It reflected in her face.

A coward stared back at him through her eyes.

I can't. It was a word he'd barred from the vocabulary of his life. Until today.

Defeat draped over his head like a reaper's cloak, weighting his shoulders down.

"Goodbye, Joel." The words scraped up her throat in a rough whisper.

Joel gave her hands one more squeeze, then let go.

He tanked across the airport lot without a backward glance. If he looked, he'd run back.

For her. For Bradley.

Move ahead. Just keep moving. Moving ahead. Don't look back, just move. Once in the lobby, Joel halted.

Spurts of adrenaline flooded his fists. They clenched a stranglehold around his neoprene duffel straps.

His uncle stooped on a bench near the lone ticket stand at the small airport. Judging by the dozen coffee cups strewn about, he'd been there awhile.

Despite the urge to flee, Joel anchored his soles to the floor. No way could Joel get across the dinky lobby to the counter without Dean seeing him. Walking out meant staying in Refuge, and he just couldn't. In fact, not another second. Joel pushed his legs forward in long, quick strides.

If he ignored the man, maybe he'd get the hint.

Apparently not. Dean rose from the bench to meet him. Somehow fifteen years had made Dean seem shorter.

"Please wait," a solemn voice said.

Joel stepped to the counter and handed the woman his military pass. She took it, peering over Joel's shoulder.

"Joel, please."

He refused to acknowledge Dean's presence.

"Please, Joel. Give me five minutes of your time, and I promise, I'll never bother you again."

Joel cringed at the brokenness in his voice. Sniffling sounds followed. Was the guy actually crying? According to the ticket clerk's raised brows as she looked from him to Dean, yes.

"Last flight boards at six-thirty." She took Joel's duffel and gestured to seats facing floor-to-ceiling windows that held the airfield in their frames like a landscape portrait.

"Three minutes. I beg of you," Dean implored.

Joel glanced at his watch—6:10. "Can't I board now?" He tried to ignore the concern in her face, the pleas behind him, and the voice within, willing him to stay.

"No, sir. If you'd like a quiet table to talk, The Balcony restaurant is up those stairs." She gestured with a pen.

Did everyone in the world have to go against him? Joel sighed.

"Sir? Are you all right?"

Joel lifted his face to tell her he'd be better if she'd let him get on the plane. Two placid eyes looked past him. Grave concern on her face made him turn.

Dean trembled all over. Sweat beads capped his hairline. When had salt-white seasoned his pepper-black hair?

"I'm fine," Dean said to her. Then to Joel, "Please, son."

"I'm not your son," Joel bit out. People stared. Security murmured. Intent to avoid a fiasco, Joel hiked his thumb sideways at a secluded table. "Up there."

Dean worried at his tie and shuffled his dress shoes. He teetered in the turn a second. Much as he hated to, Joel reached out a steadying hand.

"This way." Joel redirected him to the lower level. Hand to Dean's elbow, he seated him in a red high-back chair at one of the tall, black tables in front of the Deli Bar, closed for renovations. Joel sat himself across, marveling at two things—how frail Dean looked compared to what he remembered, and how much Sheetrock dust rested on the table.

Dean dipped a shaky, sun-spotted hand into his chest pocket and pulled out a lump of crinkled bills. "Can I buy you something to drink? You still like RC soda?"

A flash from times past hit him. Childhood images of sitting at the drugstore counter sipping fountain sodas with Uncle Dean. Joel drew in a breath, drawing whiffs of plaster and paint. Another image surfaced of summers helping Dean with home constructions. Joel freight-lined his focus to the present. "No. You've got two minutes to say what you came here for."

Dean stuffed the paper wad back in his pocket with uncoordinated motions. Currency scattered to the table, disturbing more dust. Dean either didn't notice or didn't care. His trembling worsened. Mere anxiety?

"I've waited for this day a long time. Two decades to say face-to-face that I'm sorry." Dean drew a finger across the table. A shiny vertical black line broke through the gauzy haze.

Dean drew a horizontal line across the first, near the top.

A cross.

Tears stung Joel's eyes. He refused to let them fall. He dipped his head to check his watch. Fifty-five seconds. When he looked back up, Dean placed a hand to his chest.

"From here. I'm deeply sorry, Joel."

"You see me at the church and follow me here?"

"Saw you leave. Saw how upset you were. Came here because I knew you'd try to run. I'm not just sorry today, Joel. I married regret and live with sorrow. Every. Single. Day." Dean fisted his chest with each word, leaving stark dots of white dust on his navy suit. "Since the day you left when you were little, I've woken up and died every day."

Suddenly Dean didn't look so good. His chest drooped. Color drained from his face. Too much coffee? Joel rose automatically, railed against his emotion. This was the last person he felt like helping, but as a paramedic, he couldn't ignore this.

He reached to palpate Dean's radial pulse. Dean must have mistaken it for Joel reaching for his hand. He clasped Joel's hand tight. Beneath a gritty layer of Sheetrock particles, Dean's skin felt cool and clammy to touch.

"What medical problems do you have?" Joel asked

the man who had ruined his life and his family. The man who'd caused his mother to abandon him, and who'd pushed his father to the brink of insanity. Joel wrenched his hand free.

Dean shuddered and dropped his chin, swiping tears with severely scarred knuckles. Knuckles he used to rub across Joel's forehead in a game called Scob Nob.

A mind-bulb flashed of a younger Dean yanking paper from a burning can. It hit Joel like an incoming missile. His dad had made Joel start a fire and toss artwork he'd made for his mother in one by one. Joel had cried from his gut so loud it brought Dean from across the street. Dean had plunged his hands in the fire to save the pictures.

Joel fought long-forgotten memories and rising sympathy with a vengeance. He could not, would not feel sorry for this man. He observed Dean's respirations accelerate and peered at his watch to count the rate. Joel tapped the face of it. What was the deal? Luminox watches never quit.

"Guess my time's up." Dean drummed bony fingers. "I just wanted you to know how sorry I was." He rose but grasped the table. Joel surged to steady him.

"What medical problems do you have?" Joel repeated. Dean sank to the chair. Joel maneuvered behind him, placed his palms under Dean's armpits and lowered him to the floor. He turned the chair over and draped Dean's legs over it to get blood flow to his brain and heart.

"Get an ambulance," Joel called to the clerk, who stared wide-eyed. "Now." A throng of people gathered.

Dean scratched his head. "Don't fuss over me. I just wanted you to know how sorry I... I guess I need to...should be getting you back to your studies. Now."

Studies? Joel loosened Dean's tie and top button. "Do you know the day, Uncle Dean?"

"Every day. Always have so much homework." Joel's father had never helped when he'd struggled in school. Dean had.

Airport personnel rolled a medical cart up. Joel placed a pulse oxygen cable on Dean's finger. Ninety-five percent in room air. Not perfect. Not life or death, either. "Have you been sick, Dean?"

"I saved them. Those pictures you drew. Every single one."

Images swept through Joel's mind of painting at the house on Haven Street with Uncle Dean. They'd muralled his walls and fridge. Joel had forgotten. Until now.

"I need to know what kind of medical problems you have."

"Nothin'. What kind do you have?"

An errant laugh coughed its way up Joel. "I'm not the one lying on the floor."

Dean lifted his torso. "Need help layin' floor, you say?"

"No." Joel pressed Dean's shoulders. "Don't move. You're not making a bit of sense."

Dean patted his pockets. "I have plenty of cents. Have all you want. I still got your pig bank on the shelf there. I never robbed a dime."

"Uncle Dean, do you know where you are?"

Dean looked around. His eyes paused on Joel, but a dull haze swam in them. "Yes, Jinky. I know you. I know who you are."

Joel tensed at the word. Only his mother had used it. If Dean weren't disoriented, it would have been a hard slap in the face. "Do you take medications?" Joel asked.

"Um. Oh yeah, the little yellow pill."

Joel rechecked his pulse. "What's it for?"

Dean tried to sit up. "What's what for?"

Joel held him steady. "The pill."

"Why, you need it?"

"No, but you might. What did the doctor give it to you for?"

"Ten bucks a bottle. Highway robbery I tell you—"

"No. He prescribed it why?"

"Fixes my blood pressure." Dean scratched his forehead.

"To lower or raise it?"

"Brings it down."

"Okay. That little yellow pill is all you take?"

"That's it. You sure do ask a lot of questions, boy."

"Your doctor hasn't diagnosed you with other

problems? Heart disease? Blood sugar? You don't have diabetes?"

"No."

"You sure? Because you're acting like a diabetic who's had too much sugar or not enough insulin."

"Yeah, I take sugar in my coffee. Lots and lots of it, or I do go insane."

Joel remembered all the cups. "Who's your doctor?" He flipped open his cell.

Dean's eyes bugged. "Don't mention the coffee."

"I want to see if they've checked your blood sugar and let him know EMS is taking you in."

"Taking me in? Sounds like I'm goin' to the slammer. Only I've been locked up all my life. Prison a' guilt. My only problem is regret and sorrow for the fool-hearted choices of my youth. It presses in from all sides, weighs down on a man after a time—" A mauve-blue tinge flushed the pink from Dean's mouth.

Joel leaned in, to be sure the light wasn't playing tricks.

No. Definitely cyanosis.

"Uncle Dean, don't try to talk. Rest."

The oxygen read low nineties now. Joel twisted the tank knob. Empty. "You have another one?" he asked the closest staff member. "I need it pronto."

The harried young woman ran to the back area.

Dean closed his eyes. Sweat trickled from his forehead. Joel dabbed it with his hankie, disturbing a red-spotted tissue Dean must have forgotten to remove after shaving. Some things never change. As a youngster, Joel forever plucked dime-size wads off Dean's face when they'd go to town.

"I'm glad I got to see you," Dean slurred.

Dean could have been taken to the hospital twice by now. Joel grabbed the large oxygen tank the airport employee lumbered up on a rolling dolly. They must not have had a portable. "Where's the ambulance?"

"Coming." Distress built in her eyes.

"This'll do until they get here." Joel uncurled an oxygen tube and held it in front of Dean's nose, twisting the knob to four liters. Instantly Dean pinked up and his numbers rose to normal range. Joel looped the tube around Dean's ears.

"I musta forgot my insulin this morning," Dean announced.

Joel drew a slow breath in and turned to the employee. "You have medication for insulin-dependent diabetics in that cart?"

"All the medications are outdated and on reorder. Nothing like this has ever happened here." She wrung her hands.

"I got my finger poker in my pocket," Dean said.

Joel dug the glucose monitor out and checked Dean's sugar. "It's low." Joel felt relieved. Low was easier to treat than high in his opinion, especially since he didn't carry vials of insulin in his first aid kit. Maybe he should start.

"Do you have milk or orange juice we could give him?" Joel asked the girl.

She nodded, stood and sprinted up the restaurant stairs. Joel suddenly felt awful. He hadn't noticed her being significantly pregnant before. Sirens cut through his thoughts.

The intercom announced last boarding for his flight. Joel looked at the plane—his ticket out of here. He looked down at his uncle.

Dean opened his eyes.

Joel patted Dean's shoulder. "Help will be here in a minute." Dean needed to be seen by a physician. Joel didn't think Dean's blood sugar being low should cause this much of an oxygenation problem. Better to make sure there wasn't something more ominous going on. As soon as the ambulance crew arrived, his responsibility would be met.

Then he could leave and never look back.

Except for one thing.

Dean's fire-withered finger traced the PJ motto along Joel's watchband.

The creed. It hit Joel like a house falling from the sky.

It is my duty as a pararescueman to save life and to aid the injured. I will be prepared at all times to perform my assigned duties quickly and efficiently, placing these duties before personal desires and comforts. These things I do—

"That others may live." Dean's words paralleled

Joel's thoughts. The pregnant girl trundled down the steps with orange juice and peanut butter crackers.

"Slow down," Joel called to her.

She helped Joel prop up Dean, who sipped and nibbled.

"How'd you know to bring crackers?" Joel asked her.

"I was in nursing school before…"

Joel looked where her hand roved over her protruding belly. "You can go back later." Joel laid Dean back.

He clutched Joel's sleeve. "Your mother'd be proud. So would your father. I'm so sorry I took all that away."

One part of Joel wanted to comfort and another wanted to get up and walk away.

So others may live.

Only he didn't walk away from duty. He never backed away from an assignment and this had God's signature all over it.

Don't let me do what I want. Help me do what's right. Help me do what You want. Get help here.

Joel peered into Dean's face. "How are you doing?"

"I'm just lyin' here. What are you doing?"

Joel chuckled, deciding not to correct. "Tuning in and talking to God, actually." Maybe Dean had a hearing problem.

"Good. That's right good. I been talking to Him, too." Dean's eyes glittered.

"Is that right?" Joel kept his hand on Dean's.

"That's right. For years. About you. I wanted a chance to tell you. With your mother, it only happened once. With her married, that was once too many. She felt sorry. I felt sorry. We made a mistake befriending one another in your dad's absence. I never knew where that forbidden friendship would lead, Joel. I miss my brother. I miss you. Please tell your dad I'm sorry. For your sake, I wish he hadn't sent her away."

Sent her away? Though questions burned on Joel's tongue, he clenched his mouth against the siege. He refused to put Dean's life at risk by exhuming bitter bones.

"I forgive and release you, Uncle Dean." *Dear God, now please help me mean it.* "It's all right."

"No, son. Sin's never all right. And you never were a good liar."

Joel smiled. "Neither were you." He hadn't meant that as an accusation, but hurt flashed in Dean's face anyway.

"I see questions in your eyes that I imagine have haunted you a lifetime. I don't want to leave here without giving you answers. It's the least I can do after—"

Joel pressed a hand to Dean's chest. "Let's talk after you get better."

A feisty scowl knit two salt-and-pepper brows. "I may not get better. It'd kill me to lie here and keep quiet."

"Okay." What could he do except let the man talk?

Dean gave Joel's hand a feeble squeeze. "I need ya to listen for a minute, Jinky. Will ya?"

Joel suddenly felt sick inside. He hoped this wasn't some deathbed confession. Faced with it, he wanted to run from the unknown. He hated this and wished…he wished he wasn't alone. He wished for his mom and he wished for Amber. He wished for her so bad, he'd lost his mind and imagined her grapefruity perf—

"Hey." Soft rustling accompanied a feminine voice. "What's going on?"

Joel closed his eyes. Relief surged as the voice he most hoped for sounded beside him. Her voice, in tandem with the impression that God sent her here and she listened, pulled a rip cord within. A parachute of hope opened and pulled him from the gravity of despair that had clutched him a lifetime.

Thank you for taking care of me, Father. I suspect You always have. I just couldn't see You in the fog or ashes. Like that table. Layers of mess. Remnants of renovation. Not until Your touch disturbs can truth gleam. I'd love closure and answers, but I'll settle for comfort and peace. Put forgiveness in my heart, and strip me of this vow. I want to be whole.

He turned to Amber. "I was just wishing you were here."

She smiled in her sweet, calm way and knelt. "I passed an ambulance coming this way. When I got home, I found a message on my machine from Dean, saying he'd seen us together and did I know where he could find you. I put two and two together and came here."

Speech evaded Joel. No doubt God had brought him to this moment. Maybe all of them.

An airport employee knelt. "How's he doing?"

"Better, but he needs to see a physician. What's the holdup with the ambulance?"

"It's been detained."

"By?"

"A bad wreck. Down the block."

"Can't they call another crew?"

"We did. It's been detained, as well. Paramedics from the fire department are en route."

He didn't understand this. Frustration gripped him such as when he'd watched buildings burn with his grandmother inside. A sense of helplessness took him hostage by storm. Who would rescue the rescuer?

Triage meant dealing with the most critical first, so the accident victims must be worse off than Dean. "Was it detained by the same wreck?" Joel asked.

"No. By the rain. It also detained your flight." She returned to the counter to assist other passengers.

Joel tuned his heart heavenward. *God, please hold the rain back. Speak into it as you did the Bible storm, make it still so we can get Dean to a hospital.*

Joel knew God intimately enough to understand there's a reason for the rain. Trust proved harder when looking at a victim through the eyes of a paramedic and family.

Amber took her phone out and pushed buttons. She left a voice message with her parents to pray then rested a sustaining hand on his. "Refuge has two ambulances. Paramedics will be here soon."

Dean must have heard them whispering. His eyes fluttered open and lit on Amber. "Hey. I'm down for the count."

"I see that. Some people will do anything to get attention." Amber smiled and rested her hand on Dean's arm. "What happened to you?"

Dean aimed a chin at Joel. "Your boyfriend here punched my lights out."

Amber gasped at Joel.

He lifted his hands. "I did no such th—" he laughed "—thing."

"Why, he most certainly did. Socked it to me, he did." Her gaze narrowed into slits.

Dentures clacked with Dean's snort. "Your knees hurt?"

"Why, should I be praying more?" Amber asked.

"No. Because I'm pullin' your leg. Don't get yer dress in a ruffle. He didn't lay a finger on me except to check my pulse."

"It didn't sound like something Joel would do."

Dean smiled at Joel and flicked a glance at Amber. "So, you know this one, huh?"

Joel nodded, drinking in the sight of her. "Yeah. I know her." *I know I never want to say goodbye again.*

"You'll treat her better'n the last one did, so I'm glad you found one another."

Amber shook her head. "Dean, we're not—"

Joel put a hand on her arm. "It's okay."

Mirth glittered in Dean's eyes and a smile danced around his mouth. "Well are ya an item, or aren't ya?"

Joel winked. "I say we are, she says we're not."

Dean looked at her. "What's your holdup? Hey, listen, I was just tellin' Jinky here about his mother."

Joel felt proud of Amber for tamping down her surprise at Dean's blurt.

She drew in a breath and looked to Joel. "Is that right?"

"That's right."

"Should I give you two some privacy?" Amber adjusted her purse strap.

"That's up to Jinky." Dean eyed Joel.

"I'd like you to stay," Joel said to Amber.

"I'm here then. Looks like the ambulance is, too."

The rig rumbled outside glass doors. Flashing strobes turned the airport lobby into a triage disco. Two uniformed men wheeled a stretcher inside. A cardiac monitor rested on the gurney. As they approached, Joel stepped aside.

The airport clerk motioned him. "Sir, your flight is boarded. You're the last passenger. They need to know what you plan to do."

Joel looked at Amber, then Dean, then the plane that would take him from his problems.

Then asked himself the same question.

What was he going to do?

Chapter Seventeen

So mad she could spit staples, Amber ripped her gaze away from the east airport window where Joel's tall shoulders and broad back stood a head above other passengers in line to board.

She stared out the west window where paramedics attached monitors to Dean, who lay on the carpet in his Sunday best. She knew he tried to be brave, but having come to know him from church, she assumed him scared by the way his dress shoe toes clopped back and forth.

Amber wanted to run after Joel and shake him. How could he leave? Run from his problems?

He'd regret it. She knew he would. Especially if Dean didn't make it.

She didn't want Joel to hurt any further.

Joel's face upon exiting the tarmac had reminded her of a caged animal. Like the little fawn when sedation waned. Not sure whether to run in circles, lash out, thrash, play dead or flee.

He couldn't hide from this to make it go away. It had chased him all his life, and now it had him cornered.

Remembering softened her anger. Now she wanted to run after him and beg him not to leave. She'd hug him, then slug him.

It had to be his decision, or he'd resent her.

She'd called Celia to pray but hadn't heard back yet. Celia could talk sense into anybody. And if that didn't work, Celia could slug harder than Amber.

She recalled a message on contending prayer. She'd asked God to teach her how to listen, grasp what He was up to in any given moment, then press in and contend.

She didn't remember signing up for the crash course.

Don't let Joel make a mistake he'll live to regret.

Amber followed the gurney to the front doors. Outside, the diesel engine chugged on the paramedic truck.

"Wait." Dean reached for Amber. A paramedic stepped aside.

Dean pulled a package from his suit pocket and sandwiched it in her hands. "When he's ready, give him this."

How would she know? "Why don't you get better and give it to him yourself?"

"I aim to, but just in case I don't, or in case he never speaks to me again, see that he gets it. Will ya?"

"I will." She stepped aside to let the paramedic work.

The crew opened the rig doors. Her hands trembled

as she clutched the DVD. Her gaze fell to the sprawling title, written by a black marker in Dean's handwriting. Words that jumped out and screamed through her mind.

Words that rocked her to the core.

To Joel, my son. With love.

Her mind scrambled to comprehend, to make sense of it.

By the time she'd surfaced from grappling with the words, the ambulance doors had closed. She backed onto the curb and let her gaze fall to the DVD again.

When were those words written and who had written them? Joel's father, Dale? Joel's mother? Or Dean?

Her phone rang, jolting her out of the trance the DVD had plunged her into. "Little too much caffeine today, Amber."

She hit her voice mail and listened. The words siphoned strength from her knees.

"Bradley?" *Not again.*

She flailed her arms to the wall, moving herself on numb legs to a seat by the door. Slumping down, she scrambled in her purse for paper and replayed the message. She put the DVD under her arm and transcribed the caseworker's message with trembling fingers.

Bradley's been taken to Refuge Memorial by ambulance...

Had the paintball game been too hard on him? Or Joel leaving? Maybe she wouldn't be a good mom after all.

Worse, had he been in that accident?

When they'd dropped Bradley off at Miss Harker's earlier, she'd mentioned Foster Lady was on her way to pick him up.

It could be.

The formidable thoughts shoved her to the east window.

Plane door closed.

She dialed Joel's cell. It rang and rang. No voice mail. Weird. She peered at her bar signal. One. No wonder.

She dashed to the counter. "There's been another emergency. Do you think they could hold the plane?" Amber rasped.

The woman picked up a phone. "Are you certain Mr. Montgomery will want to come back?"

She didn't know.

Before today, she thought she knew him, but he might be just like her father was at that age. Gone when tragedy struck. Gone when the earthquake came. Gone when her mother sat alone through Amber's surgery. Gone during Amber's recovery, and gone during news that she'd never have children.

Just…gone.

She'd at least give him a chance.

As she dialed, her phone rang. Miss Harker's number. Amber ended the call to Joel's cell and answered her phone, amazed a call got through. Amber scribbled information as Miss Harker cited Bradley's room and phone numbers.

"Beyond that, I don't have any other information, Amber." Miss Harker paused. "Are you on your way to the hospital?"

"Yes."

"Good, because Bradley's oncologist just mentioned it vital that you be there for legal reasons."

At least Bradley and Dean were headed to the same hospital. Amber shut her phone. No time to chase down Joel's plane.

"Thank you, but I'll notify him on the way or later," she said to the clerk. Bradley needed her now.

Amber clipped through the hall leading to the parking area. Through the glass encasement, she glared at Joel's plane as it taxied to the end of the runway, then lifted off. Higher, higher, flying over her and the small airport. She fought anger at Joel for leaving, and herself for ever thinking he'd be a good dad or husband.

A man should be there for his family. He'd left the two people she knew he cared about more than anything when they most needed him. How could she trust a man who might never be around to take care of his family? This is what life with Joel would be like.

She wanted no part of it.

Only he had already imprinted her heart. She raked her hand across her hip, but those stupid blue stains refused to come off. Giving up on the idea of a future with him would be easier said than done. Her heart had hoped behind her back without her realizing it. Now he'd made his choice, and it wasn't her.

Just like Bart.

She'd made her choice, too. Bradley. Speaking of, Joel at least needed to be notified so he could pray. She pulled out her phone, debating whether to call yet. She didn't think people were supposed to have cell phones on in airplanes. It wasn't like the pilots would turn the plane around and bring him back.

Or would they?

She felt torn between Joel, Bradley and Dean. Each headed to the unknown with no family at their side. The last two could be facing death in the next two moments and Joel could any day if deployed into danger.

She didn't want any of them to face it alone.

I don't know what to do. Please help.

At the end of the glass-domed hall, movement caught her attention. The ambulance zoomed past, heading for the highway with lights flashing and siren blaring. She'd get in her car and follow it then call Joel once she got to the hospital for word about Bradley. At the short-term parking lot exit, she pushed the electronic pad to make the front doors open, then went full speed ahead to where she'd parked. She stuck her face in her purse and dug for keys.

"You should be more aware of your surroundings."

Amber jumped at the voice, scarcely believing it.

"Joel!" She looked in the sky where the plane he had just boarded gained altitude in the clouds. "What—"

He pushed off from where he leaned against her car, grinning. "I run faster than you, remember?"

She looked at the plane. "They let you off?"

"I never got on. Let's go to the hospital." He opened the passenger side door for her.

Hospital.

She held his arm. "Joel, Bradley's sick…or something. They've taken him there, too."

At her rush of words, he pulled her close. "Tell me in the car. Let's stay calm until we know what's going on. If they gave you his room and phone numbers, he's stable. Okay?"

"Okay." Relief flooded her.

Joel closed her door then got in and closed his. "I called Dad about Dean which is why I missed you in the lobby. I had to go out a side door to get a decent call through. There's terrible reception inside that airport."

"No kidding."

He eyed the rearview mirror and backed out, clicking his seat belt. He looked over to be sure hers was fastened, too. She'd noticed that about him— very safety conscious.

"I'll call my parents so they can pray for Bradley. They already know to pray for Dean." She dialed their cell and left a voice message.

Since Joel didn't flinch when she said Dean's name, maybe he was making progress in forgiveness. He nodded, watching traffic. He seemed composed. She guessed he had to be that way as a PJ. Regardless, his presence calmed her.

"Where are your parents on vacation?" he asked. She figured to make small talk to get her mind off Bradley.

"They went to a beach in Florida. On the way back, they stopped at my dad's parents' in Missouri who stay with them over the holidays. They'll bring my grandparents back with them."

"Do you have cousins and stuff?"

"Lots. Though I was an only child, my parents have a ton of siblings and my cousins are like brothers and sisters to me. There are a slew of them." Amber suddenly felt bad for having such a large family when Joel didn't seem to have any. The person he did have was mentally absent, or hanging on by a thread.

"I'll share."

He glanced at her before returning his attention to the road. "What?"

"My family. I'll gladly share."

He blinked a couple times, looked at the dashboard as if the solution were there, then swung his eyes back to the road, seeming to soak in her words.

She needed to tell him of the DVD before reaching Dean's room. "May I drive? I have something to share." She gripped indentions into her purse strap.

He eyed her with interest and pulled over. "Fire away," he said after they'd switched places.

She steeled herself to say words that might hit Joel

with the biggest earthquake of his life. "Dean gave me something to give you." Eyes pinned to the road, she dipped her hand into her purse and tugged the DVD out before her courage faltered.

He took it in total silence. Plastic crackled as he opened the case. He had to have seen the words on the front by now. She peeked.

His palms held the circular disc. Both hands rested on his lap. He held it. Just held it. His eyes didn't blink, and other than a furrowed brow, his face didn't react. His chest fell softly with a breath he must have held, because it went on forever.

"What is this?" His voice wafted quiet, solemn. Little-boy thoughtful.

"I don't know. All he did was hand it to me and ask me to see that you got it. I didn't have a chance to ask because they whisked him away."

The most obvious question went unasked aloud. No doubt it bellowed in his head as it did hers.

Who was the DVD from?

One swallow. Two. "That's Dean's handwriting."

Tears stung her eyes. "I noticed that, too." She drew in a breath, and tried to let it out slowly, but it rode out on a shudder anyway. "I don't know what to say."

"Just say you'll be there, because if what I'm holding is what I think, my whole life has been a lie." His strong voice cracked on the last word like a guitar string wound too tight.

"I'll be there." Tears plopped on her hands. On her

knees. One right after the other. On the seat. The more she swiped, the more they persisted.

"Good, because I'm going to need a good friend to lean on."

"I don't want to be friends, Joel." Before he could take that the wrong way, she grasped his hand. "I love you."

She might have heard a moist sniff, but couldn't be certain since he faced the window. His fingers twined around hers like a zip tie pushed to the tightest notch.

"I love you, too. Have for some time now," he finally said.

Amber realized it had never occurred to her that he might not say it back. She already rested more securely in Joel's love than she ever had in Bart's.

After a moment of silence, he squeezed her hand again. "So, where do we go from here?"

"To the hospital, then hopefully to the altar where you won't leave me standing alone. Because if you do, I know a street-smart firecracker who will slug your lights out."

He jolted upright. "Amber, pull over." He looked stricken.

A scream lodged in her throat. The dilapidated car that Bradley's foster mother drove sat at the side of the road, consumed with flames. Fire trucks, police cars and an ambulance flanked it.

"Stay here," he ordered. He'd transformed before her eyes. Deliberate, militant steps took him from the car. His muscles coiled with lethal control as he approached the scene. She could see the warrior he must be in combat situations.

She almost pitied his enemy. Almost.

Learning from the deer episode, she stayed in the car. A surge of panic hit her as the charred car spit smoke from shattered windshields. Wicked flames danced over the backseat where Bradley usually rode.

He's in a room. He has to be fine. Then why did she hyperventilate, her lips and fingers numb?

Joel stared at something the officer pointed to as they spoke. Joel nodded a couple times, then shook the officer's hand and jogged back to the car. "Bradley's fine," he said as he got in. "He's in for overnight observation."

"What happened to the car?"

Joel's jaw clenched. "His foster mother decided to transport her meth lab because she sensed a home inspection, and her car took a turn for the worse…right into the path of a truck. The substances in her trunk were still volatile. Someone rear-ended her after the initial collision. The friction and combustible drug paraphernalia caused a flash fire and a small explosion."

"A small explosion? Is there any such thing?"

"The trunk took the brunt of the concussion. Foster Lady's forehead took the brunt of the collision. She lost consciousness when her face cracked the windshield. Bradley pushed his cricket bat through the protective coating and flagged down a motorist who dragged her out as smoke billowed from beneath the back bumper."

"Bradley's already a hero."

"Be sure and tell him."

"Is the foster lady going to be all right?" She turned onto the street leading to the hospital.

"The cop says she's going straight to jail after the hospital releases her, so apparently she's okay."

The implications of this hit Amber. "Joel. I hate to drop another bomb, but I'm next in line for guardianship of Bradley."

"You told me that while wearing duck slippers, remember?"

"That's why I'm bringing it up. The adoption could go through sooner. I need to know if you think there's a chance you'll ever want to be a dad. My foster care license went through. That was the last hoop to jump through in order to secure the motion for adoption. I'm just waiting on paperwork. Joel, I'm going to be a mother. I need to know how that will affect us so I can prepare myself emotionally."

Joel's head swiveled around to peer at her. Without a word, he rubbed his forehead with his thumb and forefinger. Another slow breath funneled out his lungs. His head dropped back onto the seat. Eyes stared at the underside of her convertible top.

Several excruciating moments of silence chugged by. Power poles ran past her car in a line. Seconds ticked. A grove of trees. Deafening silence. More poles. She started counting them. Hitting ten for the third time, she couldn't stand it another second longer. "I wish you'd say something."

"What are you going to do about this?" he asked in a monotone.

"About what?"

Three more poles.

He knuckled the top of the car interior. "This. Convertibles aren't exactly safe for kids."

"Is that all you're going to say?"

Arms folded across his chest. "For now."

Amber turned up the radio, giving him a chance to fully absorb what she'd told him, and contemplate what that meant for them.

As they pulled in the hospital lot, a cell rang. Joel and Amber looked at one another.

"Is that mine or yours?" she asked.

"Yours. I changed my tone."

Speaking of tones, a disconcerting amount of detachment resided in his.

Amber flipped open her phone, updating her parents. When she clicked off, Joel stared out the window unblinking. Considering his manner of speaking coupled with agitated body language, he may as well have strung yellow Police Line—Do Not Cross tape around himself.

Amber stared at him, never having seen him go this long without casting a tender glance or a teasing grin her way. Though he surely sensed her visual intensity, he didn't acknowledge or match her gaze.

Clearly, communication wasn't sanctioned.

Chapter Eighteen

"**B**radley's roommate's bathing," the nurse said when they arrived at his room. "Please return in a few minutes."

Amber stood outside in the hall, unsure how to proceed.

"Let's check on Dean, then come back." Joel's voice had softened, but she really missed his smile and playful teasing.

They reached the end of one hall and stepped into another. Joel braced an old-fashioned mommy seat belt arm in front of Amber, impeding her forward movement.

A man zoomed inches by, white lab coat flailing behind him like a flag in the wind. A stethoscope snaked around his neck jiggled against his name tag. He yanked a curtain aside on a three-tiered hall cart, grabbed a yellow kidney-shaped basin and pulled a one-eighty, heading their way again.

"Who ya here to see?" he asked, moving swiftly past.

"Dean DuPaul?" Joel answered.

The man waved his clipboard in a pitcher's arc, not breaking his stride. "Follow me. I'm Dr. James, Dean's doctor. Not James Dean's doctor, just Dean's doctor with the last name of James," the man said as they kept at a brisk pace beside him.

His voice reminded Amber of Christmas. Rush and nostalgia. Pockets jingled with his steps, voice jolly. Face full of cheer.

If she moved and talked that fast everywhere she went, maybe she'd be wheat-stalk-thin, too.

"Friends or family?" Dr. Skinny asked.

"Family. I'm his nephew." Joel stared straight ahead.

"Pardon the sprint but he's queasy. Nurses are busy." The doctor's shoes squeaked a left turn down an antiseptic-smelling hall with waxed floors. "Will the son be coming, too?"

Joel's foot screeched to a standstill. "Son?"

The doctor slowed. His bifocals slid down his nose. "Dean mentioned a son whom he hoped would come once he got word."

Joel moved full speed ahead. "He got word, all right."

They stopped in front of a sink. Dean's doctor handed the bowl to Amber, then turned on the water with a knee handle. "Is the son here?"

Joel's jaw clenched. "That would probably be me."

Hands dripping, the doctor eyed Joel over his glasses. "I'm sorry. I thought you said you were the nephew."

"I did. I am. At least I thought I was. But now I

think I might be his son." He gave the bowl in Amber's hand a sharp nod. "Have you got another one of those buckets?"

Joel looked seriously nauseated. So did the doctor.

Water splashed the bottom of the deep surgical sink as he stepped to the second door down. Amber shut the water off while the doctor rapped on the wood.

A nurse came to the door. The doctor pushed the bowl through a crack. "A little late, but thanks. He blew his IV with his stomach contents. It'll be a few minutes while I clean him up and start a new line. He's dehydrated."

"I don't know how after all that coffee," Joel said.

"Coffee?" the doctor asked.

"Whoops." Joel grinned.

"It's a conspiracy..." The words were bellowed from within the room.

"He drinks a pot a day with a pint of sugar, then forgets his insulin," the doctor said. "When he moves to the high-rise, it hopefully won't be a problem anymore."

"Moving?"

"Yes, his fiancée's a home health nurse. The high-rise is one step up from independent living. She lives and works there."

A nurse rounded the corner toting video game paraphernalia and a pair of green pediatric nonskid slippers.

The threesome stepped out of her path.

"Thanks," she said, passing. "I've got one bored to death."

"Does his name happen to be Bradley?" Joel asked.

She halted, all smiles. "Why, it sure does. Are you his adoptive parents? He informed me he's going to be adopted."

Amber swallowed past the pinecone in her throat and didn't dare look at Joel. "I am. I'm also his teacher. May I see him?"

"He's only in for observation, but his roommate is sick. I'll put Bradley in a chair and wheel him to the waiting room."

"Thank you." Why would the nurse have mentioned adoptive parents? Amber remembered his oncologist had called. There'd been a message from the case-worker, too. Her heart dipped and soared all at once and she felt torn from both sides.

Someone else besides her wanted Bradley?

Dean's doctor waved a hand toward the hallway's end. "Why don't you folks go to the waiting room? We'll get Dean settled in, then come talk with you when we find out what's going on."

Amber figured he wasn't only referring to Dean's health.

"Can I do a wheelie in this?" Bradley's voice wafted from another hall. Joel and Amber turned.

"Hey!" Bradley pushed the wheels until the nurse had to jog in her blue Croc shoes to keep up.

"I need to see a driver's license or photo ID before I release you to them," she said.

Bradley's nose wrinkled. "I'm too young to drive."

Joel laughed.

Good to hear it. Not much had passed through his mouth other than breathing since the bombs she dropped in the car.

"She means our ID, Bradley. Not yours," Amber said.

They pulled out their identification. She eyed the sheet. "I have her name listed, but I don't see yours, Mr. Montgomery."

Amber wondered if a shard of disappointment glinted through Joel's eyes with her words, or merely the flicker of fluorescent hall lights offering illusion. The waiting room door opened. Miss Harker and Dr. Riviera stepped out.

"I thought I heard you two causing a racket out here." Miss Harker grinned at Joel and Bradley.

"Is Mr. Montgomery an approved visitor?" the nurse asked.

Miss Harker nodded. "Yes. I needed his consent to add him."

Joel nodded. "You bet, but only if I get first dibs on choice of the controllers." He eyed the video game box.

Dr. Riviera chuckled, then turned to Amber. "Miss Stanton, if Mr. Montgomery won't mind keeping Bradley entertained for a few moments, may we have a private word with you?"

Joel nodded and Bradley grinned.

Amber walked like a mummy into a quiet cove off the right side of the waiting room with Dr. Riviera and

Miss Harker. Mixed thoughts buzzed around her head. What could this be about? Were they about to tell her Bradley had been placed elsewhere? She should be upset at the thought, but peace held her emotions steady.

Whatever this was, God seemed in on it. As they sat, Miss Harker pulled a bundle of papers out, handing them to Amber.

She stared down at them not seeing.

"We've pulled a few strings, Amber. A recommendation from your landlord suspended the home inspection which is why your foster care license was approved early. We called a special hearing with the judge and presented your case. In light of Bradley's acute circumstance of living in a drug house, they've expedited paperwork."

Amber stared at the forms. "I don't understand."

Miss Harker handed her a pen. "We pushed it through. When you sign the dotted line, Bradley is yours."

Tears rushed from her shoulders up. "Mine?"

Bradley is yours.

Which meant Joel might not be.

"Your foster care license approval sent you to the top of the list for adoption. The judge ordered ninety days of Bradley living with you to be certain you want to take this on as a single mom, considering his medical condition. If at the end of that you still feel strongly about adopting him, he's yours."

Mine. I'm going to be a mother. But more importantly, Bradley's going to have a family.

"Can I call my parents? They've wanted grandchildren for ten years, though they never let me know. I have a tactless great-grandmother who knows all and shares all." She smiled through a curtain of tears. "I can't wait to tell Bradley."

"One more thing," Dr. Riviera said. "You are aware Bradley passed all necessary conditions for bone marrow candidacy and we've found a donor. Two weeks from today he will undergo treatment if we can keep him in remission until that time. It's a big if."

"I know."

"Still want to go through with it?" Miss Harker asked.

"Yes. I want him. Whether it's a day or half a century. Whether he plans my funeral, or I plan his. I want him to have a mother. I've wanted children since I was—" she gulped, just now realizing the coincidence "—seven." She thought of Joel, and the year both their dreams came under fire.

Dr. Riviera smiled. "You may spoil him."

Amber tucked a curl behind her ear. "Not spoil, love. Okay, maybe a little spoiling when it comes to video games. Then I won't have to worry when it comes time for him to pick my nursing home when I'm old."

Miss Harker clapped. "That's a great way to look at it, Amber. In faith. Speaking of looking, ahem."

Amber lifted her face.

Joel stood in the corner, hands pocketed, shoulder propped against the alcove frame. "The nurse took

Bradley to check vitals. She instructed me to wait in here. I guess she didn't realize the room was in use. I hope you don't mind me eavesdropping. I'm very interested in what's going on with Bradley and Amber."

His leisurely gaze did a slow hike over the terrain of her face. "Always look as if seeing them for the very first time and love them as if it were the last."

Miss Harker and Dr. Riviera faded into shadows in the light of Joel's face. She wondered at the words that flowed from his mouth like molasses. Slow and sweet. How long had he been standing there? How much did he hear?

"That's an admirable quote, sir. Who came up with it?" Dr. Riviera leaned his clipboard on his knee.

"A navy buddy named Silas. Lost his wife and child in one fell swoop," Joel answered the oncologist, but kept his gaze pinned on Amber.

Miss Harker cleared her throat and stood. "We can bring these forms back for you to look over later, Amber. No rush. If you want Bradley to come home with you upon discharge, you'll need to sign the top two before he leaves, though."

Joel peered at Miss Harker. "When do you anticipate that?"

She looked at Dr. Riviera, who scanned the clipboard. "A day or so, if his labs come back okay. Looks like the results aren't here yet."

Miss Harker closed her briefcase. "Take as much time as you need to decide. Bradley will come home with me until we hear from you on how you'd like to proceed." The caseworker's gaze flicked from Joel to Amber the entire time she spoke.

Joel's gaze hardly wavered from Amber except to land lightly on Miss Harker, Dr. Riviera and the papers before fluttering back like a butterfly to its favorite flower.

The door creaked open. "Mr. DuPaul?"

Everyone looked at each other. Joel moved to the door. "Who specifically are you looking for?" he asked the nurse.

"The son of Mr. DuPaul."

"That would be me. I think." Joel moved toward the door. He paused, looked over his shoulder at Amber. "Mind coming with me?"

Thankfulness trickled through her.

She wanted nothing more than to go with him. Everywhere he went, in fact.

Everyone exited the alcove together.

"Hey, people! Here I am." Bradley wheeled out of the nurses' station, but the blood pressure cuff pulled tight, leashing him to the nurse. "Awww. Forgot about Mr. Squeeze."

The nurse tugged the Velcro strap off and scribbled numbers on a form. "All finished."

"Can I come with you?" Bradley wheeled up to Joel.

Joel swallowed and knelt. "Tell you what. I need a few minutes alone with my…Dean. You wait here with Miss Harker for a few if she doesn't mind hanging out a bit longer. Then, I'll come back in here. Okay?"

Miss Harker winked. "Don't mind a bit. In fact, if it's okay with your nurse, I know right where a soda machine is."

The nurse nodded. "He's cleared for takeoff in the carbonation department."

A toothless grin broke out. "Yeah! Let's go raid it."

"Why's he in a wheelchair?" Joel asked the nurse after Miss Harker wheeled him around the corner.

"Because he wants to be. Gets him there faster. Bradley's a frequent flyer. One of these days there's going to be a runway on the roof with his name painted on it."

Amber laughed with Joel. Their mingled voices sent a surge of longing through her for a future with him of days like that.

"Shall we go see your—Dean?" Amber wasn't sure how to refer to him, either.

Joel eyed the cream-colored hall and held an arm out. "After you, milady." Heat climbed her neck with his knightly cadence, but relief overpowered embarrassment. She'd bear scorched cheeks for the return of typical Joel any day.

When Dean's door came into view, Joel slowed. His eyes glittered with uncertainty. The next blink softened them with peace. He sought her gaze. "Pray." His voice pitch had dropped.

"I am." Must be contagious, because hers lowered, too.

"Let's go," he said as though she needed the pep talk instead of him. He approached the door and stopped. Head down, he ran a tongue along the inside of his cheek and let out the softest of sighs. His hand hovered a sustaining moment before knuckles tapped lightly. "Uncle Dean?"

TV volume dialed down. "Come in," a female voice echoed.

Joel entered first. Immediately Dean reached a hand out, then patted the bed beside him. Joel slowly sat.

"This is my fiancée, Millie. Millie, this is Joel. I used to sit on his bed like this when monsters came." Dean smiled.

A small laugh came out of Joel. "I remember now." A contemplative expression overtook his face, as if he remembered for the first time in a long time.

Amber sat in a light pine chair beside Joel, who took hold of Dean's hand. "But you always made them go away." No animosity palpable or detectable. Only serene kindness radiated from him.

"Maybe this time you can chase mine away?"

"I'll do my best." Joel shifted on the bed to peer at the IV fluid. "Feeling better?" A sweet sincerity carried Joel's voice across the space dividing the two men.

"Better now that I got my insulin. And my nephew."

Joel grinned genuinely. Dean's tears proved he sensed it.

Amber wanted to laugh and cry at the same time.

Whether either of them recognized it or not, she basked in the moment of the miracle. Forgiveness. God weaving invisible threads of it back and forth, back and forth, heart to heart, resecuring the parameters of their relationship. Then restoration would come.

Dean looked at the woman perched in a chair on the other side of his bed holding his hand. "Millie, this is Amber. She goes to our church now."

Millie smiled. "I thought I'd seen her there. Hadn't had a chance to introduce myself."

Dean looked at Joel. "Did you get the VD from her?"

Joel craned his neck forward. "Excuse me?"

"DVD," Millie whispered, leaning over.

"Yes, Uncle Dean. She gave me the disc," Joel said.

"Did you have a chance to watch the tape?" Dean asked.

Millie clasped her hands. "DVD."

Joel shifted, resting his heel on the bed frame. "Not yet. I'd like an idea of what it is first."

Dean eyed Millie.

She squeezed his hand. "You can do this, Dean. Just like we practiced. Now go ahead. Just tell the truth."

Joel set both feet flat on the floor and leaned forward. Hands loosely clasped, elbows resting on his knees, he waited.

Dean took in a deep breath that Amber never saw him let back out. "Truth of the matter is, if I could go back and live life over, I'd do it differently. Each day we wake up breathing is a gift from God. I'll not waste another one hiding in the shadows of my shame. I've done that for thirty-one years."

Joel's eyes bored into Dean's. "Thirty-one years. That's right about the time I would have been—"

"Conceived, yes. The affair was a one-time deal, Joel. Only it happened before you were born, not after. Not once after, in fact. Only your dad didn't believe that. Dale Montgomery is not your biological father, Joel. I am."

The constellation of emotions that orbited around Joel's face caused Amber's hand to cover his. If she could infuse strength by osmosis…

A shadow fell over Dean as Joel stood to face the window. "Do you know why she was coming back when she was killed?" Joel asked in a rough voice.

"I have an idea."

"Mind telling me what it is?" Joel's back still faced them.

"I think she was coming back for you."

Joel plunged hands deep in his pockets. "Why?"

"Because your mother loved you more than life. Nothing short of death would have kept her away. If she could have, she would have come back for you sooner. Other than my brother's temper, her love for you was the fiercest thing I've ever seen." Dean struggled for a steady breath. "Evidence found during the wreck suggested she left to make a place for you, then bring you with her where she was. A diary said she planned to give it a month for your dad to cool off. Only he never did, so she postponed it a day. Then another. Then a week. Then another. Out of desperation, she told me to have you packed for when she returned. She trusted me with you more than Dale and his rage."

Joel spun. "That means what? She postponed me right out of her life? She promised, but she never came back. Never even called." Torment tightened his face.

"She called. Several times a day. One day it stopped. No explanation. I know you don't want to believe this about your dad, but Dale made it his personal mission to punish her. He refused to let her talk to you. She was in torture. She feared he'd try to kill her and she didn't want to leave you orphaned."

Muscles in Joel's jaw rippled. "You think he had something to do with her disappearance, or the wreck?"

"Not the wreck, no. The disappearance, I hate to think so. You need to ask him that question."

Joel huffed. "I have. A hundred times square. Why didn't I know you'd tried to find her those three years?"

"Because I trespassed on another man's marriage. I didn't want you to think I was pursuing it because I wanted to continue the sin. I wanted to find her for your sake, not mine."

Dean readjusted his top cover. "Little kids need their mama. I know the missing hurt you. I watched it

pick you up, rip you to shreds, then spit you back out
and start all over again the next day. And guess what?
Staying away from Refuge won't keep the monsters
from eating you, Joel."

Joel's head snapped up. His eyes turned tumultu-
ous.

"They go where you go. You have to turn around
and face them head-on, headstrong, full speed ahead
just like you do everything else. I'm not saying fight
it in your own strength."

Dean motioned to Millie for his water pitcher then
faced Joel. "Go to God, crawl up in his lap like you
used to mine, and let him hug the hurt away. He'll heal
those broken places and restore your soul." Dean
sipped his water, then swiped his chin.

"I've kept up with you through Aaron Petrowski,
son, so don't think I don't know how you are. Apply
that stubborn streak and militant determination that
makes you a top-notch soldier and declare full-scale
war on your fear. Even if the worst thing you could
ever imagine happened, requiring your utmost trust,
God would still take care of you."

Joel's beeper vibrated. "Excuse me." He stepped
from the room looking highly annoyed at the electronic intrusion.

Dean waggled a finger at Amber. "Come here, little
lady. Listen. I see how you two gawk at one another
when you think the other isn't looking. Scratch that.
He doesn't bother to hide it. If you love him like those

stars in your eyes say you do, I need your help with something. You game?"

"If it will bring closure or help him reconcile this, yes."

"Good then. Listen up. That cassette—"

"DVD," Millie whispered.

"It has messages from his mother to him. One every day for three years. I think she sensed she was going to die. I need to be sure he watches it so he knows she didn't abandon him."

She nodded.

"Another thing, trust Him to work out the details 'tween you and him. Ultimately Joel has a choice. I know firsthand God's power to turn the heat up when we make up our minds about something that doesn't jibe with his plans."

Amber squeezed his hand. "Thank you. That meant a lot for you to say that. You have no idea."

He winked. "Maybe I do."

Amber saw the resemblance when he did.

"Pray that he won't harbor bitterness against his dad. People change. I'm a testament to that. If his father has changed, I don't want this to put a deeper wedge between Joel and his dad. They hardly speak as it is."

"You're sure Dale made her leave?"

"I know he did. I was there when it happened. But the thing I don't know, and what I've spent the last two decades trying to figure out, is what kept her away."

"Maybe she was afraid."

"Maybe for a day. A couple months at most, but not for three years. We may not know in this lifetime. But God will reconcile it regardless. Now, let's talk about something else. How's that little fella who shadows you at church sometimes? I thought I saw him go by in a wheelchair earlier."

"Yes, that was Bradley."

Dean's brows lifted. "You need to go check on him?"

"Probably." Amber stood, strumming her purse flap.

"Why don't you get the nurse to move him in here so neither one of us gets lonely at night. I ain't sick, so it won't hurt him to be in here. You and Joel can visit us together."

Amber hoped Joel would continue to visit Dean.

"I'll speak to the nurse." Amber hiked the hall to the desk and asked. The nurse called Dr. Riviera.

"He ordered the transfer," she said after hanging up.

"What transfer?" Joel asked behind her.

She jerked.

Stealthy guy. He'd tiptoed into her heart like that, too.

"Bradley's moving into Dean's room. Are you okay with that?"

He stared a few beats. "I don't know if it's a good idea."

Disappointment sliced through her. Until he grinned. "That's one more person to fight for the best game remote."

Amber smiled as the elevator dinged. The doors slid open and a fleet of familiar voices wafted her way. She spun, looking down the hall then twirled back to Joel. "Oh! They're here?"

Joel wondered who made his delight whirl in circles. "I'm so excited they get to meet you! Come on—"

Amber grabbed Joel's arm and did the fifty-yard dash toward a group coming off the elevators. "Mom! Dad! Over here. Hey, my grandparents are here, too."

Joel leaned against the wall, aware of curious glances as Amber's family filled the hallway with laughter and hugs. A man he assumed to be Amber's father stared at him with interest.

Amber waved Joel closer. "Dad, I'd like you to meet Joel Montgomery. Joel, this is my dad, Rick Stanton."

Both men stepped forth, eyeing one another with a whole lot of respect and a smidgen of curiosity.

"Why did you guys come back early?" Amber eyed her crowd.

Amber's mom looked at Rick. "It was your father's idea. We were already in St. Louis. When we heard about Joel's uncle, we agreed to drive the two hours back. We'd already started on the road home when you called back about Bradley. We stopped by the pond to drop Grandma and Grandpa's luggage off and came here."

Joel fumbled with what to say. "You came back for

my uncle?" It would be a while before his mind could reconcile the switch over from uncle to dad.

Lela smiled. "Actually, we came back for you. Any special friend of Amber's is an automatic member of the family."

Joel grinned, loving the warm hospitality in their faces and hearts. "Amber has some news she'd like to share," he said.

"You getting married?" Granny Stanton bellowed.

"Gramma! No! Bradley will be coming home with me."

Joel loved the red that swooped in on Amber's cheeks as her family erupted in jubilee around her.

"I took Joel to fish at the pond," Amber said.

Amber's dad hugged her. "I knew someone had been out there. Did you by chance bring the cat?"

"Yeah, why?" Amber asked.

"Because it would relieve me to know it wasn't Joel who pooped in my wheelbarrow."

"I assume your shirt's the one mildewing in my washer?" Lela asked Joel with a grin.

He smiled. "Amber and I seem to have issues with mildew. I assure you, sir, she was outside when I changed clothes. I have the utmost respect for your daughter. In fact, I love her."

Lela glowed. "Will you need to speak to my husband alone about anything then?"

"Mother!" Amber's face grew as red as he'd ever seen it.

Joel walked down the hall to find a seat for Amber's grandmother…and to hide his own blush.

This was a family who laughed and cried together and championed one another's dreams. One who sequestered themselves from anything with potential to rip them apart. The kind he'd longed for his to be. Not that he wanted a different family. He wanted the one he had to live out the potential of their blessings. Not crumble under opposition and leave grace under the doormat when they stepped inside.

I'll share.

The truth of her love hit like a cricket bat to the back of his knees. Maybe he should find a seat for himself, too.

I vow never to have children. No child should have to go through what I did with parents in a military marriage.

Amber's home was Refuge, and he couldn't live with the memories the town resurrected. Or could he?

He had eight years until retirement, and she'd signed a three-year contract with the school. In eight years he would be able to be there for a family. He couldn't expect her to wait eight years for him, and Bradley may not have eight years.

Joel scouted the halls for a quiet place to tune in and do some heavy-duty praying.

He had a big decision to make.

Chapter Nineteen

"I can't stay," Joel said the next day as Amber passed him leaving the hospital lobby after school. "Petrowski paged me yesterday. Something came up. My team could use a hand. That'll also give me time to think."

His words sent pangs through her. "Okay. For how long?"

"As long as it takes."

She didn't understand if that meant the mission or a decision about them. "When will you leave?"

"I needed to leave five minutes ago. But I didn't want to without saying goodbye."

"Goodbye for how long?"

"Not sure, but I need to hit the road."

"Where?"

"Can't say. I'll find you." He hugged her briefly then hoofed it toward the exit. She wanted to cling to him. Every step away seemed to take hope for a future with him. It had been foolhardy to consider he might change his mind about children. Besides that, he was right. Dr. Riviera had just informed her they might move Bradley's bone marrow transplant up a week. A man should be around to take care of his family. How could she trust one who couldn't?

God, if a dad who wants to be there but can't always is better than a dad who can but doesn't want to, how do I work this out?

Amber's mom approached. "Are you okay?"

She forced a smile. "I will be. Let's go tell Bradley the news. I hope he doesn't mind living in a single-parent home."

Lela's arm draped her. "I think Joel will come around."

She fought the sting of tears. "I almost hope he doesn't."

"Amber Marie. It's time you and I talked." Her mother tugged her into the hospital chapel.

Lela sat. "That day when you came over, I said if your dad had his life to live over he would have made better choices."

"I remember." Amber sat across from her mother.

"That doesn't mean he wouldn't have traveled with his job. It meant he would have better utilized the time he had with you while home. It's not travel, but time that matters."

Lela squeezed Amber's hand. "I think Joel would strive for quality, even when his missions wouldn't allot him the quantity he'd desire. Many military families navigate these waters fine."

"A moot point if he doesn't change his mind about Refuge and children."

"Trust God to help you two agree on a station. Because love this strong deserves a chance to sing."

Thirty minutes later had Bradley jumping and squealing in the bed. "She really wants me!"

Amber wondered what he'd break if he landed on the floor. "Yes, but it wouldn't look good if five minutes after we signed papers, I had to put you in a cast."

Bradley plopped on the bed, kicking legs back and forth. He had more energy than she'd seen in a while. He grinned at Amber's parents. "You mean I got all this family for my very own? I knew it." Bradley grinned.

Amber sat beside him. "You did?"

Bradley nodded. "Yep. I been asking God for a family. Every kid wants to be wanted. I even told my nurse someone was gonna adopt me 'cause I knew God would help someone want me. I even prayed it would be you."

Amber pushed tears back. "God didn't need help in that department. There's a lot about you to want. You're worthy and lovable. There's no reason anyone wouldn't want you."

"'Cept I'm kinda sick, so I might be lotsa trouble."

"Never trouble. Always a blessing. No one knows how much time they have. So we'll never take a day for granted."

Bradley's hand shot up. "I have a question."

"Since we're not in class, you don't have to raise your hand." Amber's laugh trailed off when she considered Bradley may ask about Joel. "What's your question?"

"What are we doing about crazy cat? I'm allergic."

"I've got it covered. Celia wants Psych."

"Psych and me, we got it made in shades." Bradley lay back, hands folded behind his head, grinning at the ceiling. "What a deal. My teacher doing my homework every night. Can't beat that." He wiggled his eyes.

Amber laughed. "Not hardly. If you can push keys on the computer, you can push a pencil across paper. You will have a different teacher next year when you move up a grade anyway."

"That's all right. As long as you keep packin' my lunches. I lo-o-ove PB and J."

She brushed fingers through his hair. "You knew?"

"Doesn't take a genius to figure out why a lunch box is light goin' to school and heavy goin' to the lunchroom. I figured you and Miss Muñez didn't want me embarrassed in front of the other kids."

"We didn't want you going without dignity or food."

Bradley hugged her neck. "Thank you, Miss Stanton."

She hugged back. "You're welcome, Bradley. Thank you for making my dreams come true, too. As much as you wanted a family, I wanted a little boy. Do you have more questions?" Amber asked.

He relinquished a sheepish grin. "Sure do. Since we're not in class, can I call you Mom?"

Amber's phone rang spitefully early a few weeks later. She ran to grab it before it woke Bradley.

"Good morning, sunshine," a masculine throat heavy with morning said.

Every muscle jerked with Joel's voice. "Hey."

"Did you think I'd fallen off the face of the earth?"

She swallowed. "I wondered. I hadn't heard from you." Never before had he not e-mailed or called at least once a day.

Left without a look back. Like Bart.

"That's hazardous to your hope," came through the phone.

"What?"

"To assume the worst. Why do you think you do that?"

She shrugged, though he couldn't see her. "Not sure."

"Maybe you base your assumptions on past experiences."

She sat straighter. How would he know about her past experiences? Unless someone told him. "Where are you?"

"Refuge."

Refuge? Not Asia? "Has Celia been blabbing?"

"Since you wouldn't talk to me, somebody had to."

Amber groaned. "I'm going to seriously scalp her."

He chuckled. "Celia didn't tell me. I've been

talking to your dad a lot while staying out here at the pond the last couple days."

Amber moved to the kitchen since Bradley stirred. "You've been hiding out at the pond?"

"Yeah, and you'll have to restock it because I used night crawlers I found by your mom's rosebushes. Caught all the big fish with them. There are only minnows left."

"Very funny."

"You know why?" The gentle question soothed her like a beautifully strummed guitar chord.

She tore open Bradley's favorite instant oatmeal. "Why?"

"Because when I fish, I dig deep." All joking seeped from his voice.

The oatmeal missed the bowl. "I have a feeling worms aren't the only thing you dug at the pond."

Several beats of silence followed. "I have some errands to run today so how about we talk over dinner at the B and B?"

Her heart rate kicked up a notch. "What time?"

"What time does Bradley eat?"

"You know he's here?"

"I know more than you think about almost everything. I've been calling the hospital every day, talking to him and his doctor. I swore them to secrecy so don't be mad at them." A thread of humor stitched his words together.

"Five." *What errands?* She hoped he'd see Dean.

"See you at five." Joel clicked off.

Amber sat still for lost moments, knowing what transpired by the end of this day would chart the rest of their lives.

Destiny spun in motion. Whether it took them tandem or solo, Joel had already made up his mind about them. Amber knew it as surely as she knew the alphabet had ABCs. Sure, she'd be fine without him. Eventually.

Why do you always assume the worst?

She grabbed her phone. She refused to let something this important walk out of her life without a fight.

"Celia? It's an emergency. I need a makeover."

The B and B ditch nearly swallowed Amber's car. She slammed on the brakes when the back bumper tilted. Great. She'd spent too long drinking in the sight of Joel's retreat. She should have paid attention to where she went instead of where he went.

After dinner and their evening hike, he said he wanted to go in and take a shower, and asked her to meet him at the pond in two hours. She wondered how he planned to get there.

Something strange was going on. Now that she thought about it, this whole day had contained a *Twilight Zone* element.

Celia'd been a no-show. Mom hadn't returned calls, and Dad had surfaced without warning at dinner to pick up Bradley. "Taking him for ice cream," he'd said. "Pick him up at the pond later." Bradley had just eaten cake, but Dad had insisted.

Now she'd have to deal with a missing makeover, a ditched Mustang, and a munchkin surfing a major sugar high.

Life couldn't get any better.

She put her transmission from Reverse to Drive, and pressed the gas. No traction. If she kept pressing, she'd flood the engine. She must either be high-centered or her back wheels were too far in muck. She reverse-forward rocked it, to no avail.

She swiped hair from her face. "At least he went in to shower before he saw this crazy stunt I pulled." Amber threw the door open, and climbed from the car.

Mud up to the wheel wells. "Great." She stared at the bumper. Her tires had dug themselves in deeper when she'd pressed the gas to get out before Joel saw. She'd acted foolishly.

Fingers dented both temples. "Okay, think."

She had it. Idle it out, or put it in Neutral and give it a push, whichever worked. That ditch appeared one step up from a gator swamp, so she hoped the first one would.

She got in, put her in Drive and let it idle without pressing the gas. "Yes!" Stang girl drudged out, albeit slowly.

Five minutes and four inches later, Mussy stopped.

"Stang! Don't do me this way." She clunked her head against the steering wheel.

Bimp-bimp.

Great. If he heard that and came out here right now, he'd think her a total dweeb. Hopefully the walls and the shower spray would impair Joel's hearing. Finger-nails tapped her temples. "Think."

If she called Dad, Bradley would want to see Joel. If she called a wrecker, the flashing lights would attract attention—the last thing she wanted right now. Especially from a six-foot-four V-shaped soldier who sent her world into a magnetized fog every time he came within inches. What could she do?

Either take a dip in a muddy ditch known to house snapping turtles, or call in a disco truck.

Of course, the most logical thing to do would be go to the desk and have Joel come out here and help her.

"Who has use for logic when your face-saving re-putation is on the line?" Amber exited the car, hiked up pant legs and sleeves, and slogged through water to the back of her car. She pushed the bumper hard, harder. Nada. She turned, back against bumper, feet levered against dirt wall, pushing with all her might. Those squats and leg presses weren't a total waste of time, she realized when it finally got traction and inched out.

Wait. That seemed a bit fast for Neutral. Neutral?

"Oh, no!" She took off out of the ditch the same time the car did. She hadn't taken it out of Drive! She scrambled up the slippery embankment only to slide right back down. Great. Her down here mud-wrestling with ditch dirt, and Miss Stang headed across the road all by herself. Could be worse. At least Bradley or Psych weren't in the car.

"Help!" She clawed herself up by weeds and cattails, crawling on hands and knees, finally crested the ditch ridge, and chased the car. Depending on the speed and steering wheel angle, Stang would hit between the main porch structure and the first cabin, or—

"Oh!" Wrecking the rail would be the best thing that could happen, she realized, as the car gained momentum down the hill, turning at a sharper angle than originally. Unless that open door caught the banister railing and it held, Miss Stang was taking a midnight swim in the stream behind the building.

A horrendous crash actually brought relief.

Until seconds later when every resident of the place barreled outside in their jammies. Joel being the first one.

He scratched his wet head while blinking at the spot where her car rested up to the middle of its hood through the side of the splintered wood cabin wall. He looked terribly confused for a moment until his eyes tracked the yard to where she stood in the road dripping with ditch water, mud up to her knees. Now would be a good time to run, but her feet were cemented to the earth.

He jumped the rail, sprinting over. "What happened?"

"I—I—I had something in my eye. It distracted me." Mortification hit Amber as the owner knelt, surveying damage on the two-hundred-year-old house. "I somehow ended up in the ditch."

When Joel hugged her, she realized two things— her tears, and his dishevelment. He stood, T-shirt inside out. Barefoot. Shorts thrown on backward. Half his face covered in shaving cream, the other in scruff.

He drew fingers across his dripping forehead. "But… Your car isn't in the ditch. It's in the middle of my bathroom."

Chapter Twenty

"You sure your parents won't mind me crashing at their place?" Joel asked after the police had gone, and the insurance adjusters brought Amber a rental.

"They might if your definition of crash is like mine. Since it's not, and the bed-and-breakfast is booked solid, they won't mind. Mom suggested it when I called anyway. Dad said a wrecker is on the way."

"Dean's construction company can handle the B and B damage. I'm sure he'll give us a break financially."

"Us? Joel, I crashed the car. I'm the one who should pay for damages. Please don't even consider paying for my mistake."

"Hey, sunshine, I don't think of us as two units anymore. I haven't for a while. So your crash is my consequence." He grinned. "I was right about another thing, too. You're adorable with a tree frog on your head."

She patted her crusty hair but only came back with

clumps of mud. "I might find humor in that mix of verbiage later but right now, I'm awfully confused. You sound as though you think we still have a shot as a couple."

His mouth twitched but he clamped down to defuse the grin. He looked at his watch. Not time yet. "Let's drive by the park district to check on Bambi and Bambina before heading pondward."

"Actually, it was a Bambo. The warden said the vet put pins in the knee. Though I don't know why since it's hunting season. Anyway, so far both deer are thriving."

"The deer in the road was a buck? No way. Too small."

"Yes way. Unless the game warden needs an anatomy lesson."

"That's so strange," Joel said as they left the facility thirty minutes later. "I didn't think to check. I just assumed she—he—was a doe. But I wonder where the fawn's mother—" A horrible feeling of guilt washed over him as they got back on the road.

Amber put a hand to his forearm. "I know what you're thinking. That the doe was probably in the trees watching us and you took the fawn away from her. But they went looking for her."

"I don't know the nature of deer. If we take the fawn back, will she abandon it?"

Amber shook her head. "I don't think so."

"You're not a good liar, either," he said. "I feel terrible for breaking that family apart." Joel realized what he said as the words came out. Amber must have, as well, because she sucked in a breath. He looked at her and she at him.

"Dean," she breathed.

"I know. And these are just deer. I guess I never stopped blaming him for the destruction of my family long enough to consider the toll one bad choice had on him."

"I'm glad you're reconciling this in your heart, Joel."

"Speaking of reconciliation, I have great news." He tugged the kerchief from his pocket, washed but stained with layers of blood, tears and sweat from various people, including Dean at the airport.

"What's that?"

"This is what I handed Nolan during our last mission when he needed something to wipe his face with."

"Mission?" Amber asked. It surprised Joel how calm her voice held. She'd probably assumed him in Asia doing humanitarian stuff. Better off for her to believe that.

"Yeah. Afghanistan. We were in an urban warfare situation providing cover while another team rescued a diplomat. Out of the blue Nolan asked me to pray with him to accept Jesus."

She bounced in the seat like Bradley. "That's awesome!"

"Yeah, he cried like a baby, and so did I for about three seconds. Then testosterone kicked in and we both got embarrassed. We wiped our faces with this.

Nolan's salvation melted unforgiveness off me regarding Ma." Joel put his face to the kerchief and breathed deep the scent of true repentance.

He squeezed her hand. "You're good for me. Thanks for being such a great friend, and praying for my team. It's working already, so stay tuned."

Amber's hand went lax in his. Her freckles grew dark against skin that paled.

He braked. "What did I say that upset you?"

"I'm probably still shaken from the wreck."

"Try again. You weren't in the car when it crashed."

She drew a breath. "I…I'm…in deep here."

Good. That's good. "Yeah? So what's the problem?"

"Because of Bradley and Refuge, you want to be friends."

"That's right, I do." *But that's not all.* Joel pulled the car around the corner. Amber's driveway came into view.

She leaned up. "Looks like they're having a Bunko party."

Joel snickered.

She eyed him. Then the cars. "Do you know what this is?"

"That depends on you. Could be one of two things." *My pity party, or her engagement party.* "I just want to say one thing in private before we get out of the car. I will never pull a Bart. Okay? Just so we're clear." He didn't want fear of abandonment to alter her decision.

Her eyes widened. She fumbled with the belt clip,

looking severely dazed. He grinned. She'd started to understand. He went to rescue her from the seat belt's clutches.

The audience of family and friends leaning over the rail of her parents' wraparound porch sent her equilibrium into a spin.

Her feet slowed, mind hazed, heart hoping this was what she thought, but scarcely believing it possible. A day that big girls dream about from the time they're little.

He led her to the new white SUV, pulling a set of keys from his pocket. "Want to drive?"

She eyed the Expedition. "This yours?"

"Ours?" A star of vulnerability glittered in sky-blue irises.

If he intended to propose, did the man actually think she'd say no? She reached for the keys, wrapping fingers around his. He held on, so both their hands embraced the silver ring.

"There are two sets of keys here, Joel."

"Dean deeded the house on Haven Street to me."

"You're making a home in Refuge?"

He pierced her with the kindest of eyes and the most tender expression. "My awe will remain as if it were the wonder of the first time I ever caught sight of you, but hold tightly as if it were the last."

"My mind is a blitz, Montgomery. Could you interpret that?"

He huffed a chuckle. "I told Silas it wouldn't work."

Joel dropped to one knee. Her mother's muffled sob emanated from the porch.

Joel pulled out a crinkled note, unfolding it.

She gulped a breath. The letter Bradley had scrawled his wish on. The one Dream Corps forwarded to Joel. The one she'd written her e-mail address on. This paper had set it all in motion. Joel handed it to her.

A laugh escaped her. He'd penned a message in the erasable blue ink. Fitting. This knight in a shining Expedition left indelible imprints on pages of her heart.

She read through a blur:

When I ran errands looking for a family car I saw this Expedition. It reminded me of our talks about life being an adventure. I'm asking you for a lifelong expedition. Let's stay tuned together. Be my sunshine every morning, AMS—AOSD. Marry me? Love, JMM—USAF

She gulped again. Air ran in short supply here today. Amber covered her chin with her hand, both trembled.

Someone tugged it down. Amber had no idea when her best friend had moved from porch to driveway.

Celia planted a hand on her hip. "Soldier Cutie asked you a question, *chica.* You gonna answer him or not? He's starting to sweat over here." Celia pressed something in Amber's hand. "I cleaned him up for you. Bleached his mold out. He'd make a great cake topper."

Amber looked through a curtain of tears at the toy parachutist then to Joel. Maybe his strength would bring her voice back. She gulped again, starting to feel like the fish on her desk at school. "Wh-what about Bradley?"

Upon hearing his name, Bradley skidded around the car, game controller in hand. "Look at my engagement gift Joel got me!"

"Engagement gift?" Amber asked.

"Yeah! I'm engaged to be adopted by him."

Tears flooded her eyes. "Is this true, Joel?" If she thought she couldn't breathe before, she suffocated now.

"You're right about Bradley being a tech genius. He managed to hack a way into my vow and secure a domain in my heart, Amber. We'll have to redo the paperwork to add my name to make it legal, but I've already adopted him here." Joel placed a hand against his chest. She placed her hand there, soaking in the sure and steady beat.

Just like Joel. Strong. Steady. Sustaining.

Not flighty and winsome like double-minded Bart.

Joel smiled at Amber. "Come on. There's treasure to explore inside." He tugged her toward the vehicle's running board.

He opened the door. "Hop in."

She stepped up, lifting up a puzzle box wrapped with a camouflage ribbon while Joel moved the case of Mountain Dew with yellow bows on it to the other seat. She fell into soft leather the color of sand. It smelled of wax and new upholstery. Something crinkled beneath her feet. She reached for a gift bag.

"My team sent it from the Paris airport for you when I told them I intended to propose."

Her heart melted at the thoughtfulness of guys who really didn't know her. Then again, they were like Joel's family, so they'd be hers soon, too. Silk swished up the sides of the lavender bag with embossed yellow flowers as she slipped stylish white brocade material from it. She fingered the raised yellow design on the stylish scarf... Scratch that. No scarf.

A gorgeous—and tiny—silk dress. Amber's face flamed when she considered the conversation that had probably accompanied the purchase.

"This looks like it would be tight on a Barbie doll." She looked at the tag. Size two? Wherever would he get the idea she wore a size... Amber dropped her head to the steering wheel.

The horn honked.

She looked up to face her music. "Um, Joel, I think you should know Miss Harker fudged a little on my size."

He laughed. "That's okay. We'll just exchange it when we—" His words trailed off and he bit his lip, grinning like a clown but watching her like a hawk. "Start the car."

She inched the key in the ignition but it clinked

against something. A solitaire diamond sparkled at her from the keyhole. She peeled the Steri-Strip holding the inside band of the ring to the ignition and tugged the silver from the key slot.

Joel pushed it onto her ring finger. It fit. Someone must have told him her size. Joel tilted the visor down. Something landed in her lap. She laughed at the package of blue erasable pens. She opened the yellow envelope taped to them. Two plane tickets to Paris spilled in her lap.

She blushed. "This is for?"

"Our honeymoon…if you ever say yes."

"I guess I haven't answered yet, have I?" She pushed the passenger door open for Bradley, who scrambled in.

He peered above the case of soda at her hand. "Day— I-I mean honk! What a rock!"

"Honk?" Amber looked from Bradley to Joel.

"I told him whenever he felt like saying a word we've deemed off-limits, he should try and catch himself, or substitute a safer word. We decided on honk."

"Not bimp?"

Joel grinned. "My boy might beep, but he won't bimp. Real men honk."

"Granted this comes from a man who practically skydived in diapers. From a woman requiring sedation to go up the St. Louis arch, he's not a man yet. Can't he beep for a little while before he honks?"

Bradley flopped his head to the seat. "Oh, brother.

I can see it now. I'll be the only kid on the block whose mom wears a parachute to change a lightbulb."

Joel laughed. "You kill me, Bradley."

"Gee, I hope not. I'll be the one having to rig her chute, *and* deal with the shriek-and-flail all the way down."

Amber pointed a finger at Joel. "You told me I did fine—"

Something caught her eye as Bradley bounced in the back of the SUV. "Is that a new booster seat?"

Joel nodded. "Technically he doesn't need it since Illinois law states up to age eight. Dr. Riviera suggested he use one until he gains ten pounds since he's small for his age."

Amber peered around the interior. "Two booster seats?"

"Four. I want us to adopt as many orphans as we can. Bradley'd like brothers and sisters."

Bradley grinned. "I told him that when we transplanted my flower at the school yard."

Joel grinned. "I asked Mr. McCauley when would be the best time for him to give you a couple weeks off. I'd like my team to be at our wedding. You should see how vibrant Bradley's flower is with sunshine, proper care and rooted in healthy soil."

Amazement filled her. "Is there anyone besides me who didn't know about this, or anything you hadn't thought of?"

He swallowed. "Yeah, how long I'm going to have

to kiss you senseless in front of your dad if you don't answer me pretty soon."

She laughed, but he grew stone serious. It took her breath.

"What do you say, sunshine?" The wind of his words and his compelling eyes disabled her power of speech.

She took his hand and found her voice. "I say from now on I'm going to keep my eyes open all the way down. I'll laugh when the ride takes my breath away. I'll trust when I don't remember how to land. I'll dig deep, stay tuned and watch where I'm going from now on. I don't want to wreck our Expedition."

Her mind numbed as Joel dipped his head and drew her close for a kiss. His lips closed over hers in warmth, sealing their love in sweet assurances. She knew he'd never break a promise.

* * * * *

Recipe

Mountain Dew Apple Dumplings

INGREDIENTS:
2 cans crescent rolls
2 apples
2 sticks butter
2 cups sugar
2 teaspoons cinnamon
1 can Mountain Dew

INSTRUCTIONS:
Preheat oven to 350. Core and slice apples. Wrap each in a crescent triangle. Line up in a 9 X 13 pan. Melt butter, cinnamon and sugar together. Spread mixture over dumplings. Pour soda around perimeter. Bake 45 minutes. Dive in. Dig deep. Stay tuned.

Dear Reader,

You're holding in your hands the fruition of a little girl's dream—my debut novel, *A Soldier's Promise*. I hope you never lose sight of God's dreams for you, promises He's made to you. In this story, Joel Montgomery faces a difficult past to pledge allegiance to a promise spoken to a little ill boy he doesn't yet know or love. Your Heavenly Father knows you intimately, and loves you to the utmost. He always keeps His promises. Thank you for skydiving with me into the realm of imagination, where we soared together on winds of story to Refuge, invading the lives and hearts of Joel, Amber and Bradley. I hope you enjoyed their journey of love and faith.

I absolutely love hearing from readers. You may contact me at anavim4him@gmail.com or write me at P.O. Box 2955, Carbondale, IL 62902-2955. Drop by my Web site, www.CherylWyatt.com or www.scroll-squirrel.blogspot.com to blog. Leave a comment and sign up for my newsletter if you like. I will personally answer every correspondence if you leave contact info. If you liked Joel's story, pick up Manny's story, *A Soldier's Family* in March 2008.

Praying you fulfill God's destiny in your life.

Cheryl Wyatt

QUESTIONS FOR DISCUSSION

1. Amber feels her mission is to make the rest of life matter to a dying child. In her mind that means setting her own hopes aside to help Bradley's dreams come true. Has there been a time in your life when you've had to make great sacrifices to help an ailing friend or loved one? Did you consider that a hardship or an honor? How do you think God views it?

2. Bradley has two wishes: to meet a real Special Forces soldier, and to have a real family. If Jesus were standing before you right now, asking you what your two deepest desires are, what would you tell Him? Do you think He already knows the dreams of your heart? Do you think He planted them there? Why or why not?

3. Amber felt God promised her He would spare Bradley's life. Her faith was severely tested because Bradley seemed to get worse instead of better. Has there been a time when the circumstances looked completely opposite of a promise God made to you? How do you think we can choose faith over fear?

4. Has there been a time when God didn't give you the answer you longed for? A time when all hope

of a dream was lost? For instance, has someone you loved lost their battle with cancer? How did you cope with the loss? Did you feel abandoned by God? Or did you feel buoyed and covered in tangible peace and comfort?

5. Joel finds himself facing the hardest mission of his life: returning to the site of his mother's abandonment and his uncle's betrayal. Has there been a time in your life when you've had opportunity to face a deep hurt of your past? How did you deal with it? How did you feel afterward?

6. Joel and his teammates surprise Bradley and Amber by parachuting and fast-roping to the school lawn one day. Has there been a time when you've had an unexpected and pleasant surprise? Can you think of a way to do something profound and unexpected for someone that they would remember for the rest of their life?

7. Do you think God loves to surprise us with outlandish and lavish gifts? Give us things we did not expect, or ask for, or feel worthy of? Have you experienced a blessing like this from man or God? If so, explain.

8. Joel promised Bradley he'd come back to see him because he knew that would give Bradley the will

to fight his cancer. But his promise was severely challenged by circumstances beyond his control. Has this happened to you either as the giver, or the recipient of a promise? If so, please discuss.

9. Amber was afraid to get too close to Joel because she wanted a family so much, while he claimed he wouldn't make a good father. Have you ever been with someone who had such different life goals from yourself? Did that bring you closer together or further apart?

10. Finally, Joel comes to terms with his past when he aids his uncle during a diabetic episode, and the truth comes out. How did Joel react to the news his uncle gave him? How do you think you would have reacted? Where was God's hand in this?

LOVE INSPIRED HISTORICAL

Powerful, engaging stories of romance, adventure and faith set in the past—when life was simpler and faith played a major role in everyday lives.

Turn the page for a sneak preview of
THE BRITON
By Catherine Palmer

Love Inspired Historical—love and faith throughout the ages
A brand-new line from Steeple Hill Books
Launching this February!

"Welcome to the family, Briton," said one of Olaf's men in a mocking voice. "We look forward to the presence of a woman at our hall."

Bronwen grasped her tunic and yanked it from the Viking's thick fingers. As she stepped away from the table, she heard the drunken laughter of the barbarians behind her. How could her father have betrothed her to the old Viking?

Running down the stone steps toward the heavy oak door that led outside the keep, Bronwen gathered her mantle about her. She ordered the doorman to open it, and he did so reluctantly, pressing her to carry a torch. But Bronwen pushed past him and fled into the darkness.

Dashing down the steep, pebbled hill toward the beach, she felt the frozen ground give way to sand. She threw off her veil and circlet and kicked away her shoes.

Racing alongside the pounding surf, she felt hot

tears of anger and shame well up and stream down her cheeks. With no concern for her safety, Bronwen ran and ran, her long braids streaming behind her, falling loose, drifting like a tattered black flag.

Blinded with weeping, she did not see the dark form that loomed suddenly in her path and stopped dead her headlong sprint. Bronwen shrieked in surprise and fear as iron arms pinned her, and a heavy cloak threatened to suffocate her.

"Release me!" she cried. "Guard! Guard, help me!"

"Hush, my lady." A deep voice emanated from the darkness. "I mean you no harm. What demon drives you to run so madly in the night without fear for your safety?"

Release me, villain! I am the daughter—"

"I shall hold you until you calm yourself. We had heard there were witches in Amounderness, but I had not thought to meet one so openly."

Still held tight in the man's arms, Bronwen drew back and peered up at the hooded figure. "You! You are the man who spied on our feast. Release me at once, or I shall call the guard upon you."

The man chuckled at this and turned toward his companions, who stood in a group nearby. Bronwen caught hold of the back of his hood and jerked it down to reveal a head of glossy raven curls. But the man's face was shrouded in darkness yet, and as he looked at her, she could not read his expression.

"So you are the blessed bride-to-be." He pulled the

hood back over his head. "Your father has paired you with an interesting choice."

Relieved that her captor did not appear to be a highwayman, she sagged from his warm hands onto the wet sand. "Please leave me here alone. I need peace to think. Go on your way."

The tall stranger shrugged off his outer mantle and wrapped it around her shoulders. "Why did your father betroth you thus to the aged Viking?" he asked.

"For one purported to be a spy, you know precious little about Amounderness. But I shall tell you, as it is all common knowledge."

She pulled the cloak tightly about her, reveling in its warmth. "Our land, Amounderness, once was Briton territory. Olaf Lothbrok, my betrothed, came here as a youth when the Viking invasions had nearly subsided. He took the lands directly to the south of Rossall Hall from their Briton lord. Then, of course, the Normans came, and Amounderness was pillaged by William the Conqueror's army."

The man squatted on the sand beside Bronwen. He listened with obvious interest as she continued the familiar tale. "When William took an account of Amounderness in his Domesday Book, he recorded no remaining lords and few people at all. But he did know the Britons. Slowly, we crept out of hiding and returned to our halls. My father's family reoccupied Rossall Hall. And there we live, as we should, watching over our serfs as they fish and grow their meager crops. Indeed, there is not much here for the greedy Normans to want, if they are the ones for whom you spy."

Unwilling to continue speaking when her heart was so heavy, Bronwen stood and turned toward the sea. The traveler rose beside her and touched her arm. "Olaf Lothbrok's land—together with your father's—will reunite most of Amounderness. A clever plan. Your sister's future husband holds the rest of the adjoining lands, I understand."

"You've done your work, sir. Your lord will be pleased. Who is he—some land-hungry Scottish baron? Or have you forgotten that King Stephen gave Amounderness to the Scots as a trade for their support in his war with Matilda? I certainly hope your lord is not a Norman. He would be so disappointed to learn he has no legal rights here. Now, if you will excuse me?"

Bronwen turned and began walking back along the beach toward Rossall Hall. She felt better for her run, and somehow her father's plan did not seem so farfetched anymore. Distant lights twinkled through the fog that was rolling in from the west, and she suddenly realized what a long way she had come.

"My lady," the stranger's voice called out behind her.

Bronwen kept walking, unwilling to face again the one who had seen her in her humiliation. She did not care what he reported to his master.

"My lady, you have a bit of a walk ahead of you."

The traveler strode forward to join her. "Perhaps I should accompany you to your destination."

"You leave me no choice, I see."

"I am not one to compromise myself, dear lady. I follow the path God has set before me and none other."

"And just who are you?"

"I am called Jacques."

"French. A Norman, as I had suspected."

The man chuckled. "Not nearly as Norman as you are Briton."

As they approached the fortress, Bronwen could see that the guests had not yet begun to disperse. Perhaps no one had missed her, and she could slip quietly into bed beside Gildan.

She turned to go, but he took her arm and studied her face in the moonlight. Then, gently, he drew her into the folds of his hooded cloak. "Perhaps the bride would like the memory of a younger man's embrace to warm her," he whispered.

Astonished, Bronwen attempted to remove his arms from around her waist. But she could not escape his lips as they found her own. The kiss was soft and warm, melting away her resistance like the sun upon the snow. Before she had time to react, he was striding back down the beach.

Bronwen stood stunned for a moment, clutching his woolen mantle about her. Suddenly she cried out, "Wait, Jacques! Your mantle!"

The dark one turned to her. "Keep it for now," he shouted into the wind. "I shall ask for it when we meet again."

* * * * *

*Don't miss this deeply moving
Love Inspired Historical story about a medieval
lady who finds strength in God
to save her family legacy—and to open
her heart to love.*

THE BRITON
*By Catherine Palmer
Available February 2008*

And also look for
HOMESPUN BRIDE
*by Jillian Hart,
where a Montana discovers that love
is the greatest blessing of all.*

Love Inspired® SUSPENSE

RIVETING INSPIRATIONAL ROMANCE

Watch for our new series of
edge-of-your-seat suspense novels.
These contemporary tales
of intrigue and romance
feature Christian characters
facing challenges to their faith...
and their lives!

Steeple
Hill®

Visit:
www.SteepleHill.com